Pride Publishing books by Bellora Quinn and Sadie Rose Bermingham

Elemental Evidence
Breathing Betrayal
Burning Boundaries
Surfacing Secrets

I0681393

Elemental Evidence

SURFACING SECRETS

BELLORA QUINN &
SADIE ROSE BERMINHAM

Surfacing Secrets
ISBN # 978-1-78686-349-2
©Copyright Bellora Quinn and Sadie Rose Bermingham 2018
Cover Art by Erin Dameron-Hill ©Copyright March 2018
Interior text design by Claire Siemaszkiewicz
Pride Publishing

SURFACING SECRETS

Dedication

Sadie and Bellora dedicate this book to Angel, and to Scott, for your continual support and enthusiasm — even when we are at our most contrary — and in spite of you both having super busy schedules too. We love you both loads.

Sadie also dedicates this volume to Julie, with thanks for enthusiasm and feedback, and for your endless patience. Trying to keep a paranormal romance writer focused on the real world is bloody hard work. Bless you.

Chapter One

The persistent pounding on his apartment door pulled Jake out of bed. He stumbled, bleary-eyed and yawning, into the living room and managed to stub his toes on the coffee table. "Ow, son of a— Hang on, hang on, I'm coming already," he grumbled, and yanked the door open. Early morning sunlight slanted through the windows in the hallway. Framed in the golden halo of rays was Detective Inspector John Cordiline, looking like a fallen angel crumpled from the long descent, a haggard expression on his face, along with at least a day's worth of stubble.

"Detective, what brings you by at"—Jake squinted at the clock—"six in the morning?"

Cordiline raised a finger to scratch his temple, just where his dark brown hair was fading to a softer shade of gray. It was a nervous tic, one of a very few that the generally self-assured Fitzrovia DI possessed.

"Official business, I'm afraid, Chivis. Do you mind if I come in? It's to do with the bloke that lived across the hall from you."

Leaving the door open, Jake backed into the apartment then wandered over toward the kitchen. This was going to require coffee, he could tell. The pot was set up to go off on its own in another half hour anyway so all he had to do was hit the brew button. As the door clicked shut, he turned back around.

"Coffee'll be ready in a few minutes. What's going on?"

Cordiline perched on the edge of one of the sofa cushions with his forearms resting on his knees. The shadows under his eyes said this was the wrong end of a long night, but that cloudy blue gaze still traveled over Jake from head to toe. A small smile tugged at his lips for a moment, then was gone.

"Did you know Mr. Sullivan?"

"Jim? I talked to him a few times in passing. I didn't know him well. What happened?"

"Guy that runs the grocery store downstairs called in a complaint when he came in early to supervise a delivery. Said there was water coming through the ceiling and he couldn't get anyone to come to the door. The PC that responded found Mr. Sullivan in the bathtub, water still running, head under the surface."

"Aw, shit," Jake swore softly.

"Yeah, that it is."

"I take it the boys in blue found something that didn't fit with an accident, or suicide, if they called you in?"

"Did you see Mr. Sullivan last night?" Cordiline asked, instead of answering. "Or see him with anyone new lately?"

"No. It's been a few days since I last ran into him. I've never seen him bring anyone home. Our conversations were, basically, 'good morning' and 'nice day'."

Cordiline heaved a sigh. "I figured that might be the case, but I had to ask. We're going to have to talk to everyone in the area just to see if anyone noticed comings and goings from the apartment at odd hours. You were closest. Sorry about that." He rubbed his face with both hands, scratching at the shadow of stubble on his chin, the dark flecks dotted with silver. "Did I wake you?"

Jake made a dismissive gesture. "I would have been up in another half hour anyway. I like to run before it gets too busy."

Cordiline grunted. "Did you say something about coffee?"

Jake nodded and turned, which was all it really took for him to reach the cupboard in the tiny kitchen. He pulled down two mugs, poured the coffee and set them out on the counter along with sugar and milk.

"Help yourself," he said, sipping from his own mug.

Cordiline dumped a couple of sugars and a good splash of milk into his and knocked back half of it, seemingly immune to the heat.

"Good cuppa," he said with a sigh of approval. "Not supposed to take sugar but I reckon I need it this morning." His gaze wandered toward the half open bedroom door behind Jake. "I'm not interrupting anything, am I?"

Jake snorted. "You think Mari wouldn't be out here already? He stayed home last night."

Cordiline raised an eyebrow. "School night?"

"Wait, wait, what's the right phrase? Ah, cheeky cunt. Yes. That's the one," Jake told him. "No. He's starting his new job today."

"He's a bad influence on you. I thought you were such a polite young man." Cordiline chuckled. He sobered quickly though, taking another good swig from his coffee. "So long as he's still being good to you. You back at work yet after that Birthright business?"

"They offered to extend my leave another couple of weeks but I told them I'd rather get back to it. I go back tomorrow."

The DI nodded. "Yeah, you don't want to leave it too long, it's harder the longer you stay away, so I hear. Speaking of getting back to it..." He drained his mug and set it down with a sigh. "Glad you're doing okay, Chivis. You take care of yourself."

"Let me know if there's anything I can do to help," Jake said.

* * * *

The website was called yourdirtylittlesecret.com and Mari figured he could hardly be surprised that it wasn't dedicated to the domestic habits of those who didn't like to wash. There was a part of his brain which registered disgust that he even bothered with sites like this, but its objection was processed and shut down in short order by the sectors that controlled his libido. After watching several video clips that made his eyes bigger, if not other parts, he concluded that this small, stifled part of his brain had a point and clicked on one of the links to similar interests in the hope of something, anything at all that could be helpful.

His relationship with Jake Chivis had progressed in leaps and bounds these last few months, and was starting to move past the stage of friends with benefits to something deeper. He knew that Jake had some very serious intentions and while he wasn't sure if he was ready for such an intense involvement this early, he was drawn to him in a way that went beyond his good looks. Although, admittedly, Jake's dark curls and big brown eyes, and that honest to goodness *amazing* body, were certainly not a small factor in the attraction. Just thinking about Chivis in a state of undress had him more turned on than a hundred smutty video links.

So, it was frustrating that he still wasn't able to relax enough with the man to make love to him. Or at least, to let Jake fuck him. He had ridden his lover's sexy backside plenty and very tasty it was too, but Jake hadn't yet managed to return the favor. Not for the want of trying.

Mari's therapist called it dyspareunia, caused in all likelihood by performance anxiety, and said it was treatable. His ex, Tomas, had been blunter, telling him — in front of the entire office where they had both worked — that he was frigid and if he wanted to play his 'ice queen games' he could play them with someone else. That had been *after* Mari discovered he also had a wife and children, of course. With hindsight, it would have been easier not to make a fuss, but he had never been that sort of boy. He'd used his interface gift on Tomas' phone before they'd split up, and after that morning of revelations he'd used the information he'd copied over from his SIM to send pictures to Tomas' wife. Pictures that she was hopefully still giving him grief over.

That had been his last hurrah before handing in his notice and coming back from Barcelona to London to start again. Once he had landed here he'd promised himself that workplace romance was off the cards indefinitely. At least this time he'd kept that promise for almost three years.

Jake Chivis had melted all of his resolve. It was those puppy dog eyes, he told himself. He never could resist a cute pup. But he already knew that Jake wanted more from him than tickles and a walk in the park.

The thing was, Mari wanted it too, more than he could put into words. It just terrified him that one day

Jake might get as tired of waiting for his arse as Tomas had. He didn't think he could stand to hear those words thrown at him again. At this stage, failure was simply not an option.

Hence the videos, or *extreme therapy*, as Mari preferred to think of it. He'd done a lot of reading on the topic of the male sexual response and he had been busy trying to find out about people who had suffered similar problems to his own, to learn if — and how — they had conquered them. He already knew, from extensive experimentation with other partners, that certain factors relaxed and stimulated him in equal measure. He and Jake had played around with his love of physical chastisement, though he knew that Jake was less enthusiastic about spanking him hard than he was about receiving the punishment.

The website called straponbitchez.uk was eyewatering, if not entirely satisfying. Their sister site iputacollaronyou/sle.ez proved intriguing, though Mari was more interested in the collar and cuffs element than any kind of puppy play. Some of the acts suggested by the video links were most certainly illegal in at least a hundred and forty countries. Another link led to lagriffe.com, where an incredible amount of money must have been spent on their CGI in order to turn their actors from human into various shapeshifters, though some of them were incredibly — and disturbingly — hot, even in their beastly forms. Mari didn't want to analyze that thought too much.

He clicked on another link, deciding that this would be the last one. It was late and he was meant to start a new job in the morning. As the scratchy home-made video clip began to play, he considered that it might turn out to be more promising.

The young guy was cute and the man standing behind him, though he didn't show his face, had a reasonable body. Mari settled down and made himself more comfortable on the bed as the top tied the younger man's hands in front of him and secured him to the bed with his ankles fastened apart to the footrail. The sex was quick and rough but the bound man seemed to be into it. Then the top slid his hands over the bottom's slim shoulders and around his neck, and began to squeeze. Mari caught his breath and his hand slid lower as he watched, moving over the flat plane of his own belly toward the waistband of his briefs. Where it stopped.

His eyes widened as he took in the scene. When the playback stopped, he reached out and took it back a few minutes, watching it again, just to be certain.

By the time he reached the end he could barely breathe. His stomach was tied in painful knots and the screen blurred through the shimmer of tears in his eyes. Fake. It had to be fake. But it looked so damn real. Horrifyingly, shockingly, real. He shut the laptop down and took some deep, cleansing breaths. *What if it wasn't faked?*

With a shaking hand he turned out the light and huddled under the duvet, but the image of the man being choked would not let him be still, no matter how hard he tried. Every time he lay back and rested his head on the pillow he saw the light go out of the eyes of the man on the bed and he fought the urge to throw up.

Chapter Two

When Jake was about sixteen he and his best friend had goaded each other to walk into an adult store. After furtively checking out the videos and snickering at the toys, they'd snuck past a curtain and into a booth where they could drop quarters to watch porn. He could have watched the same thing at home on the computer, but the back room of the store had been more exciting. The risk of getting caught, the semi-public setting, and the fact that he had caught Mark checking out his boner when he'd thought he wasn't looking, just added to the thrill.

That was about the extent of his excursions into adult stores. It just seemed like a waste of time when he could get anything he wanted online and have it shipped. His problem with online shopping, though, was no matter what something looked like in a picture, it didn't guarantee what it would look like when it showed up on his doorstep. He didn't want to drop a big chunk of change on a bunch of leather straps and buckles riveted together and get cheap junk.

He was not relishing the idea of walking into a sex shop and looking stupid, but he figured he couldn't be the only one to have ever done so. Also, it just so happened there was a shop only a couple of blocks from his building. At least it would be a short walk if he left utterly humiliated.

A tiny chime sounded when he went inside and he had to blink a couple of times before his eyes adjusted to the dark interior. It smelled like a saddle shop. Maybe he should have just eaten his pride and gone to see Colm. The professional Dom would no doubt have told him exactly what he should get, *and* how to use it. Hell, Colm would have been overjoyed to give him a personal demonstration. Which was another reason why he was here instead.

To his relief the shop was pretty much empty. The guy behind the counter looked up from his phone. "Hiya," he said, smiling.

Jake gave him a nod then glanced around, trying to give off a casual vibe like he knew what he wanted without looking too closely at anything in particular.

"You after something special or just browsing?" the clerk asked.

"Uh, just looking." Jake shuffled further inside.

Some of the stuff was pretty self-explanatory. Shelves of pocket pussies, cock rings and pornos were standard fare, he guessed. It was the bondage gear and other kinky shit he was interested in. He snaked his way past a display of flavored lubes and vibrators. Why had he thought it would be any easier to shop in person?

The clerk set his phone down and came out from behind the counter, trailing him at a discreet distance.

A slick of copper-brown forelock kept falling into his eyes and he wore small, rectangular rimmed spectacles that reminded Jake of the reason why he was here. Not that the guy looked anything like Mari otherwise. He didn't look old enough to work in a place like this, for one thing, but Jake figured he had to be at least eighteen. He suddenly felt ancient.

"If you can't find what you're after, just give me a nudge," the clerk said in an irritatingly chirpy voice. He began tidying a shelf of butt plugs, no doubt on purpose.

Jake considered just leaving, but he wanted more than anything to make Mari happy. He took a deep breath and turned toward the kid with the glasses.

"Look, my boyfriend likes to get tied up and spanked. You got anything for that?"

The assistant straightened and peered over the tops of his glasses. "You say that like it's a bad thing. Chill, man."

He came around to Jake's side and crooked a finger, indicating he should follow. "What are we talking here? A little slap, or something more hardcore?"

Aw, geez. Did he have to actually quantify it? It wasn't that he was a prude, he was just a private person. He didn't really want to be standing in a shop discussing the intimate details of his sex life with a stranger.

Fuck it. He was already embarrassed, he might as well wallow all the way down to the deep end and get what he needed. "Definitely not just a little slap."

"O-kay," the cheery young man said with a nod. "We can do that. Come and take a look."

He led the way past a wall of dildos in every size, shape and color imaginable. At the very back of the store were racks of clothing and displays of naked torsos in a variety of leather harnesses, some with lots of chains and loops and D-rings for attaching wrist and ankle cuffs. On a pegboard hung flails, straps, paddles and whips.

Jake fingered the braided leather tails of a flogger and wondered if Mari would like the feel of it. He'd bent him over his knee and spanked him, even smacked him with his belt until his ass had glowed bright red, and Mari had come like a rocket going off. How much was too much, though?

"That one is pretty heavy duty," the clerk told him. "If you're not careful with it you can break skin. If you're going to get it make sure you practice first so you know how much arm to put behind it."

"Right," Jake said. "How about something that I'm not going to accidently scar him with?"

"Try this one."

He handed Jake another flail, this one with wider tails. He tried to imagine himself using it and all he could picture was a peg-legged pirate on a ship deck flinging curses and whipping backs.

"Maybe not."

"Or this one." The assistant gave him something sort of like a leather strap with a handle. The end was long and swishy, but stiff. He gave it an experimental swing, landing the end across his thigh to see how much sting it had. Quite a lot. It made a loud, satisfying slap sound too. He pictured Mari's expression, the way he would squirm and moan when he smacked his backside with it and smiled. "Yeah, I think he'll like this."

"That's a nice one." The clerk's voice dropped to something smooth and low. "Feels really good. Did you want any of the restraints? These are good." He showed him a pair of long, leather bracers that fastened with three buckles and had extra straps to hook them together or to something else. "They're very comfortable to wear. But impossible to wriggle out of." He grinned and practically batted his eyelashes.

Jake wasn't blind to the flirting but he didn't give him any encouragement in that direction. He got the restraints as well, along with another set that could be attached to the ankles or thighs. The flirty clerk threw in some flavored lube and a vibrating cock ring. The whole lot was neatly packaged up and supplied in a neutral, high-end, matte-black carrier bag. Which was fortunate, because he had arranged to meet Mari at his favorite Malay-Chinese restaurant at six-thirty and his diversion left him with just fifteen minutes to get there on time.

Jake spotted Mari at their usual table, and before he took more than two steps toward him he could tell something was wrong. Mari was suited and groomed, straight out of work probably, a picture of sartorial elegance as was his customary fashion, but his hair was slightly disheveled and there was a slump to his shoulders. Maybe he was just exhausted. Jake reached the table and Mari looked up from the menu with a thin smile that didn't quite reach his eyes.

"Chivis! You look good enough to eat." He exhaled, his eyes flickering to the carrier bag then back. "I'd forgotten what it was like to go into work for a whole day. It's hell!"

"Aw, my poor baby." Jake leaned down and kissed him tenderly, placing his hand on the back of his neck for a moment before taking the seat next to him. "That bad, huh?" he asked. "You look tense. I figured they'd go easy on you your first day at least."

"Ah, you know what it's like. First day, new boy, I got the induction spiel and the meet and greet and the grand tour. I feel like I've walked the length of the Thames and back this afternoon alone." Mari hesitated and offered a smile to their waiter when he brought a couple of bottles of beer and a jug of water. When he had gone again Mari leaned back in the banquette seat and the smile he turned on Jake was warmer. "You consoled your back-to-work blues by going shopping, huh?"

Jake smiled back. He'd had a chuckle on the way to the restaurant that the first expensive-ish present he'd bought for his lover was a pile of leather straps from a sex shop and wondered what that said about their relationship. He had decided that considering his dismal record with past relationships, this was probably a move in the right direction.

"I did. I decided you needed a present to celebrate your new job." He picked up the bag and set it beside Mari. "You might wanna wait till we're back at the apartment, but you can take a peek if you want."

Mari's eyes glittered with mischief, some of the weariness melting away as he ran a finger along the edge of the carrier.

"You are a very naughty boy. I recognize the bag. And whatever this is, it wasn't cheap." He chuckled, a husky undertone creeping into his voice. Rather coyly, he tucked one edge of the bag down and peered inside. Those pretty blue eyes widened, then slid back up to meet his own, with more heat in them. "Mmmhhh, I think I'm only going to need a light lunch this evening, Jake Chivis. A boy shouldn't work out on a full stomach."

Jake gave him a look that was full of smolder and promise. "Sounds like a good plan. Make sure you eat enough to keep your strength up, though."

Mari didn't normally need encouragement to eat. He had an appetite that was surprising given the whip-thin lines of his body. Despite his claim to want to eat light, Jake still expected him to order half the menu and was surprised when he asked for an appetizer portion. He did seem preoccupied, picking at his Sambal of fresh shrimp and ribbon noodles. After a while, Jake was beginning to feel self-conscious about the way that Mari watched him eat, an odd expression on his face as he played with his chopsticks and took his time over one medium-sized shrimp.

The feeling that something was wrong plagued him. Should he ask, or wait until Mari brought it up? He didn't want to spoil his dinner but Mari was barely picking at his food anyway. "Something on your mind?" he asked.

"I just like watching you eat," Mari said.

Uh-huh. He somehow doubted that Mari had developed a food fetish overnight, but Jake knew from experience that calling his bluff rarely got him anywhere. Instead he gave him his best skeptical cop look.

Mari sighed. "It may be nothing, but, eat your dinner. I'll show you later. I can't tell you about it. This is something you need to see, trust me."

Jake arched an eyebrow. "Why don't we pack the rest of this up to go then. You don't look like you're having much fun. We can go back to mine and you can tell me what's bugging you, okay?"

"Okay." Mari shrugged, with such an uncharacteristic lack of resistance that Jake was seriously worried.

Chapter Three

The restaurant staff were politeness incarnate when Jake asked them to make up a bag so they could cut and run. Five minutes later the bill was paid and they were in a taxi. Ten minutes after that they were in his apartment again, and Mari locked himself in the bathroom for a short while, where Jake heard him trying to throw up quietly. His face was pale when he came back out, the shadows under his eyes even more conspicuous than earlier.

"Sorry," he said.

"Come here." Jake coaxed him toward the couch and pulled Mari down into his arms, snuggling him close. He ran a soothing hand over Mari's hair and kissed his temple. "Do you have the flu maybe, or food poisoning? Or is this from stress?"

"I feel terrible," Mari said. "After you bought me such a fabulous present and everything. Jake, I really need to show you something, but if I hadn't already just spilled my guts in your toilet, I'd have said it would probably kill the mood."

"The presents can wait. You are really starting to get me worried. What is it you want to show me?" Jake said.

Mari reached down for the messenger bag he'd dropped by the sofa when he ran for the bathroom. Extracting his tablet, he plugged in one of the innumerable flash drives that went everywhere with him and with a few deft flicks of his fingers called up a video download.

"I've been terrified all day. I really shouldn't have downloaded this but I was scared that I was imagining it. I need you to watch it and tell me it's not real, that I'm not seeing what I think I saw last night when I first found it," he said, talking without stopping for breath.

He hit play and passed him the tablet.

Jake watched in silence as a young man made kissy faces and flirted at the camera, then started to take his clothes off. He glanced at Mari with a puzzled look but where he might have been amused if Mari had wanted to show him some porn, he knew this couldn't be all there was to it. He returned his attention to the screen as things started to get steamier. Hands were groping and the guy was moaning in a soft, hungry voice which might have got him going if he hadn't been so concerned.

"Mari—"

"Just watch." Mari cut him off, drawing his knees up to his chest and hugging his legs to his body in a defensive posture.

Jake watched. He was trying to be clinical about it because Mari was so obviously upset, but it was pretty hot. Right up until hands that had been stroking the man's cock a moment before moved up to his neck. Normally this wouldn't faze him. A little breath play could be exciting. But the way those hands wrapped around the other guy's throat and squeezed was not in the least bit sensual. Jake frowned as he continued to watch the scene, as the man's face started to turn red and the veins stood out on his forehead, then he started to claw at the hands around his neck.

"Jesus," he murmured under his breath. A lifetime of Hollywood horror movies told him this had to be faked, or at the very least any second he was going to let go. He didn't let go. It didn't stop. If this was acting it was done so well Jake couldn't tell if it was genuine or fake. It looked real. It looked very real. It went on and on even after the man stopped struggling and Jake knew why Mari was so upset. It was horrific.

Do people get off on this?

The camera pulled back, panning over the body, lying still with his eyes open and unblinking, a streak of glistening semen still on his belly.

"Jesus fuck." Jake exhaled a tremulous breath.

He heard the air catch in Mari's throat, a sound somewhere between a gasp and a sob, then Mari buried his face in his hands and clutched at his hair, pressing his forehead down against his knees. For a few seconds he seemed to be struggling to breathe, then without looking up he whispered, "It's real, isn't it? The bastard killed him. And filmed it!"

"I'm not sure. They can do some very real looking shit with nothing but a camera and makeup. Fuck knows why anyone would make this but—" Jake shook his head. "There is no way to be certain if it was faked or real. Why you were looking up snuff porn to begin with?"

"I wasn't looking up snuff porn. It was just there. All I did was click a link, Jake. It was there and once I'd seen it I couldn't unsee it."

"Were you just looking for regular porn and you happened to come across that vid?" He asked it in as nonconfrontational a tone as he could manage. It wasn't like he cared if Mari looked at porn. They could probably find something they liked together.

"I wasn't looking for porn, regular or otherwise," Mari said. "I wanted to…to find a solution to my, um, problem, that's all. I'd been reading up about something. Do you remember the auto-erotic asphyxiation case in Hampstead? The one that got us arrested."

"Like I could forget? Please tell me you're not thinking you should try it."

"It's not as dangerous as it sounds, trust me. Phil died because his psycho girlfriend wanted him dead. It can be fun. The shortness of breath, it makes everything else so much more intense, forces muscles to relax. I was trying to find a technique that would loosen me up, that's all."

"It *is* as dangerous as it sounds." Jake said. "At least the auto part of it. Every year you hear about several deaths from 'the choking game'."

"I don't need a lecture, Chivis."

"I'm not trying to lecture you, Mari. You're an adult and you can look at or experiment with whatever you want, I'm just saying that if you read something that said it wasn't dangerous, that's total bullshit." He stopped, not liking the stubborn set to Mari's jaw at all. "I'm serious, Mari. If you want to try breath play I'll do it with you, but promise me you won't try auto-erotic asphyxiation. Please?"

Mari seemed to mull it over for a moment, then nodded once. "Okay. I give you my word. I won't try it alone. So long as you keep to your promise to help."

Jake heaved a dramatic sigh. "I will somehow endeavor to persevere through all the kinky sex you throw at me." His lips were twitching and he stroked Mari's hair with infinite tenderness. "Not tonight, though. I don't think I could put my hands on you like that after watching that video."

His boyfriend looked up at him, eyes huge and red-rimmed. Mari could be theatrical but he wasn't normally over-emotional, and this had freaked him out. Jake couldn't blame him. He felt a bit sick himself.

"I haven't slept." Mari exhaled. "I couldn't eat, or think about anything but that video all day. Should I go to the police, do you think? Will they just arrest me again? I don't know what to do."

"You won't be arrested," Jake assured him. "For one thing, you work for the government. Nobody is going to arrest James Bond." He tried for levity because he couldn't stand to see that haunted look on Mari's face. "And yes, we need to show this to the police. It doesn't matter how you got it, if we turn it over to them it'll be up to them to figure out if it's real or fake and start investigating."

Mari was beginning to get his breathing back under control and he leaned against him, resting one cheek on his shoulder. Shutting his eyes, he murmured, "I will never surf fetish sites again. I swear."

Jake put his arm around him and petted his back, kissing the top of his head. "Is that what you were doing?"

"Not in the sense that you think." Mari tilted his head back to look up at him. "I wanted to find out if there were people out there who'd, um, who'd had any success using the choke method to overcome—you know—tension." A hint of color returned to his pallid cheeks.

Jake had given up telling him that it didn't matter to him, that he was perfectly happy with everything they did in bed, because this one thing seemed very important to Mari, and Jake could understand his frustration.

In a careful tone, he said, "I can't say I'm unhappy you didn't find anything to suggest that would work, babe."

Mari reached across for his tablet and unplugged the flash drive, shutting the sleek machine down with a sigh.

"You can't deny, it got rid of his tension," he said grimly.

Jake looked hard at him but his expression said it was not a joke. Mari stared back, his features defiant, but he dropped his gaze first and tucked the tablet back into his bag, muttering, "I'm going to have to scrap all my tech. It feels...dirty."

Jake did not try to tell him that reaction seemed way over the top. Given the mood Mari was in, it probably wasn't the wisest course of action. Instead he asked, "Do you want me to turn the flash drive in?"

"Will you? I mean, you have a tame police dog and everything. It might be easier for you to give it to him. He doesn't like me."

"He doesn't *dislike* you," Jake said. "Speaking of Cordiline, he was here this morning. They found my neighbor across the hall dead. They haven't determined yet if it was an accident, suicide or murder."

"Is that supposed to cheer me up?" Mari asked him, his lips twisting around a mirthless smirk. "You cops have the strangest sense of humor sometimes." He shivered. "Poor sod. Did you know him?"

"Um, not really. We said hi a few times, is about it. I didn't mean to sound blasé about it, it's just—that's how we talk about a case. Sorry, I probably shouldn't have brought that up tonight. I'll give the video to Cordiline, see what he makes of it."

Mari was quiet for a moment or two, which was unusual. He seemed calmer now that Jake was on board, as if that somehow settled his fears.

"I've been thinking. Before you do," he mused. "Last night I was so freaked out that I just copied the thing and shut everything down. But, look, I know it's a recording and everything, but if I can get back to the webpage it came from, maybe I can trace it back. Maybe find out where it came from."

He looked up at Jake, his expression wary again.

Jake had been afraid Mari was going to suggest that. He had a better understanding of what Mari did with computers, what he did when he was using his elemental ability and not just doing standard IT work. Slowly, through asking Mari and poking around on his own, he'd found out that Mari's brand of interfacing was addictive. Even if he wasn't doing anything illegal, it still wasn't good for him to do it too much. If he flat out told Mari no, it was a sure-fire way to start a fight.

"Okay, just, be careful," Jake said.

Mari seemed reluctant as he retrieved his laptop, yet another weapon in his traveling arsenal, from the messenger bag and settled down on the sofa with it. He wriggled back against Jake as the machine powered up and locked on to his Wi-Fi signal.

"Hold me. I feel like I need an anchor for this. I have no idea what I'm going to find. Maybe it was just shared, maybe I'll have to chase it halfway around the world," he said. "The guy that strangled him had kind of a London-Estuary accent though, I'm pretty sure. He didn't say much but it was enough. He's English, or he's lived here long enough to pass, at least."

Jake moved over on the sofa, drawing up one leg and sliding around so Mari sat between his legs. It was enough to be distracting, or would have been, if they hadn't just watched a possible murder.

"A half hour max, okay? If you don't find anything by then there probably isn't anything to find."

"Okay." Mari half turned in his embrace and his lips brushed Jake's in a sweet kiss before he returned his attention to the machine in his lap. His fingers danced over the keys and, as Jake watched, he brought up the laptop's history, to find the last site he had visited. A tap on the touchpad opened the page and he rested the fingers of one hand against the glowing screen. Then Mari took a deep, tremulous breath and went very still in his arms.

Chapter Four

The webpage filled his screen again, the video link still open. Mari didn't click play this time but took his fingers off the keys and touched the screen. Jake's arms tightened around him, and Mari shuddered as he let go of his body and pushed into the tangle of communications spilling into and out of his laptop's internal router.

This was his gift, it was what he did, what set him apart from most humans he knew, Jake excepted, and what had brought them together. Mari was a Human/Cyber Interface. When he switched out like this, his mind logged into the network of communication technology that was racing like a virtual pulse around the planet, every second of every day.

It was both exhilarating and terrifying to him, and as addictive as crack cocaine.

Mari loved it. He had been riding the Ethernet links since he was a child and they had grown up together, in synchronicity. As the communication infrastructure grew ever wider and faster, so Mari's interfacing skills improved, and he'd learned how to hop from one wireless network to another, passing through businesses and personal chatlogs, bank accounts, phone networks, firewalls, military defense — there was practically nothing that could keep him out. He moved like a ghost from system to system, invisible and leaving no trace of his passing.

That gift made him invaluable to governments the world over. In Catalunya and here in London he had worked with some of the world's top security organizations developing software that could be used for spying or keeping enemies at bay. Even though he worked for them, those organizations weren't naive enough to believe that Mari didn't have the potential to become the enemy.

Hence his current post with MI5, where the British Government and the military could keep an eye on him.

He was not gone long this time around. According to the clock on his laptop screen, about twenty minutes had elapsed between falling limp in Jake's embrace and the sudden jolt to his physical senses as he came slamming back into his body, gulping for breath. Jake retrieved the laptop when he almost threw it to the floor as he regained the use of his limbs. Mari lay back, flexing and twitching for a few moments as he remembered how to move, to think, to speak like a human being and not a computer network.

"I need a drink," he slurred.

Jake must have known he meant something stronger than water but when he extracted himself and went to the kitchen that was what he came back with.

"Drink some of this, slow sips," Jake instructed, sliding back around him.

Mari gulped it down, ignoring the advice, and as he got proper control of his tongue he asked, "Have you got anything stronger?"

"What did you find?" Jake asked, making no move to go get the liquor, even though Mari knew there were still a couple of fingers of brandy left in the bottle he kept in the kitchen. Jake also knew that Mari was no better on strong liquor than he was.

"The ISP of the poster is in Hackney, not a million miles away. But the video, there's something odd there. A lot of threads link into it, and back out again, message streams going out all over the country, all over Europe. They're not all connected to the porn industry. There are threads from medical institutes, political organizations, all sorts of places. This is a big network and most of it is probably irrelevant to our search. I need some time to process the information." Mari set the glass aside and pressed the heels of his hands to his eyes. His vision was still blurry when he lifted his head. "I think this could be bigger than one person, but I need to find out more about the poster first."

"Mari, let's turn this over to the police. Let them do the digging." Jake's tone was rigid.

Mari turned and glared at him so Jake held up his hands in surrender. "I'm not saying drop it, I'm just saying you don't have to solve it all in one night. Or by yourself."

"I can do it," he argued. "I can follow every strand like I did with the Birthright chat threads. I can find everyone that's posted in or out to that ISP and we can narrow it down, tonight. Move faster than the police ever could."

"Baby, you are exhausted. Look at yourself," Jake said, still touching his face with gentle fingers. "Yes, you can do it, but I don't want you to kill yourself in the process. You're gonna burn out if you do this all at once. Get some rest tonight. We'll tell Cordiline about this in the morning. He can get their IT people onto the initial ISP and you can work on the traces they think are most interesting."

Mari wanted to argue, but at last he subsided and pulled himself closer, resting his forehead against Jake's shoulder and letting his body mold itself to Jake's. He was so weary that he could feel how close to the truth Jake had been when he warned against burning out. Mari cursed the maker of that video to a fiery end, and not just because of what he had done to the guy who'd been strangled. He could not let this go, and he knew from previous experience that it was a one-way street. The only way to recover from interface-related exhaustion was to rest and abstain. Completely.

The difference between Jake's gift and his was that Jake's contact-visions came over him whether he wanted them to or not. Jake had no choice in the matter, so he was naturally more cautious, limiting himself in situations that might leave him open to a 'flashback'. On the other hand, Mari had never exercised such caution. He had spent so much time exploring the limits of his gift that he could immerse himself in just about any communications network that he chose. And he loved to do it, which was part of the problem. Jake already understood that it damaged him, sometimes in small ways, sometimes larger ones, whenever he interfaced. And Jake did not like that, he had made it plain.

"All right," Mari conceded. "I've got the general area already. In the morning I'll zero in on the location and go take a look."

Jake sighed and kissed his temple. "Fine. Are you staying over?"

"I'm afraid my mood's tanked."

"You don't have to be in the mood for anything. Stay here. I'll go with you in the morning."

That offer was a hundred times better than walking home and failing to sleep alone. Mari curled around him and pulled him close, reveling in his warmth. "You have a deal."

Chapter Five

The Hackney Picturehouse had been built in 1907, originally to house the Central Library and Methodist Hall. Today, the imposing, copper-domed sandstone façade loomed over its corner of Mare Street and Paragon Road like an ancient palace, trading glares with the brutalist cube-cum-baroque wedding cake hybrid of the Hackney Empire across the road. When Mari strode down the main road from Hackney Central overground station, with Jake at his side, they were the primary buildings to catch his eye. It was the first time that either of them had ever set foot this far east. Or at least, this far east of Marylebone. A few streets further still, the main thoroughfare carried them into a vastly different neighborhood, more tower blocks and twenty-four-hour Tescos than Theatreland. Outside the Globe on Morning Lane, Mari stopped and checked his phone. He'd mapped the traces he'd found of the IP address where the apparent snuff film had been uploaded to this neighborhood but was still working on pinpointing the location. That was easier said than done, given the preponderance of high-rise blocks off Morning Lane. When there were more than thirty separate residences on a relatively small plot, it complicated matters.

"What are you going to do, even if we find the damned place?" Jake asked, his words almost drowned out by the rumble of a passing juggernaut laden with rubble. "Ring his bell and ask if the occupier has made any snuff films recently?"

"Don't be an idiot. We're not going to say anything about what we saw, we just want to get a feel for who the poster is, that's all. We can decide what to do about him once we have a better idea who we're dealing with," Mari admonished, gesticulating with his phone in the direction of a five-story block of modest maisonette flats that stood nearby. "I think it must be this one. We should go inside and I'll try again, see if I can get a better fix on where the recording came from."

"You are overdoing it again," Jake warned. "You know that too much interfacing will make you go blind."

"Do you have a better idea, Detective?" Mari asked. He delivered the retort without animosity though, so that it was barely an insult. Or at least he hoped Jake wouldn't take it that way after last night.

"Yes," Jake answered. "We give the video to Cordiline like we planned last night. We let the police do their jobs, and find out if there was even a crime committed. It could all have been staged."

"And what if it wasn't? What if the police think it was all an act? He gets away with it?" Mari looked irritably at him, still turning his phone in his hands as if it would give him special powers to change Jake's mind. "Do you think that's fair? We're not going there to arrest him, just to get a feel for whether he was the killer or just passing it on."

Jake turned his head but Mari still saw him roll his eyes, although he didn't continue to argue. This only made him angrier. He'd rather have Jake tell him off than treat him like he was only humoring him. If Jake didn't trust his instincts, if he didn't care about seeing justice done, if he didn't want to be supportive—

Mari stopped that train of thought. Okay, perhaps that was unfair. Jake wouldn't be here with him if he wasn't supportive, and he hadn't dismissed Mari's concerns. He just wanted to follow different steps. Do what he was trained to do.

"How will it hurt to ring the bell and shake his hand, see what you pick up?" he asked, trying a more pacific tack.

"I'm not you, I can't turn it on and off, Mari. There's no guarantee I'll get anything off him at all," Jake said.

Mari turned and set off in the direction of the nearest block. He looked over his shoulder at Jake. "Well, if you don't try you'll never find out. And you wanted to find out if you can hone this gift after getting your booster. Now's as good a chance as any."

Jake's eyebrows met in a brief frown, then his expression smoothed into a careful blankness. It was eerie. He was still Jake but Mari suspected this was the first time he was seeing Jake's 'cop face'. The expression gave away nothing of what he might be thinking but Mari could still tell he'd hit on a nerve.

"Lead the way," Jake said in a neutral voice.

Mari leaned in and kissed his cheek, before activating his phone again and touching his fingers to the screen. "This way."

With no more warning than that, he set off in the direction of the housing block but actually wandered around the estate a few times before selecting a different building and heading off up the stairway to the second floor, with Jake at his heels.

He swerved to a halt outside a half-painted door part way down the walkway and consulted the phone again. "Here, I think."

Jake studied the door, then looked around, assessing the situation. Mari lifted his hand to knock but Jake rested a hand on his arm to stop him.

"Just a sec." He reached out tentatively and ran the backs of his fingers over the door handle. Mari already knew from Jake that he was unlikely to get anything from either the door or the handle, despite the fact that lots of people had likely used both. It was just one of those odd, unexplainable things. It was metal, and it was touched frequently—both of those things suggested it should hold on to memories, but for some reason doorknobs seemed immune. Whenever Mari asked him if he had any theories about why that was, Jake just shrugged and muttered something about thresholds having weird energy.

As expected, Jake released the handle and shook his head. Nothing. At least he had tried. Mari couldn't fault him for that.

He steeled himself and knocked. When no one answered after about half a minute, he lifted his hand to knock again, but just before his fingers made contact with the panel in the front door, a shadow fell across the glass from within and he heard the latch slip back.

A small woman looked up at them both, dark eyes glowering with suspicion from under a heavy, mousy fringe.

"Are you Jehovahs? We're not into any of that god squad bollocks," she said.

"No, ma'am, we're not peddling religion, or anything else," Jake answered before Mari could open his mouth. "We're looking for someone, actually. Does anyone else live here?"

"We only just moved in," the woman said. "Just me and him, my other 'alf. What d'you want? We're not registered to vote yet, so you can fuck off if you're with the Tories too. We don't want none of that lot neither."

Jake smiled, a big, friendly, disarming smile. The same one that made all the twinks at that bar he lived over flutter their eyelashes at him. Mari felt fluttery himself looking at it.

"Do I sound like I'm about to spout politics? I'm sorry, I didn't mean to give that impression at all. We really are just looking for someone. Would you mind if we talked to your husband for a moment? I'd just like to ask if he'd maybe spoken with the previous tenants."

"We didn't know them. Never met them," she said in a flat, unconcerned tone. "Place was empty when we took it. A wreck. Whoever had it before was a pig. He's sleeping, my husband, I mean. Working tonight. You can talk to me."

Her words came out staccato, like bullets from an automatic weapon. When her eyes moved to Mari, he pressed a smile on his lips, though he was conscious that he was not nearly so good at charming people as Jake.

"How long have you lived here, Mrs. — ?"

"Selma. Ms. Five days. Look, I got stuff to do," she said with a scowl.

"Thanks for your time. We'll be off then," Jake said, taking a step back. It was quite obvious to Mari that

Jake was thinking the same thing he was. If they'd moved in five days ago it was very unlikely that they were the ones to have uploaded the incriminating video. It was possible, but it was more probable that whoever lived here before them had been the one to put it online.

"May I ask who you let the flat from?" Mari asked, refusing to be deterred.

She looked at him with an odd frown for a moment but he held her stare.

"There was — that is, we're looking at some incidents that have happened on the estate recently," he said, improvising off the cuff.

"You're from the council then? We've nothing to do with any of that. We keep ourselves to ourselves," Selma told him.

"I wasn't suggesting anything." Mari held his hands up to deflect her ire.

"If you could just tell us the name of the rental agent, we can go ask our questions there and won't be a bother to you any longer," Jake coaxed her.

"You're coppers, aren't you?" Selma said with no less suspicion or loathing than when she'd thought they were Witnesses. "That bitch next door said he did a runner, the bloke before us. Didn't pay his rent and he just cleared off one night an' didn't come back. She's a junkie cunt though, dunno if you can trust anyfink she tells you."

Mari glanced at Jake, whose expression hadn't changed as he listened to her. He didn't confirm or deny her suspicion, just said, "The letting agent, ma'am?"

"Wimbush and Lewis on Mare Street," Selma told him, stepping back and making to shut the door.

"Thank you, Ms. Selma, you've been very helpful," Mari told her in a faux-cheerful tone.

She made a rude noise and the door closed between them, though at least it wasn't slammed in their faces. Although this was probably more in deference to her sleeping husband than their finer feelings.

"What a charming lady," Mari demurred, giving way to an undertone of sarcasm. "I wonder if her neighbors are as delightful as her."

"I didn't get that impression somehow," Jake said, his voice flat and neutral again.

"Maybe we should find out." Mari took a few steps over to the next apartment along. There was a board over the glass panel beside the front door. Someone had sprayed the word SKAG on it in red aerosol paint. Under it was written HORE in black magic marker. Loud rap music was playing somewhere deep inside the building, a pulsing, driving beat that reverberated through the concrete underfoot.

Jake ghosted along beside him and Mari was gratified that he didn't try to talk him out of speaking with the neighbors. His first knock was ignored and he rapped again, harder this time, moments before a shrill voice inside yelled, "Cameron! *Door*!"

"No shrinking violets in this block," Mari muttered.

Still there was no diminution in the volume of the music but, just as he was about to give up, the sound of several bolts being wrestled back from within brought him and Jake back to the door.

A skinny woman stepped out, possibly in her mid-thirties, possibly older. She was white, with long dark hair scraped back from her face and hanging in a limp tail from the back of her skull. Very pale, almost colorless eyes scrutinized them from head to toe. Her pupils were pinpricks. Ms. Selma's astute assessment seemed to be correct in one respect at least.

"Good morning," Mari said politely. "Sorry to bother you, miss. We're looking for the man who used to live next door to you."

He pointed back toward the flat they had just visited for clarification. Her eyes followed the direction of his finger then came back to his face. She looked him over again.

"Figures," she said disparagingly. Then, "He's cleared off. And good fuckin' riddance. Nonce!" Without stopping to draw breath, she turned her head and bellowed, "*Cameron*! Turn that shit *down*!"

Like a magic spell, the sound level dropped to zero and she turned back with a brief moment of pleased surprise on her face, arms folded across her insubstantial chest.

"Do you know where he went, ma'am? The guy next door?" Jake asked.

"No idea, sweetheart. Does he owe you money? You won't see it." Her eyes rolled up and down him in an approximation of seduction.

Mari stifled a snort of humor. Before Jake could work any magical sweet talk on her the spell broke, as a wave of sound from within the flat rolled over them, and the woman on the doorstep turned to harangue the invisible Cameron over a soundtrack of Lupe Fiasco.

Jake waved a hand and went into retreat, turning to stride back down the walkway toward the stairs, and Mari made his apologies and left in his wake.

Chapter Six

Behind them the door banged shut, but they had only gone the length of the walkway when it opened again and a tall, dark-skinned youth in straight-leg, dark blue jeans and a sleeveless shirt exited the flat and came striding after them, tugging a cap down over his dark curls.

"Now see what you bought us," Jake said in the same mild, unruffled tone he had used on Selma's neighbor.

"Oh, I see all right," Mari agreed, admiring the cut of the lad's low-slung jeans and the waistband stripe of the black Nick + Campbell boxer briefs that they exposed.

"Behave. You'll get us knifed, Mari," Jake warned, as the youth caught up with them on the stairwell. He inched back though, deliberately putting himself between Mari and the boy.

"Is the bitch right? You the po-lice?" the lad asked, coming straight to the point with them. Though he was a match for height with Jake, he had the lean build of a teen, not yet grown into the full bulk of a man. His eyes were pale like the woman's but there the similarities ended. There was nothing drug-addled about his stance or his gaze. "You lookin' for the batty man?"

Mari rolled his eyes. "Your neighbor? The man who lived at fourteen-C?"

The young guy narrowed his eyes, jaw set and limbs loose. Suspicious, yes. Wanting to establish his dominance, for sure. Still more cautious than aggressive, though, as he eyed them, taking in the way Jake positioned himself like a bodyguard.

"You must be Cameron? We're not police. We just need to ask your former neighbor about something, that's all," Mari said keeping his delivery soothing and resting his hand briefly on Jake's arm as he moved to stand beside and not just behind his lover.

The boy's eyes flickered to that touch, missing nothing. His stance relaxed too though.

"No. You not the police," he agreed more quietly, his pale stare coming back up to level with Mari's.

"Do you know where he's gone? The man in the flat next door?" Mari asked again.

Cameron shrugged. "He just cleared out one night, innit. My mate reckoned some of the local gangstas put the frighteners on him, told him, you run or we burn you, right."

"Why would they do that?" Mari asked, though he had a guess.

"Because Clifford said he was a fuckin' nonce and a perv. We don't want none of that in this hood, right. Why you lookin' for him?" Cameron asked.

"Who's Clifford?" Jake asked.

Again, those pale eyes danced from Mari's face to Jake's and back again.

"My mum's friend. He comes over sometimes, when she's scored." Cameron's tone was disapproving. "Clifford said he knew Wade from way back. He said Wade had been banged up for touching kids. Well, that got my mate Shaq's back right up. He got some of the lads round and they set 'im straight, didn't they?"

"You said 'they' did. Not you? You didn't get involved?" Mari asked, keeping his tone curious and gentle.

"I wasn't 'ere. I was at my dad's. He lives in Birmingham. I go up to see him sometimes." Cameron sounded defensive.

"We aren't here to judge anyone," Mari told him. "I'm not interested in whether you thought it was wrong or right. We just want to learn more about the man who lived in that flat. That's all. Where does your mother's friend live? This Clifford guy?"

"He's got his own digs, a flat over on Chatham Place," Cameron said, shifting from one foot to the other. "So, there's not going to be no bother, over what the boys did, right?"

"Not from us," Mari said.

"Is Clifford his first name or his last?" Jake asked.

Again, those lucid eyes darted to his face and back.

"Dunno. The old cow just calls him Cliff. He only comes when there's something handing round, you know."

"Did you ever see Wade coming and going from the flat with anyone else, Cameron?" Mari asked.

"Never saw no one else go in there." Cameron wore a doubtful scowl.

"But your mother's friend did? Or one of your mates?" Jake pressed him and he began to look edgy again.

Mari fired a narrow-eyed look at Jake, trying to warn him without words to back off a bit. He stopped short of touching Cameron but poured that soothing voice over him like cooling gel over an inflamed sore.

"Did they see something? It could be important."

"Shaquille said he saw Wade at the Globe with a bloke. Not anybody local, he didn't recognize him," the boy said at last.

"What do you think?" Jake asked Cameron. "You think he was a perv?"

"I dunno," the boy replied uncertainly. He looked at his feet for a moment, shoving his thumbs through the belt loops on his jeans. "He was a private sort of bloke. He stared at you a lot though. You know, not saying nothing, but you'd look over at him and he'd be watching you. A bit creepy like. Just watching out the window and stuff. He got his windows broke a lot."

Jake was frowning again and he turned toward Mari. "Can you pull up a screenshot of the vid? See if Cameron can identify anyone for us?"

"But it never shows his face," Mari said.

"Just show him, Mari."

Jake shot him a look but Mari wasn't sure what it was supposed to mean. He shrugged one shoulder and swapped his phone for the tablet in his messenger bag. He plugged in the flash drive and tapped on the screen a couple of times, keeping one eye on the stairwell and the other on the walkway at all times. At last, satisfied that he had the clip least likely to get him beaten up, he turned the device and showed it to Cameron.

The boy's ice-gray eyes opened wider. He looked back at Mari with a curl of his lip. "You faggots like this shit?"

"No," Mari told him, ignoring the epithet for the time being. "Does he look familiar?"

Cameron tapped the screen and moved his fingers apart, expanding the image with a growl of disgust. "Perverted cunts! Yeah, that's him."

"The top? That's Wade? Are you sure?" Mari asked, his eyebrows rising at the certainty in the boy's voice.

"No, not the bloke with the tat. I don't recognize him. But the guy on the bed with his hands tied, that's Wade. Is that sick cunt bummin' him or something?"

Mari turned the tablet and killed the screen, detaching his flash drive and tucking the lot back into his bag with a glance at Jake.

"I think we can knock this search on the head then," he sighed. "When did you last see Wade, Cameron? Think hard, it's important."

The boy was staring at them both, lip still curled but also like he might run if they tried to grab him. "Somethin' bad happened to him? Right? And I don't just mean that perv knobbing him."

"We have no idea. That's why we're looking for him," Jake said. "Anything else you can tell us about Wade or Cliff?"

Cameron looked at Mari again, a glint of a different sort coming into his eye. "So, you two fags looking for your fag friend? You like that? Getting that pervy shit done to you?"

"Just answer the question, Cameron," Mari said in a warning tone.

"Clifford used to live over Hammersmith way, maybe he knew Wade from there, or just from when they was banged up together," the boy mused. "Do you reckon that's where he got to like it, when he was in the slammer?"

"I reckon you think too much, Cam," Mari told him.

"I think that's all the questions we have. Thanks for your help," Jake said, giving a meaningful look toward the stairs.

"No biggie." The boy touched the lip of his cap and his eyes were on Mari again as he said, "Watch yourself round 'ere. There's a lot of folks would hurt you without thinkin' bout it too much, you know what I'm sayin'."

"I don't take threats too seriously, Cameron," Mari told him, turning back to look him in the eye.

"You wanna do. It'd be a shame to mess that face up, right." The boy pointed a finger at him, then wheeled about to walk back to his flat again like nothing had been said.

Mari made a move, as if he might follow him and give him a bigger piece of his mind but before he'd even taken a step Jake took his arm and steered him away.

"Let it go, you won't do any good trying to make a point. We've got all the info we're going to get here."

Mari fumed in broody silence, but after a last glance at Cameron's retreating back he let himself be hustled down to the ground floor. For three blocks he did not speak at all. Only when they were back outside The Globe pub did he finally explode.

"Jumped up piece of shit! Who do these kids think they are, the fucking Terminator or something? Ridiculous! He's what? Sixteen?" He was shaking though, and only now did he feel the adrenaline of their encounter kicking in hard.

Jake put his arm around him, his expression and demeanor far calmer. "Exactly. He's sixteen or seventeen, one caretaker is absent, the other is a junkie, and he lives in a place where he's in constant danger of a beating or worse for expressing the wrong point of view. He's just trying to survive, Mari."

Jake's quiet assessment of the situation took Mari by surprise. He moved out of the protective circle of Jake's arm quickly though. He might not be easily cowed, but he was taking the threat of violence to heart for once. Although a part of him didn't really believe that Cameron would have attacked him, not right then, when it was two against one. Maybe not even had they been in a one on one situation.

Had he been with his friends and trying to prove himself a hard man, the conclusion might well have been different, though.

"I don't know whether to feel sorry for Wade or believe he got what was coming to him," he said, still angry but determined to focus on the task in hand. "I'm kind of thinking that if the guy in the video clip didn't kill him then someone from this lovely neighborhood did. Can you imagine? But the video clip was posted from that flat. Which means that if he was killed there, the sick bastards that did it to him calmly uploaded it and posted it before they left the flat. And they got rid of the body because the gossip squad would have been all over it if he'd left in a body bag."

"All true," Jake said with a smile. "You'd make a good detective, Dr. Gale."

He mellowed for that gentle praise and returned the smile. "So where do we take this investigation next, partner?"

Jake glanced at him from the corner of his eye. "We take the video to Cordiline, and tell him we've confirmed the last known residence of the apparent victim, and see if he can get the tech boys to figure out if what is on the video is what it appears to be, or if it's just some very good acting."

Mari thought that even an Oscar winner would struggle to act 'blue in the face' to the degree that the late Wade *Whateverhisnamewas* had done, but he kept that observation to himself and nodded mute acceptance. "Okay. Let the Met earn their wages. But if they don't find a link I'm not letting this go."

He set off toward the railway station and Jake fell into step with him as he walked, not touching but close enough that their arms brushed against one another from time to time. Mari moved his hand so that the backs of his knuckles skimmed Jake's hand, but he didn't go any further. It was still in his mind that Cameron had been calling him out and Mari loved a challenge, no matter how dangerous. He also hated feeling as though he needed to hide anything about what or who he was. In this day and age, in a supposedly enlightened country, he refused to pretend for anyone.

Jake must have read his mind, or perhaps just his body language, as he ventured, "What he said really bothered you, huh?"

"What? That kid? He was just flirting with me. Couldn't you tell?" Mari said, unable to contain the small, bitter edge to his words.

"Yeah, I didn't miss the way he looked you up and down a couple times," Jake said, a shrewd smile tugging his lips. "And I'm sure he didn't miss the way you looked back, until he started playing the thug. Is that the part that bothered you? His act?"

Mari looked sidelong at him with a sigh. "No one should need to put on an act. This is the twenty-first century, not the Dark Ages. I bet he fucks his bitches up the arse." He chewed on his lip, annoyed with himself for resorting to childish name calling.

Jake laughed. "I can't figure out if you're jealous or just pissed off he didn't make more of an effort with you."

"Oh puh-leese!" Mari uttered a bark of mirthless humor, shaking his head. "He's a child! You really think I'm that incorrigible a tail chaser? I'm disappointed in you, Chivis."

"No, you're not. You're disappointed in him. Haven't you *ever* been in the closet, Mari?"

"Closets are for clothes," Mari told him, with a sniff. "I only go in mine if I need to pick a matching tie for my suit."

Jake smiled ruefully back at him. "It's not so easy for some of us. It's hard to be yourself when who you are means you're despised by the people around you."

Mari turned his head, meeting that soulful, dark-eyed gaze.

"Fuck 'em," he said with a casual disdain that didn't quite run to his core. "It doesn't matter what other people think. Letting them believe it does only reinforces stale, hidebound attitudes that should have sunk with the ark, Chivis. You have to be hard to change the way things are. Not just pretend to be. I know you think I'm a precious diva sometimes, but I'm made of granite."

Jake grinned. "You're not anyone's pansy, Mari. And yeah, I understand, hiding isn't the way to change people's perceptions. I'm just saying it takes some people longer to figure that out, and it's a lot easier to get to that place if you're not in constant fear and survival mode."

"Jake, I lived in a sixty-percent majority Muslim country until I was twelve years old," he said levelly. "I've seen survival mode and trust me, Hackney doesn't touch it."

His fingers twitched between Jake's as they walked and he smiled at the burst of warmth that brief contact sent through him.

Jake sighed and squeezed his hand, letting whatever point he was trying to make go. "Feel like finding some lunch? Then I'll ring Cordiline."

Mari withdrew his fingers and wondered at himself that the merest mention of the DI's name cooled all the warmth out of his body. Was he really so jealous of the man? Jake had already said that he wasn't interested, but the guy was like a terrier. He was always sniffing around. And he was a cop, which gave Jake something in common with him.

"Yes, to the former. Absolutely," he said, bestowing his most beaming smile on his mate. "I am ravenous."

Chapter Seven

The scent of spicy chilies, curry, tamarind and turmeric had Jake's mouth watering as the server set their plates in front of them. He'd ordered the Tandoori chicken and Mari got a delicious smelling Tamil dish. Neither of them had eaten much since yesterday afternoon, and for several minutes they both focused on feeding their hungry bellies.

"This is divine." Mari juggled a sambhar-dipped crayfish segment into his mouth, munching happily.

"Mm," Jake agreed, still busy with a tender, juicy piece of perfectly seasoned meat. When the gnawing in his gut let up enough for him to do more than grunt between mouthfuls he slowed down, watching the way Mari tucked the food into his mouth and licked his lips.

"We never did get around to opening your presents," he said.

Mari stirred the spicy sauce on his seafood platter with his chopsticks and put the tips in his mouth, sucking them lightly. "No. I suppose we should do that sometime soon."

Jake grinned and took a bite of his own food. "We've got plenty of time, and this is really good."

Mari pinched a piece of chicken from the edge of his plate in the tips of his chopsticks and popped it into his mouth.

"Mmm, exceedingly good." His suggestive tone rather implied he'd prefer to have parts of Jake in his mouth.

There were two guys at the adjacent table, who Jake had pegged as business associates, and one of the men was giving them an odd look. Not unfriendly, but curious. Mari blew him a kiss and the guy quickly pretended he hadn't been staring.

Jake stifled a chuckle. He knew how the guy felt. There was just something about Mari that grabbed attention.

"We should plan a night out again."

"Hopefully we won't set the place alight this time," Mari told him, bringing to mind what had happened the last time they'd gone out on a date.

"Yeah, I was hoping we could avoid that too." Jake chuckled. "The Vault is doing their official grand re-opening this weekend, I thought you might like to give it another try."

"That would be cool. I enjoyed myself last time, at least I did until the place went up in smoke," Mari agreed. "They were a good crowd as well. Very friendly."

He popped a small, spicy shrimp in his mouth and made a great show of savoring it, complete with satisfied noises that did uncomfortable things to Jake's groin.

"Manny says they are going to be doing some, ah, activities downstairs. They've redesigned it with more sections. I'm sure what's-his-face will be there."

One of Mari's tawny eyebrows tilted upward. "You mean Colm, of course? Are you sure that you even want to be in the same building? Last time you two were in a room together things got ugly."

"That was because he was being an asshole, and he knows it. He's apologized." Jake watched Mari's eyebrows climb higher and wondered if he could get them all the way to his hairline.

"When was this? You didn't say anything."

"It was only a couple of days ago." Jake shrugged. "He said, if he'd realized how 'territorial' I was, he wouldn't have put the moves on you so heavy. I told him, if he ever laid a hand on you again, I'd put him in the hospital. We came to an agreement." He took a bite of chicken.

The guy on the table opposite was looking at them both with some astonishment as well. Mari made a soothing gesture with one hand.

"You are such a smooth operator, Chivis," he said. "I'm glad to hear that no bones got broken this time around, at least."

"Uh-huh, well, he's still a pusher. He said as a peace offering he'd let me strap him into his cross and give him a thrashing, if I wanted. I think he's just angling for a spanking session."

Mari shifted in his seat, distracted from his food, which was something that practically never happened.

"What are you trying to do to me, Chivis?" he murmured, leaning forward, his gaze half shuttered by long, golden lashes. "When we first met, I practically had to grab you by the chin to make you talk to me and now—"

Jake cast a look around the restaurant, where the majority of lunchtime clients were still filling their faces, blissfully unaware of their private game. The solitary diner at the opposite table was looking back at them, but blushed and lowered his eyes to his plate when he caught Jake's eye. The two guys adjacent to them were leaning forward too, engaged in a hushed war of words. Mari smiled when Jake turned back to face him.

"I'd think it would be obvious what I'm trying to do to you." Jake grinned at him. "But you don't blush easily, so I have to up my game."

"You are a wicked man. If I'd realized that seeing me flustered and helpless got you so hard, I'd have invested in a crinoline and a fan a long time ago." Mari snickered. "Seriously though, not many men get through my firewall, Chivis. And you were such an ingénue when we first met. Or was that all an act as well?"

His expression sobered, growing more curious.

Jake looked down at his plate and contemplated what was left of his meal as he thought about how to answer. "No, not an act, more like…conditioning. Survival."

He glanced up and saw that it clicked for Mari, that when he'd been talking about the hostile youth earlier, he was talking not just about Cameron, but himself.

Mari hesitated, then put down his chopsticks and reached over, laying his right hand over Jake's unoccupied left. There was a brief flicker of sadness in his gaze, there for a moment then gone, replaced by something more tender.

"You were ashamed of what you felt?" He said it carefully, and Jake wondered if he was trying not to instigate an argument when things had been going so well between them. "Ashamed of me? You don't need to lie, Chivis. I can tell there's some truth in that. I'm not angry. Not in the way that you might think, anyhow."

Jake held his gaze. "No, not ashamed, not of you. I wished I could be more like you. It wasn't shame. I never bought into that religious bullshit. But, I was...afraid." That was harder to admit than Jake had thought it would be, and once he'd said it he realized it was true. The way he'd tried to keep his private life and his sexuality separate for most of his twenty-nine years was very much about fear.

Mari squeezed his hand tighter. Dismay widened his eyes and softened the cynical line of his kissable mouth.

"My sweet Jake! I am so very glad that you are not more like me. I don't even think that I could feel the way that I feel about you, if you were. You were so strong, so stoical. What on earth were you afraid of? You'd cut your ties. You were free. Maybe for the first time ever. What did you have to lose by being yourself?"

"Nothing. It just took my brain a while to catch up to that fact. It's not just about being gay, although that was a large part of it. It's a cultural thing too. Strength and stoicism are admired in our culture. Any sign of weakness is looked down on. Showing affection openly for anyone other than your mother or grandmother, even toward the opposite gender is—it's like blood in the water. You learn quick to bury all of that shit deep."

Mari chewed on his lips, his expression intent. He was very still for a moment after this admission had been made, the warmth of his hand on Jake's the only sense that he still lived and breathed, and cared.

"You were like a wolf, raised in a cage," Mari said at last, his voice soft and raw with emotion. "Learning all of your life to be dependent on creatures who were not like you. To obey their ways and hide what you were, a wild, proud, beautiful creation. And when you got the chance to come here, it was like someone opened that cage. Suddenly you were free. Only you didn't have any idea what to do with that freedom, did you, my handsome wolf?"

Mari leaned across their table, clearly unfazed by the proximity of so many other diners around them. He cupped Jake's face in both hands and kissed him full on the mouth.

Jake didn't pull away. It didn't even cross his mind to pull away. Maybe he might have with someone else, with anyone else, but not with Mari. He kissed him back, sliding his own hand up to touch Mari's face as well. The wolf in the cage analogy was perhaps a shade melodramatic, but it wasn't really wrong. It was pretty much exactly what had happened, and he was more grateful than he had words to express that Mari understood that.

For a short time, as they kissed, it was like the rest of the world slipped away from them, leaving them in a vacuum where they were the only creatures in existence. When they broke that kiss, at the same moment, the world came slamming back, too loud and too bright. Most of the diners were pretending not to notice, but a few stared openly. The casually dressed man at the closest table who, with his friend, had been most distracted by their conversation earlier, surprised

Jake by rising to his feet and applauding. He smiled at Jake and winked as if they shared a secret.

A few other diners joined the ripple of applause and murmured, "Awwww"s, before the room settled back down again to its former bustling rhythm.

Mari arranged his chopsticks on his nearly empty bowl in a St. Andrew's Cross formation and murmured, "I think this is the point where you throw me over your shoulder and drag me back to your lair, Mr. Wolf."

"That sounds like an excellent idea," Jake agreed with a laugh.

On the way to his apartment, they stopped in at the police station to leave the memory stick for Cordiline. Jake waited until they were back outside his block before he tugged Mari closer and hoisted him in a fireman's lift, ignoring Mari's laughter and protests as he carried him into the building and up the stairs.

Chapter Eight

Jake muffled Mari's bubble of laughter with a kiss as he set him back on his feet just past the threshold of his apartment. He slid his hands up Mari's thighs and hips, over the swell of his buttocks and halfway up his back.

Considering that he'd been awoken early on the previous day with the news of death, only to be confronted with more death that same evening, it seemed remarkably easy for Mari to take his mind off those things. It wasn't that he didn't care, but if nothing else, being a cop had taught Jake how to compartmentalize so he was able to still function under pressure. Right now, he was functioning very well, he decided.

Mari broke the kiss and Jake gripped his upper arms tight and nudged him toward the sofa, tumbling him down and settling one leg between his.

Mari made a small sound and lifted his hips, grinding up against his thigh.

"That feels good," he growled, as Jake kissed down the side of his neck.

Jake nipped the base of his throat where the skin was tender, then kissed and sucked the spot gently. "I wonder what your new boss will say if I send you into work tomorrow with a few love bites."

"She'll say I'm one lucky bastard," Mari responded with a hiccup of laughter. "Ghislaine is fairly cool with personal stuff. I like her. Makes a change from Karden, anyway."

"I thought you were working with Darren," Jake murmured into his ear.

"I was, at first, but a job came up in another unit that needed his expertise, so they've started me with Ghislaine Macq. She's worked with Elementals before." Mari ran his hands slowly down Jake's back to the waistband of his pants and carried on, sliding them under his belt and into his boxer briefs. He squeezed his ass. "You've lost weight, Chivis. Need to get you back in the gym."

"I haven't dropped that much. Have I?" Jake asked, bemused by the observation.

He'd slacked off on his gym routine while he'd been off work. He supposed after the Birthright business, being kidnapped by a bunch of wingnuts who wanted to experiment on him, he should feel more traumatized. The truth was he could have gone back to work right after the doctors released him, but with Mari between jobs he'd taken the opportunity to be a bit lazy.

"You've not lost *too* much but your pants are looser than normal," Mari observed, still kneading his glutes. "I think you're pining for Damien and the post room boys."

Jake snorted. "I am definitely not pining for Damien Nolan. That fucker would do well just to stay out of my way." He punctuated this statement with a kiss and when Mari responded with lips *and* tongue, Jake ground his hips against him. Mari was breathing considerably harder when they broke off again, and Jake flashed a smile at him. "So, do you want to go into the bedroom, or do you want me to try out that new paddle on you here?"

"Hmm, if you take me to the bedroom you can strap me up in that nice set of cuffs you bought as well," Mari said, rolling his eyes upward as he pretended to think about the proposal. When his gaze returned to Jake's face there was a definite glint of mischief there.

Now there was a tempting mental picture. The thickening bulge pressing against his thigh told him just how excited that idea got Mari too. He knelt back and pulled Mari up by the hand, then led the way into his tiny bedroom, scooping the black bag full of new toys up on his way.

He dumped the contents on the bed so he could sort things out. Mari picked up the vibrating cock ring while Jake worked out what to do with the buckles on the restraints.

"The guy at the store was nice enough to throw that in," he told Mari with a smirk.

"Of course he was. Darling!" Mari chuckled. "Was that for me or for you, do you think?"

He pushed the first two fingers of his left hand through it and turned it around, setting off the inbuilt vibrator motor.

"Oh, I think that's definitely going on you." Jake winked at him. "*After* I get you tied up and helpless."

He didn't need a verbal response to that suggestion because the filling of Mari's pants crotch told him everything he needed. Those big blue eyes widened and Mari caught his breath in a rush.

Jake held out one of the long leather sheaths invitingly. Mari stopped playing with the cock ring and stripped out of his shirt before sliding his arm in, and Jake laced it up. He did the same with the other but didn't move to hook them together just yet.

"How's that feel?"

"Amazing," Mari crooned, playing with the buckles and straps, testing their resilience. "They're so supple. But really strong too. Fasten my arms behind me, Jake. I want to feel the pull. Make me feel helpless."

Jake's stomach fluttered at those words, and it wasn't entirely desire. He knew Mari wanted this, but the level of trust Mari put in him was almost as unsettling as the thought of trading places with him. He turned Mari around and rested both hands on his shoulders, kissing the back of his neck as he slowly stroked his hands down Mari's arms and took hold of his bony wrists, pulling them behind him. There were clips at the wrists, running up the forearms, and at the elbows. He hooked up the first set, then the next. If he did them all up Mari would have his arms pulled back like wings.

"Too tight?" he asked, kissing just below Mari's ear.

"No," Mari answered in a husky voice. "That's okay. A little higher, Jake."

He turned his head to rub his cheek against Jake's face.

Jake clipped the next set and the last ones that brought his elbows right together. He kissed Mari's temple, his cheek, the corner of his mouth.

"I thought that would look uncomfortable, and it kinda does, but it also looks very sexy," he murmured. He brought his hands around to caress Mari's chest and down his tight abs and popped the button on his trousers, cupping his hand over the solid bulge straining Mari's zipper.

"It's not uncomfortable," Mari whispered, his lips moving feather-light against Jake's. His ashen hair brushed like coconut-scented silk on Jake's cheek and forehead. Mari rolled his hips, thrusting that hot hardness against Jake's stroking hand. "Mmmhhh, that's so good."

Jake slid his zipper down and pushed his hand inside, pressing his palm flat at first, then curling his fingers around, gripping him over his underwear, stroking him slowly. Mari inhaled a long breath and Jake could feel a fine tremor running through him. Oh yeah, that was working for him.

He turned Mari back around to face him and pulled his trousers down, dropping in front of him as he did so to kiss and nuzzle his belly, lipping his skin and breathing in his scent, clean and spiced with arousal. He loved the way Mari smelled, a mixture of almond soap and sea air. Jake couldn't resist a taste, licking up his shaft and sucking the head into his mouth.

Mari pulled in a harder gasp and tilted his head back, his pants and briefs around his hard-muscled thighs, shoulders pulled back by the restraints. He looked so beautiful like that, all sleek skin and sculpted muscles, like a renaissance sculpture. The way Mari's breath hitched and the soft, barely heard sounds he made turned Jake on like crazy. He slid his lips down on Mari's dick, taking him deep and sucking hard, but only a few times. Jake pulled off him and let Mari's cock spring back to hit his belly with a wet slap.

"You are fucking delicious," Jake told him, licking his lips. He tugged the rest of Mari's clothing free and gave him a nudge to sit down on the bed. Then he shed his own shirt and pants. He could tell already that this was not going to be a marathon kind of night. Mari's eyes actually looked glassy, even without the brandy he'd wanted earlier. For the time being, Jake didn't bother with the paddle or the other restraints. Instead he stretched the band of the cock ring around Mari's straining dick, settling the vibrating part right under his glans.

"That's gonna to get your motor going." Jake chuckled.

"You are a very bad man, Chivis," Mari panted, his voice and body trembling with need. "As if my motor wasn't running already. Oh my, that's, uhhh! Were there ankle cuffs?"

His eyes were a luminous cobalt, huge and glazed with need, gazing through the tumble of his pale forelock. Muscles twitched in his lean thighs and his sleek, flat belly as he struggled to control himself.

Jake was already enjoying this far more than he'd anticipated and all the awkwardness of having to deal with the clerk at the sex shop seemed worth it now. He pulled over the cuffs for Mari's ankles and put them on him, but he didn't spread him and attach them to the bed. Rather, he bent Mari's knee up behind him and attached the ankle binding to Mari's thigh, creating a modified hogtie.

Mari flexed his leg muscles against the supple leather but it held him nicely. His lips parted around a breathless smile and he gasped. "I've not been tied up this tightly for a long time. It feels amazing. Oh, my stars, I'm so hard, Jake. Please!"

Jake pushed his thighs further apart, lowering himself between them. Mari wasn't the only one hard and needy. He placed a line of kisses down the underside of Mari's shaft, whisper-soft, and licked around each of his balls.

"Please what?"

"Uuhhhhhhh!" Mari groaned deep in his throat, writhing and pulling on his bonds. "Don't tease me. Jake, please spank me. Spank me and finger me. I am sooooooo fucking horny!"

Jake thought about ignoring that plea — there was an imp in him that wanted to tease until Mari was out of his head — but he could tell that no matter what he did it wasn't going to take long for Mari to come, and Jake wanted to give him his heart's dark desire.

With a deft movement, he flipped Mari forward, onto his knees, shoulders down on the mattress and that adorable ass up in the air. Jake caressed him, warming up his skin before he tested out their new toy. He slapped Mari's ass with one hand before picking up the paddle and giving him a harder swat that sounded quite loud in the small room.

Mari uttered a sharp yip as the leather cracked down across one cheek. He moaned sweetly, but didn't tell Jake to stop, still wriggling and panting. His perky bottom swayed from side to side as he lifted it higher, offering himself, eager for more.

Jake trailed his fingers down Mari's back and over the crack of his ass, making him wait for it. He'd bought the bondage gear because he knew Mari would like it. He hadn't thought about how fucking hot Mari would look all trussed up in it, on his bed. He only took a moment or two to appreciate it, though, then gave him another slap, loving the breathless sound it coaxed from Mari's throat. That was a noise that would never fail to make his dick harder. Jake lifted the paddle and dropped another fast, light stroke across Mari's blushing cheeks, settling into a steady rhythm, increasing the force behind each swat as Mari's moans grew louder.

He was already turning quite a nice shade of rosy pink when Jake drizzled a trail of lube between his cheeks and pressed down on his tight pucker with a fingertip. This much Mari could take without a struggle. They had experimented with lots of different objects in the last few weeks. Mari owned a slim, curved glass dildo, which he sometimes used on himself in the bath tub. Jake knew that so long as he got Mari really turned on first, used plenty of lube and didn't rush things, he could get a finger, or a small vibrator, inside him.

"Ohhh, mmhhhh, yes. Punish me, Jake. I've been so bad," Mari crooned, turning his head so that he could look back at his lover, evidently wondering why the paddling had stopped. If Mari Gale's MI5 colleagues could only see their clean cut, sartorially elegant new boy, sprawled on his shoulders and knees, feet in the air, buttocks raised invitingly, it would bring some heat to their cheeks too. Mari was gasping harder again at the pressure on his clenching ring, nudging back on Jake's probing finger, trying to mount it in his enthusiasm.

Jake let him hump and twitch and push back, then sank it into him, feeling his muscles squeeze down hard, impossibly tight. This would be the point, had Jake been with any of his previous lovers, where he took things to the next base. He wanted to move on with Mari as well, but he didn't dare risk a failure when Mari was so desperately in need of reassurance and relief. He eased his finger in and out for a few moments, then withdrew and lifted the strap again, laying further vigorous slaps across his buttocks.

His sexy lover cried out, hoarse and breathless, and Jake eased up on him at once, still worried about hurting him. They had a safe word for these games but he still didn't quite trust Mari to use it.

Mari whined, a small, urgent sound. "Don't stop. So close. Ohh fuck. Fuck. Jake—please!"

A huff of laughter escaped Jake and he brought the strap down again with a fierce thwack that virtually had Mari in convulsions. Jake squirted some more lube down between those pink, glistening cheeks and pressed his slippery middle finger back in, working it with more vigor in his lover's hot little asshole.

Mari cried his name, gulping air between each yelp, over and over like a mantra as he struggled and wormed around on the bed. His body jolted with each touch on his prostate as Jake fingered him harder. He did not beg him to stop, though, and Jake decided to take the plunge. Drawing almost all the way out of him, he applied a second digit and oh so slowly pressed his first and second fingers into Mari's thrashing body, taking his time, letting Mari tell him if it was too much.

Mari quivered like a plucked harp string but he didn't fight it, tight as he was. A small, horny growl rose up in his chest as he went still, eyes closed, breathing hard through his nostrils, taking it determinedly.

Jake reached under him, rolled off the cock ring and curled his hand around Mari's shaft, stroking him quick and hard.

A small, quavering sound escaped Mari's throat and his cock lurched in the curl of Jake's rapidly pumping fingers. Mari's whole body tightened up for a second, then bucked in the confines of his bonds, as he came hard and for once, almost in silence, bar the huffing of his frantic breath.

"Ohhh, Jake," Mari exhaled at last in a tiny whimper, his body falling still. Even the grip around Jake's thrusting fingers was suddenly much less. Jake flexed the two digits inside him, recovering the sensation in them, able to feel the slippery warmth of Mari's sexy ass around them once again.

He was pliant enough that Jake considered fucking him. His cock was telling him it would be fine, if he moved fast enough he'd slip right in before Mari even realized it wasn't his fingers inside him. Of course, Jake knew better. Mari would feel the change, and he would get upset and angry if he couldn't do it. Instead he leaned over him and kissed the spot at the base of his tailbone, laving the dimple, about an inch above his glistening ring, with his tongue. He kissed his way slowly up over Mari's bound arms, arching over him as he continued to caress him inside.

"Mari," Jake whispered in his ear, his front fitted along the slope of Mari's slender back. He pulled his fingers out and his cock nudged Mari, between his cheeks.

"Don't stop. Feels too good." Mari groaned. His slender arms and legs flexed against the leather sheaths and strapping.

There was ample lube, Jake was hard as a rock and Mari as relaxed as he ever got. All the elements were combined in just the right way for Jake to slide into him with his next gentle nudge. It was so smoothly done it took Jake a second to realize he was in, then the sensation of having the head of his cock squeezed tight was enough to make him shiver and groan as he pushed himself deeper.

"Ohhhh, fuck, Mari!" He kissed his nape and his shoulder, one hand braced on the bed and the other on Mari's hip as he rocked in short thrusts, barely moving within that ultra-tight grip.

Under him, Mari moaned harder and uttered a soft chittering noise that could have been a Finnish epithet or just the sound of a man coming apart at the seams, unravelling slowly as he let himself be invaded. He pushed his hips back in response, trying to get down deeper on the shaft of Jake's dick. Jake let him wiggle and squirm but kept to a smooth, steady glide, sinking into him, one centimeter at a time, until he was all the way inside.

It felt amazing and it was sheer willpower alone that let Jake keep his head and not rush. The tingling in his balls begged for something faster and harder but Jake took his time. He slid his left hand down Mari's thigh and flicked the clasp that was keeping his ankle fastened a couple of inches below the curve of his rose-striped cheek, releasing his foot. Then he reached with the other to undo Mari's right ankle as well, giving him more freedom to move those long legs.

Mari unbent his knees but otherwise didn't shift. Jake figured he would tell him if things got to be too much, and stopped worrying. He didn't have any room left in his head to worry anyway. It felt too good and he'd wanted this too long. Mari shuddered under him. His breath became ragged when Jake started to move.

"God, that's amazing," Jake exhaled, gripping Mari's hips and drilling him faster.

"Mmmhhhh," Mari whimpered again, just a tiny, fragile sound. He buried his face in the bedclothes and bumped his forehead against the mattress, once or twice, knees spread, braced hard against the quickening thrusts. Jake heard his name, spoken in that same frail, breathless note. Mari's body flexed around his cock like a fist clenching, then released, then gripped hard again.

The feel of those inner muscles enfolding him so tight was enough to tip an already over-primed pump. He slid his hands up under Mari's heaving chest, pulling him closer as that wonderful pulsing spiral of pleasure towed him under and made him burst. That was way quicker than he was used to, but he chalked it up to months and months of foreplay.

He avoided pressing Mari flat into the mattress by rolling over to one side with him, still holding on as if he wasn't sure he'd ever be able to let go.

"I can't feel my hands," Mari whispered, when he had stopped huffing like the world's smallest steam train and was just nestling against him in the curl of his slightly larger body.

Jake reached between them, slipping out of him as he moved, and quickly undid the clips holding Mari's arms back. To his relief, they were really easy to get undone, just a push and a tug and Mari was almost freed. He untied the laces holding the bracers on as well, letting Mari roll onto his back so that he could tug them off. Jake felt cold without Mari pressed up against him, wrapped around his cock.

"Sorry, is that better?" Jake wanted to rub Mari's arms between his hands to help massage the circulation back but he wasn't sure if Mari would appreciate that so he contented himself with just pulling him close again.

A little nod was the only response at first, then Mari twisted around in his embrace to deliver a quick, soft, shy kiss. His cheeks were flushed and his eyes too bright.

"Wow," he exhaled softly. "Just, wow."

Jake could feel the grin tugging his lips and tried hard not to look too smug. He tipped his head so their foreheads touched.

"I love you, Mari. That was amazing."

"I hope I didn't hurt you," Mari said. He glanced down as if he expected to see gore and looked relieved when there was not a spot of blood in sight. "I can't quite believe that happened. Oh my goodness."

Jake laughed, he couldn't help it. He just had such an adorable look of relief and awe on his face. "No, you didn't hurt me. I was more worried I was hurting you, and I promise you, if we ever get to do that again, it won't be so quick. Unless you don't want to do it again."

Mari shook his head and reached up to touch his cheek. There was sudden tenderness and worry in his eyes. Jake felt his heart quicken. It had been amazing, that was not a lie. He wasn't sure how he would feel if Mari said he never wanted to try it again. Then he felt like a total jerk after everything he had promised Mari before, about it not mattering whether he got to fuck him in the ass or not. He would love Mari and care about him no matter what he decided.

"I do. I totally do want to do it again. But yeah, I feel sore. It's…it's been a long time," he said, still sounding apologetic. Jake's heart sang with hope though.

"Maybe quick is good. I'm happy that I could do it for you."

Jake covered Mari's hand with his own and drew it down to kiss his fingertips. He was trying hard not to read between the lines but he couldn't help the feeling that Mari was happier about achieving his goal than he was from any real enjoyment of the act.

"We will definitely take it easy on your backside for a few days," he agreed, kissing him again tenderly.

"My backside, although grateful, is glad to hear it." Mari chuckled then, and some of the tension left his features. He slid his arms around Jake's neck and rested his head on his chest, beneath his chin, cuddling up. His breathing slowed and Jake could feel the stillness that overtook him as they held one another in the warm afterglow. He pulled Mari closer and tried not to think so much.

Chapter Nine

Sunday morning, they slept in hours past their usual time. Hunger drove Jake out of bed and he threw on some sweats and went to make breakfast. Mari followed him out, donning Jake's discarded shirt from the back of a chair and settling on the sofa with his laptop. While Jake cracked eggs and got bacon sizzling, he kept glancing over at Mari, enjoying the sight of him, long and lean and barely dressed. The phone rang and Jake snared it, a spatula still in his other hand.

"'lo?"

"Chivis, I didn't wake you, did I?" John Cordiline asked him.

"Not that it would have stopped you anyway, but no, I'm up. Do you have news already?" Jake asked.

"The IT team have been taking a look at your dirty film," the detective told him cheerfully. "That was a nice one for a Saturday night, thanks for that."

"Sorry to be the bearer of bad news."

"The guys in the web-crimes team reckon you've hit gold. It's the real deal, unfortunately."

"I thought you might come up with that." Jake glanced over at Mari, then back down at what he was doing. He poked at some bacon with his spatula. "Seeing as how he's not just missing, but you have video evidence of his murder, is it a safe bet you'll be moving this one up to the top of your priority list?"

Cordiline chuckled without humor. "Do you have any idea how much I already have on my plate?"

"Considering the sheer amount of people crammed into this city I have a pretty good guess. C'mon, John, this guy is a sick fucker. Can't you pull some strings and get the case moved up?"

Another glance toward the couch showed Mari had one hand over his mouth and was watching keenly, his laptop forgotten as he listened to the exchange, his mind no doubt filling in the missing comments from Jake's reaction.

"Have you got any idea how many of these bastards there are out there getting up to this sort of bullshit?" Cordiline asked in a grim tone. "We'll move it up but the more information we have the better chance there will be of catching the buggers that filmed it."

Mari mouthed, "Tell him about Cameron."

"The vic's name was Wade," Jake said, and gave him the address of the apartment they had visited. "He had a record. He was in lockup at The Scrubs with someone named Clifford. Dunno if that's a first name or surname. You might wanna question this Clifford guy about any connection he has to the case."

There was a long silence on the other end of the phone before Cordiline said, "And just how do you know that?"

Jake chuckled. "Magical divination? How do you think? Just look him up. Could be a dead end but it's all I've got for you."

"I'll run him through the system, Chivis. See what bites." Cordiline sighed. "Do I want to hear about why the fuck your crazy boyfriend was looking up snuff porn? Should I be worried about you?"

Jake glanced over at Mari and smiled. "That's a good question, I'll be sure to ask him. Thanks, John, let me know if you dig anything up."

"Was that a joke, Jake? Given the circumstances that's most likely how he'll turn up, poor sod. Do us a favor, don't download any more of this shit."

"I'm not planning on it," Jake said.

After they disconnected Mari asked him, "Why didn't you tell him about Cameron?"

"Because if I had he'd just go around there to ask the same questions we did and it would be a waste of everyone's time. He barely talked to us, he's definitely not going to talk to a cop. Besides, I told him the most important part of what Cameron told us."

That seemed to mollify Mari, at least for the time being.

"It was real then?" Mari asked.

Jake knew he already knew the answer to that, but he seemed to need a solid confirmation. "Yes. It seems that way."

Chapter Ten

After eating breakfast with Jake, Mari went home to make lunch for Mama and catch up on laundry. He made a mess of pressing two shirts, until Anni shooed him out of the kitchen and did it for him. Chastised, he retreated upstairs, where he took a shower then went to his room to check email and do some work on a program he was writing to defend against potential attacks on his operating system by similarly gifted interfaces.

With the important jobs done, he took his laptop and lay on the bed, just surfing in the ordinary way. He skimmed who was hot and who was hotter in the current media, then expanded, chasing links and hopping from site to site. He was still pleasantly sore from Jake's attention last night and it didn't take much to distract him from his laptop. His buttocks were striped with heat still. Even a long shower and the application of copious amounts of cooling moisturizer hadn't taken much of the sting out. It was a glorious reminder of the fun they'd had with the straps and the flexible leather paddle, and he moved a pillow under his backside to cushion it.

The more unusual sensation was the open feeling of his ring. Even after several hours, his backside still felt stretched. It wasn't sore, or at least, not in an unpleasant way. Jake had been thorough but very gentle and he was not in pain, much to his amazement. Mari unfastened his pants and carried out a careful exploration, with his fingers at first, nudging the middle one into the wider-than-usual dimple between his cheeks and touching himself there. He still felt wet from the shower. The moisture helped him to slip the searching digit inside and touch himself deeper. Tingles of pleasure that raced straight to his balls conjured a breathless sigh from his lips and he withdrew the finger with some reluctance and sat up to wriggle out of his pants, then crossed the room to lock the bedroom door.

Back on the bed, he stripped out of his sweater and retrieved the bottle of lube from his drawer, using it to slick up his sensitive ring before he grabbed his slim glass dildo. The glass was cool and soothing on his skin as he lay back and slowly pushed it inside, but it warmed up soon enough once he had it buried in him.

He felt guilty doing this when he already had the sexiest guy in London in his bed on a regular basis, but even Jake had gently observed that he had a very high sex drive for a man who struggled to get laid. Jake had made him feel so alive last night that he just wanted that fizzy feeling to go on and on. A part of him thought that he must have dreamed it. He'd been so sure that they would never make love that way, but Jake was his magician. He had a way of making things happen and Mari loved that.

Closing his eyes, he concentrated on recalling how Jake's cock had felt, pressing deeper and deeper into him, rubbing and nudging against the bundle of sensitive nerves behind his balls, as they'd fucked last night. It was impossible to recapture the sensation perfectly, but he gave it his best shot. Thinking of the pull of the cuffs on his wrists and ankles upped the tremulous excitement to another level, even if it wasn't as arousing as actually being bound and helpless. Tied, he couldn't do this to himself though, so he had to concentrate on remembering the caress of Jake's fingers and lips and rub of his gorgeous cock.

He glided his fingers and thumb up and down the length of his hard shaft, nudging the toy with the other hand, just pressing it deep then letting his muscles push it back out, over and over. His jacking fingers quickened until he was moving them in short, staccato strokes on his cock, feeling it respond to the sweet friction and the weight of the dildo on his prostate. Mari kept up the stimulus until he began to shoot, with a strangled cry of relief that he drowned in the pillow, turning his head and burying his face in the soft linen until his heart slowed and his body stopped shaking.

Once he had enjoyed the languid feeling of coming down from the explosion, he cleaned up with some wipes and sprawled on the bed again, retrieving his laptop. A tiny kernel of guilt niggled at him as he touched his fingers to the screen. Still, with no hesitation, he went sliding back through the system the way he had gone the other morning to track a route to Wade's flat.

He found the ISP easily enough, but the video was gone. It had been taken down. Which meant either the poster was still out there, moving his sordid clips from page to page so that they couldn't readily be found by the authorities, or he'd panicked and erased his web presence. That would be a nuisance. By the time the poster re-emerged from hiding, the film-makers could have killed any number of people.

Mari backtracked, exploring different routes into the same server, but still found no trace of the video. He then pulled back further, following the ISP route he'd tracked to the flat in Hackney. If he could not find uploaded content, he reasoned, he would go back to looking for the uploader himself. If he was posting videos fresh from the homes of the men he killed, that meant he had no single location to trace. But Mari was running his metaphorical fingers over a spiderweb of data rather than individual ISPs. He didn't need to find out where the poster lived or even where he was filming. He could use the information left behind each time the bastard posted something to follow him around the internet.

You promised you wouldn't do this, his conscience reminded him, in his great-grandmother's clipped tones.

No. I promised I wouldn't look for snuff films, he corrected it sternly. *I'm not looking for snuff films. I'm looking for the filthy pig that made them.*

His trails kept running cold though. At last, he pulled out of the web and resorted to a more mundane method, typing in the search criteria he had used the night before when he found the video. After approximately three quarters of an hour spent following irrelevant links, he hit gold again.

The clip was not the same one, but the guy in the mask sitting talking to the young redheaded man on the bed was the same as in Wade's final fling. As he watched it, he noticed what Cameron had seen, but he had not really paid attention to when he first saw Wade's movie. The killer had a small, square tattoo on his right biceps. He blew it up on the screen to reveal a pattern that looked like a SIM card, with rounded edges and one corner missing. He took a screenshot.

Could be useful.

The movie followed a similar pattern, with the lad joking nervously with his killers as he was tied up tight on the bed and the masked man gripped a double handful of his shaggy hair, using it to pull himself into the boy's mouth where he began performing oral sex. The cameraman, who had a light, almost adolescent-sounding voice, exhorted him to make the redhead gag, telling him it looked good.

Mari's stomach churned.

He paused the playback and touched screen again, pushing his mind deep into the web, sliding back down the trail of data from the video back toward its source. The trail took longer to follow this time and, by the point where he had a fix on the sender's ISP, Mari was beginning to feel faint. He kept on it until he was sure of the location though, then pulled out wearily, copying the web address and pasting it into another, offline document so that he had a record of it this time.

Then he lay on the bed for a while. The imp of the perverse that lived in his skull was urging him to find out if the redhead had met the same fate, but Mari had no desire to know. He just wanted to discover where the killer was. And he had that information. St. Albans was a long way from Hackney though, socially *and* geographically.

You need to tell Jake about this, his inner detective counseled.

That was not a conversation that he was relishing.

* * * *

Just after seven p.m., Jake's phone rang.

"Can I take you out to dinner to say thank you for last night?" Mari asked him when he picked up.

"You don't need to thank me, but I'm not going to turn down dinner. I got busy after you left this morning and forgot about lunch so I'm starved. Do you want to come over or meet somewhere?" Jake asked.

"I can meet you at Leo's," Mari said. "Say, half an hour?"

Leo's was a small, friendly Mediterranean café close to Jake's apartment and they stopped there for coffee on a regular basis.

"I'll see you there." Jake said and disconnected.

Mari was already seated at the counter when he arrived, and looking rather delicious in a pair of pale blue slacks, a roll neck sweater and a darker jacket. His blond curls looked windblown and perfectly disheveled in a way that he was sure models spent hours trying to achieve. He was wearing his reading glasses, and when Jake got close enough to kiss his cheek he could see shadows under his eyes and a tightness around his mouth.

"How was your day?"

"Okay." Mari turned his head to deliver a rather chaste kiss in return. "I fail completely on the domestic front. Don't ever expect me to wash and iron for you. I fancy the rigatoni, nothing too heavy. I'll never sleep. What do you want?"

"I think I'll have the kofta pitas," Jake answered, sliding into the seat next to him. Even though the small talk was innocent enough, Jake saw through the veneer. Mari was twitchy and distracted. He looked drawn. The clipped, almost defensive sentences sounded at odds with the happy, sated mood he'd left in that morning. Jake fiddled with the silverware while they waited, twirling a spoon in his fingers. Nothing. No memory of a business lunch or date jumped out at him. It was weird.

Mari nodded toward his hands, his face half hidden behind the large glass of white wine cupped in his own long fingers. His next comment echoed Jake's thoughts.

"When I first met you, there was no way on earth you would have done that? Not without having nightmares about what you might see. We've eaten out twice in as many days and the first time you even suggested it." A faint smile curved his lips. "Is that something to do with the shots that Corrie gave you, do you think?"

Jake controlled the urge to frown, keeping his expression carefully blank. He didn't think the remark was meant to blindside him, but he knew Mari didn't like it when he sidestepped talking about his experience as an unwilling guinea pig for Roy Corrie. He supposed a shrink would read something into that, but he just didn't see a need to obsess about something he had no control over. They'd given him the experimental drug against his will and he'd managed to live when others had died. He didn't know why. He was just thankful. Except for that one nagging thing that kept creeping up on him. He licked his lips, still uncertain.

"I don't know. The EQ10 serum was supposed to enhance ability." Jake cleared his throat. "I haven't picked up a single memory off of anything since that night, when I couldn't make them stop. Nothing."

Mari's eyes widened. "Did it burn you out, do you think? Have you told Weston?"

Professor Weston had been their handler when they'd both first come to London for the Six Elements Program. He had been testing their elemental abilities in his department at UCL ever since.

"I'm not sure, and no, I haven't," Jake said carefully. "If that is the case, I might very shortly be without a job, or a visa."

The look on his lover's pretty face said that wasn't a possibility he wanted to consider too closely. "They can't just kick you off the job, surely? You're doing important work with the security team, whether you can still get impressions or not. That's the official reason why you're here."

He seemed upset though, which was gratifying, if not exactly the reaction Jake wanted to provoke in him tonight.

"No, they probably won't can me, not right away. But you and I both know any actual work I do for the department isn't really important to them. They want me for the research, and if I can no longer 'perform', I'm no longer useful." Jake blew out a short breath and looked down at the spoon he was twiddling between his fingers. He set it down again and picked up the salt shaker, turning it slowly in his hand. "I used to wish I could do this, pick something up that hundreds of strangers had handled and not worry about what I might see. Now, well, you don't realize how much you rely on a sense until it's gone, do you."

"Perhaps the effect is only temporary. Give it time," Mari counseled. "But in the interim, it is rather lovely to be able to take you out like this and not worry about you freaking out over a spoon."

He slid his left hand under Jake's right and lifted it to his lips to kiss his fingers softly.

Jake smiled at him. He hadn't wanted to take the mood down to so somber a level, and hadn't intended to share his worry about not being able to use his psychometry anymore, at least not yet.

"I suppose it is better than being assaulted with other people's memories whenever I touch anything at all," Jake said. That would have been a far worse fate, had he remained stuck the way he had been on the night when Corrie had exposed him to the drug. Having to live like that would have made him into a recluse, if not driven him right out of his mind.

The waiter brought their food then and they both tucked in with ravenous appetites. Mari still seemed oddly quiet though. The absence of his usual torrent of words made Jake wary. Ever since Jake had met him, Mari had seemed to be incapable of saying nothing, so it was unsettling for him to be so reticent. He knew better than to try to pry it out of him, though. All he had to do was wait. Eventually Mari would tell him what was wrong.

Chapter Eleven

Neither of them felt like lingering over drinks when they'd finished with dinner, so they headed home soon after they were done eating. For all that he was quiet, Mari didn't seem to be reluctant when Jake put an arm around him, pulling him closer as they walked. He led them into the apartment and turned on the light.

His resolve to be patient ebbing, Jake finally asked, "So, what gives? You're awfully quiet tonight. Is everything okay?"

"I'm not sure," Mari responded, his lips practically touching Jake's as he gave his answer. "Something happened this afternoon, something that I feel bad about and I don't know how to start making it right."

Jake felt a weird swooping sensation in his middle as Mari spoke. He was not generally one to imagine the worst, which was an unusual trait for a cop, but those words put a chill in him.

Something happened. That was exactly how Alex had put it when he'd confessed to cheating. Maybe Mari didn't look so tired because he'd been taxing his ability after all.

"Well, how about you start by telling me what happened?" Jake said, containing the surge of sick dread as best he could.

Mari took hold of the front of his sweater and towed him to the sofa, making him sit down there. When Jake was seated, he knelt astride his thighs and sat in his lap, cupping his face in both hands and kissing him hard. Only when their lips parted from the kiss did he murmur, "Jake, I can't stop. I can't make myself stop once I have a phone or a keyboard in my hand. It's like a hunger, chewing away inside me. Like addiction."

He bent his head, looking thoroughly ashamed, resting his forehead to Jake's, his hands under Jake's warm jersey, touching his chest.

Jake let out a slow breath. Not what he'd been braced to hear, thankfully. How horrible did it make him, that he was giddy with relief to hear Mari wasn't fucking around with someone else, for even a few seconds, when Mari had just confessed to a far more serious problem? That he was even willing to admit to it — Jake wasn't sure if that was good or bad. It was an addiction, but it wasn't like any normal craving. He wasn't sure there was a treatment for it, especially considering it was part of Mari's job.

"I know, Ilmari," Jake said, keeping his voice quiet and steady, though it took a supreme effort. "I know. I've realized for a while that you can't stop. I didn't want to admit it any more than you." He brought his hand up to brush the fall of Mari's hair from his forehead. "I don't know how to help you. I had hoped just making you promise — but I guess that was pretty dumb."

Mari pushed his spectacles up into his hair and rubbed his eyes with his thumb and forefinger like they hurt. After seeing him so bright and positive this morning, it made Jake's chest ache to watch him come so low, but whatever he had been doing during the afternoon had sucked so much energy out of him that he seemed smaller for it.

"What happened?" he asked helplessly. "What did you find?"

"Wade wasn't the only one." Mari heaved a sigh. "This could be a production line. They post from different locations. Today's video wasn't even posted from London, but the guy in the mask was the same man, I'm pretty sure. I have a lock on the data trail they left behind but they're clever. I don't think they're posting the videos from their own address. This one doesn't match the first. They uploaded the new video onto a different site to Wade's film and from a different machine. The ISP for the new one was for an address in Hertfordshire. I think they're locating their victims online and the killers go to them. I could track back to the sender's machine and look through all his online messages but it would take time, even doing it my way. And I have a headache," he complained, pinching the bridge of his nose.

"Babe, I know you don't want to hear this but you can't save everyone. You just can't. You have to stop."

"I'll stop when they're behind bars," Mari said with a tired smile. "Have you got any aspirin?"

Jake dislodged him to get up and go into the small kitchen, where he retrieved a blister pack of tablets and a glass of water and brought them both back. He waited until Mari had swallowed.

"And what happens if they don't catch them? Are you just going to keep going until your brain fries and leaks out of your ears?"

"That isn't going to happen," Mari said stubbornly. He drained the glass and leaned forward, setting it on the floor at his feet. "And if it saves lives it's worth a few headaches. But if I don't keep tabs on them we'll never find out who they are. The police obviously can't be all that bothered, if you have to nag them to even look into it. What does it matter to them if a few queers get bumped off?"

He slumped back against the sofa cushions and shut his eyes, breathing slow and deep.

Jake crossed his arms on his chest and leaned back on the counter, watching him. He wondered, not for the first time, if trying to get him to see reason was utterly pointless.

"That's not how Cordiline is," Jake said. "He's gay, so he's hardly going to hold it against the victims. If he didn't think this was important he wouldn't have had that video analyzed as soon as I gave it to him. You need to let the police do their job, Mari."

Mari opened one eye and made a rude noise. "Jake! Don't be stupid. He's after you. That's the only reason he calls. He wants to fuck you. I bet no one on his unit would even guess he likes cock. This will get filed away and sod all will get done unless it winds up on the evening news."

Jake sighed. "It doesn't matter how many videos you come up with, Mari. Even if they are ninety-nine-point-nine percent sure they show a real death, they still need to find a body before it's officially a crime. Turning your brain into mush before they do that isn't going to help anyone."

"In that case, we need to find a body," Mari said in that infuriatingly practical way that made Jake want to shake him. "Preferably before they make any more. I didn't come here to argue with you about this. It would be good if you wanted to help, but if you don't I'll do it on my own."

He pushed himself forward with another sigh and levered himself to his feet unsteadily.

Jake ground his back teeth together, trying not to lose his temper, but it was already sparking. He hated when Mari did that.

"Don't fucking turn my words around like that. If I didn't care, if I didn't want to 'help', I wouldn't have turned the video over to Cordiline, I wouldn't have let you drag me across the city to interrogate some thug kid, and I wouldn't be trying to get you to see reason and slow your ass down before you get hurt."

"I think I'm the best judge of what hurts, Jake Chivis. I'm not a child. Stop treating me like I'm made of fucking glass. For crying out loud, I ask you for a pill and you go all Nurse Jackie on my fucking arse. Anyone would think I was asking you for help breaking into the Pentagon." Mari threw his hands up. "What the hell is it with you? I wish I'd not said anything."

"Right. You wished you'd not said anything so you can plug your head in whenever you want and not have anyone tell you you're being stupid and doing it too damn much. Look at yourself, Mari. You look like you're about ready to drop with exhaustion. You can't even wait one damn day for the police to get on it before you're right back in. You're not pissed off because you think I won't 'help' you. You're pissed off because you don't want to hear you're overdoing the interface shit and you just might need to put the pipe down for five minutes."

Mari's lips pressed into a thin line and his eyes narrowed. "Oh yes. Because the killers are going to take a day off while I get some sleep. I imagine they're very considerate like that. And if someone hadn't kept me up half the night I might not be quite so ready to drop. Nobody else can do this, Chivis."

"And yet, somehow, detectives manage to solve crimes without your help every day."

"Oh right, be sarcastic about it. You know damned well what I mean. Stop trying to twist things yourself, Mr. I've-been-there-and-done-it-all. If they can do it, why aren't they doing it?" He rubbed a hand across his face, turning away. "I can't do this tonight, Jake. Fuck it! I'm going home. I don't want to fight with you about this."

He grabbed his jacket from the back of the sofa.

Jake caught his arm before he even thought about it, not roughly, but enough to turn Mari to face him. "Mari, please, just listen to yourself. You have no idea what the police are or aren't doing, but you've convinced yourself they are doing nothing so you have an excuse to plug back in and go hunting. Nothing else seems to matter to you."

"If you really think that, you don't know the first thing about me," Mari said in as cold a voice as Jake had ever heard him use. "Just because I don't put myself first doesn't mean I don't care about anyone else. If I stay here, one of us is going to say something that we'll both wind up regretting. I don't want that to happen. This weekend has been" — he made an expansive gesture with both hands, his tone softening—"amazing, in a lot of ways. I really don't want it to end like this, Jake."

Jake let his arm go. "That's what you want? You don't hear what you want to hear, you don't get your way, so you call it quits?"

One tawny eyebrow tilted upward cynically. "Are you trying to tell me you get a kick out of fighting with me? Because I don't."

Mari wriggled one arm into his jacket and managed to dislodge his glasses from the top of his head in the process. He cursed under his breath, trying to catch them one handed and sending them skittering across the living area floor instead.

Jake retrieved them and handed them back, but didn't let them go when Mari took a hold. "I don't get a 'kick' out of fighting with you. You do whatever you want, you're going to anyway. But don't stand there and try to make out like I just want to fight and you're being the reasonable one."

"You're the one that's making me *have* to fight you just to see where the fuck I'm going." Mari flicked his wrist, trying to wrest the light-framed reading glasses from him. "And this morning I thought you liked the fact that I did what I wanted. Let go."

He aimed a slap at the back of Jake's hand with his free one and pulled again.

Jake let go. "Fine. Don't listen to anything I have to say. What do I know? The junkie always knows better."

Mari had just about repositioned his glasses on the bridge of his nose and he fired a look through the narrow, rectangular frames that could have iced the Thames over. Jake had good reflexes but even he didn't see the hand coming that smacked him sideways.

"What did you call me? What. The. Fuck. Did. You —?" Mari came after him and rained blows down furiously with each word. "Take that back!"

Jake brought his hands up to protect himself but didn't try and stop him. When he paused on his own he grabbed Mari's wrists lightning quick, forcing him back a step.

"Okay, that was an ugly name." Jake conceded. He met Mari's glare without flinching. "You're addicted, Mari, and I'm scared to death you're going to cook your mind or kill yourself."

Mari huffed, making determined efforts to get his hands free and looking like he could commit bloody murder himself at the moment. Jake saw a flicker of something else in his gaze though, briefly there then gone again — bewilderment, desperation and fear.

"Let me go," he said, the words more neutral than the wildness in his ocean-blue eyes. "Let go of me, Jake."

Slowly, feeling like he was letting go of far more than just his wrists, Jake released him. To his surprise and relief, Mari didn't try to hit him again. He wrestled the other sleeve of his jacket on and glared at him, eyes narrowed, as if he suspected Jake might fight him to the floor if he moved another muscle.

"I'm sorry," he said, at last, lowering his eyes. "I shouldn't have hit you. I'm sorry. I'm going to... I'm just going to go. Okay."

He inched toward the sofa again, one small step at a time.

Jake didn't stop him. He bit his tongue as Mari snatched up his messenger bag and was at the door in three longer strides.

"Mari."

His lover didn't pause or look back. He was out of the door and gone.

"God fucking damn it." Jake cursed after the door slammed shut. He ran a frustrated hand through his hair. He wanted to throw something, or kick something. The heat inside was rising along with his temper and he took a deep breath. He went into the bathroom and flicked the light. A glance in the mirror showed a big red mark on his cheek, nothing more serious, but Jake couldn't care less about that. He had a more pressing concern.

Opening the medicine cabinet, he took out a digital thermometer. He turned it on, stuck it under his tongue and in about ten seconds it beeped at him and he looked at the read out. 101.5 Fahrenheit. In the days that had followed being injected with the drug that Roy Corrie was sure would enhance elemental abilities, he had run a fever. The physicians monitoring him had gone from concern to alarm as his temperature had steadily crept up, rising until it peaked at 105. At that point they had figured he was in the most danger of bursting into flames, as Corrie's other guinea pigs had done. Instead the thermometer reading had slowly dropped down to normal. Checking it had become something of an obsession, and Jake had noticed a clear connection between his emotional state and the infrequent spikes in his body temperature.

He splashed some cold water on his face, then went to his bedroom and changed into sweats. It wasn't a good idea to go running at night, but he had no choice. The energy had to go somewhere, and if he ran himself into the ground maybe the iron bands squeezing him would ease up.

Chapter Twelve

For about three quarters of an hour after he stormed out of Jake's flat, Mari just walked in a half-blind daze of dread and mindless rage. It was rare for him to lose his temper. He knew that he had a short span of patience but even when that ran out it wasn't normal for him to lay into someone so viciously. Now, with the cool night air on his face, he could imagine that he had helplessly stood by and watched as some furious entity possessed his body and used it to berate and batter his poor Jake until he could barely string a sentence together.

What in the world were you thinking? He hadn't struck anyone in anger since he was seven years old and another boy at the day center — where Papa used to leave him two days a week while he was working, thinking to socialize him that way — had taken the puzzle he was trying to solve and mixed it up again. Li Chao had given him such a thrashing for that.

Papa had never laid a hand on him, not once, even if he was bad. Professor Troy Gale was an ardent pacifist and he did not hold with corporal punishment. But he left the running of his household to his assistant, the very capable Song Li Chao, who was not only a doctor of mathematics but a wizard with finances and administration. He also believed very firmly that to spare the rod was to spoil the child.

Suffice it to say that Mari had *not* been spoiled rotten at his hands.

He slowed his pace as he reached the house. It had been many years since he had thought about his childhood in Selangor and when he did it was usually with fondness. Even Li was remembered with affection. Mari had adored him and happily forgave him every beating just to earn the handsome young Chinese Malay's benediction. In return, Li had taught him Mandarin and meditation, and also to count to three in his head before he responded to perceived injustice. The theory was that if he still held on to his rage after three deep breaths, it was probably justified.

That advice had gone unheeded tonight, though, and he was bitterly ashamed of himself. The voice of reason in his head told him that Jake was, without question, correct in his assertions. The tablet in his messenger bag whispered to him like a siren on a rock, luring him to his doom. Though every muscle in his neck and shoulders was tight as a bowstring and his head was pulsing again, he wanted to follow that lure, to leave his stupid body and swim through the endless waves of the Net until he lost himself there.

He stopped at the front door and rested one hand against the dark blue wooden panels, fighting the impulse to rush in, to lock himself in his room and log in. When he put the key in the lock and pushed the door ajar he was more in control. Tonka ran to meet him, his tail wagging furiously, and Mari made himself take off his jacket, hang it up, crouch and make a fuss of his mother's loveable, elderly Staffie until the chunky terrier felt appreciated and trotted back to the kitchen where he slept.

Though it was not late, Mama had already gone up to bed. He climbed the stairs quietly but the light was still shining in her room and he tapped at the door and waited for her voice before entering.

"You're early, Ilmari. I wasn't expecting you back for ages," she said, looking up from her book. Her pale eyebrows came together briefly. "Is everything all right?"

He nodded and ran a hand through his unruly hair. "Fine. I'm just tired, that's all. I have a headache coming on. Thought I should come back and get an early night before my first proper day at work."

She responded with a look that he knew well enough. That excuse flew like a brick.

"How is Jake?"

"He's—" Mari paused. *Battered, probably bruised, bewildered and bloody angry too, no doubt.* "He's fine."

Her lips pursed and she took a deep breath through her nostrils and exhaled it as a sigh. "Good. I'm glad to hear it. He's a very decent young man."

"I know. I'm— I'm going for a quick run before I turn in. Clear my head. I'll see you in the morning," Mari told her, feeling too confined.

"Be careful," she told him. "Take Tonk, he's not been out all day except for the garden." And just before he ducked back out, "I love you, Ilmari."

"I love you too, Mama," he said softly, and closed the door.

He dumped his bag in the bedroom and went straight to the closet so that he didn't have to think too hard about how his laptop would feel in his hands, his fingers on the keys, delivering the password that would open up an escape chute into which he could slide. His skin itched and he peeled off his shirt and the tank beneath it. Next he shed his pants and small, blue briefs.

Five minutes later he was clad in midnight-blue Lycra with a luminous lime-green flash along the sides of his thighs and the sleeves of his light, hooded sweat top to alert motorists and errant pavement cyclists to his presence in the dark, and let himself out through the kitchen door, with Tonka on a chain leash at his heels. *Well that was easy enough. Junkie, indeed!*

He was deliberately not letting himself feel. Li had taught him that too, a quiet, simple meditation that focused his mind, shutting out emotional responses, concentrating on the rational and methodical processes of intellect alone. His brain kicked off with some basic multiplication and long division, reeling off consecutive square numbers then dividing and subdividing until he came back down to one again. He worked up and down this numerical scale like a child at the piano, adding and subtracting, throwing in geometric probabilities as his trainer-shod feet pounded the pavements and the breeze blew his hair back from his face and cooled the heat in his cheeks.

Maybe this will work. We'll see who's a fucking junkie, Mr. Smartarse Chivis.

And just like that his head unraveled. One moment he was striding along Hampstead Road with Tonka scampering beside him and the next he was on his knees with his face in his hands, sobbing fit to choke. The faithful dog came right back to him, snuffed his hair and tried to lick him, sharing his young master's distress.

Oh, you idiot! You stupid, stupid moron! What have you done? He's smart and sexy and patient as all get out with you, and you've just rubbed his face in it and left him standing there like he didn't matter. What is wrong *with you?*

For ten minutes, he knelt in the middle of the pavement and wept his heart out and, because this was London and the middle of the night, not a soul intervened. When, at last, his breath stopped hitching enough for him to crawl to his feet and return to the house, even Tonka seemed to be taking it as a done deal that this behavior was perfectly normal.

Back home he showered, running the water as hot as he could bear then turning it to icy cold and forcing himself to stay beneath the spray until his muscles could no longer stand it. Once he was dry, he wrapped himself in his dressing gown and curled up on the sofa to try to settle down somewhere that he was not surrounded by the temptation of technology. Even then the peace of sleep eluded him. He was still tossing and turning at five a.m., fighting to steer his thoughts away from anything but the idea of going online, just for a short while until his head settled. And, when he had mastered that, to think of anything but the disappointment on Jake's face before he'd stormed out of his flat.

He curled around one of the soft, cream-furred cushions and buried his nose in it, crying quietly there so as not to disturb Mama, until his eyes and throat hurt and he was utterly exhausted. Then, and only then, did he sleep at last.

He was running again, only this time by the sea, the clean white sand shifting under his feet and the crystal blue ocean shushing on the shore. The hibiscus was in bloom and the scent filled his nostrils but he could not stop and enjoy it, he had to keep running. The terror at his heels was nameless and faceless, a dark, crawling thing that threatened to envelop him every time he stopped. He dared not look around. If he saw it he was lost. If he could only reach Jake's hut he would be fine but the refuge of that palm-fringed sanctuary remained frustratingly out of his reach. Every time he lifted his head it was further away.

His chest hurt as if he had breathed in fire and he struggled to run on the softer sand, trying to steer toward the shoreline and the wet, firmer surface. Each time he did, something made him shy away and at last he went down, gasping raggedly, struggling to get up, to keep running. The darkness was coming, it was reaching out for him…

Mari woke with a violent start. There was a warm presence at his back that in a moment of confusion he thought must be blood. As his blurry vision registered the familiar surroundings of the sunlit day room his heart stopped thumping quite so hard and he twisted about, waking and dislodging Tonka, who had curled up against the small of his back and slept there, on the forbidden sofa, guarding him. He reached down and played with the terrier's ears then dragged himself to the kitchen to decant dog food and put the coffee on.

Forty minutes later, having taken Mama tea and a warm brioche roll and kissed her goodbye, he was on his way to the north embankment, trying to set his brain into work mode. He wondered for a while if he should go to see Jake and apologize for last night but worried too that Jake wouldn't want to deal with him just yet.

Unable to reach a decision, he took himself straight off to work and tried to lose himself in the bustle of a new and strange environment.

Chapter Thirteen

Jake showered and shaved and tried to make himself as presentable as possible but he needed a haircut again, there was a shadow of a bruise on his cheek, his eyes were bloodshot and he looked like he hadn't slept in a week. This was not the impression he wanted to give on his first day back at work, especially considering that at some point he was going to have to confess that he didn't seem able to use his psychometry anymore. Instead he'd picked up the useless and considerably more worrying ability to – maybe – burst into flame if he didn't keep his temper in check.

After Mari had left he'd run for two hours, come home and still had to pull out his old mat and meditate like his grandmother had taught him. He'd gotten out of the practice since he'd learned better control of his temper. For the first time in many years he'd felt the pang of missing her and wished he could still talk to her. A dozen times he'd picked up the phone to call Mari and put it down again, afraid that if he didn't give

Mari time to cool down and think, he just might decide to break it off once and for all.

Jake liked his job at the University. He'd done his IT Security training while still on the force in Detroit, but IT crime was the same in any language. His skills had transferred seamlessly to academia and he enjoyed drawing up security training programs and even preparing risk assessments, but his patience was thin today, and he struggled to focus. At lunchtime Professor Newberry took pity on him and said perhaps a half day was good enough for his first day back. Jake wanted to protest that he was fine but he also really just wanted to get the hell out of there. As soon as he cleared the doors, he also gave in to the urge to call Mari. Maybe he would let Jake take him to lunch so they could talk. His phone only rang once though before voicemail kicked in and Mari's usual, cheerful voice was telling him to leave a message.

"I was hoping I could take you to lunch. Call me when you have a chance." He paused, then decided against adding more and hung up.

Jake went home, and when Mari still hadn't called a half hour later, he changed clothes and headed to the gym.

* * * *

Mari got a call midmorning from Mama to say that she'd been contacted by her oncologist about a new trial, and was going to see him and talk things over. For the last three years, she'd been receiving increasingly experimental treatments for what her many doctors all told her was multiple myeloma and most likely incurable.

What his mother liked best about that diagnosis was the 'most likely' part, because she was of the bloody-minded nature that liked to meet a challenge head on. He had inherited that trait from her, his Papi often assured him. 'Most likely', in Annabel Gale's lexicon, meant 'not certainly' and, she had informed him, so long as no one was one hundred percent certain that she was going to succumb to this wretched disease, she saw no reason to accept that as a terminal prognosis.

Her current oncologist — she had already dismissed five of them — liked the way she thought. He had been a research scientist in a former life and still had connections in the medical research world. Anni wasn't kidding herself that he was less interested in making a name for himself than making her well, and Mari was inclined to agree, but if he achieved the former in the process of doing the latter, it was a win-win situation, so far as they both could see.

Mari was more skeptical, though. He thought that the specialist, Landon Barnard, was in all probability the modern-day equivalent of a snake oil salesman, but Mama seemed to like him. Even so, Mari had no intention of letting her get talked into anything that sounded dangerous. His mother might have trained in medical science but that didn't mean she always applied logic to her own treatments.

His line manager was very good about him disappearing just three and a half hours into his first full day on the clock. According to Ghislaine, Mr. Ashcroft didn't care what hours he kept so long as he hit his targets. And his old boss, Dr. Karden, had rather surprisingly assured them he was quite capable of that.

He was at the hospital with Mama when he got his second call of the morning.

"Oh no, not now!" He exhaled a testy sigh and flicked the sound on his phone off, letting the call go to voicemail. He felt sick as soon as he did it but was in neither the right place nor the proper mindset to talk to Jake at that precise moment.

"Was that work?" Anni asked, looking up from a half-completed Sudoku on her tablet.

"No."

"Was it Jake?" she persisted.

"Mama, it's not important."

"Go and talk to him. I'll probably be waiting ages yet," she said, with a solemn look.

"It can wait. You're my priority, Mama." Mari wagged a finger at her.

"I'm an old lady who's had her shot at love. It's your turn, Ilmari. He's so good for you, and you don't seem to realize it," she admonished more gently this time.

Mari shook his head. "Mama, you are not old, for one. And, there are plenty of guys out there that think you're hot. Nice guys, not like this creep here. You don't know anything about Jake. I wonder sometimes if I do. He certainly knows nothing about me."

"Oh, Mari, what's happened?" she chided, setting down her tablet. "Did you fight? You two seemed so good for one another. What have you done?"

"I haven't done anything, Mama. I don't want to talk about it. Okay? Hush!" He was saved from further interrogation by the arrival of Mr. Barnard and they were ushered into the oncologist's office to learn of his latest experiment.

* * * *

Okay, maybe Mari was right, Jake thought. It had been too long since he'd visited the gym. He'd had to go down twenty pounds on his presses. He finished his set though, even if his arms were screaming. Working the legs was easier. Legs were always easier for him, though, and he chalked that up to running. A lot of guys that spent half their day in the gym hated working on legs and struggled with it, and those always seemed to be the same guys that wouldn't step on a treadmill to save their lives.

He moved on from the leg press machine back to the free weights and contemplated the fact that Mari wasn't taking his calls while he did about a million curls. Maybe he was just busy at work and couldn't talk. There was always that possibility. He couldn't imagine that Mari couldn't find ten seconds to send him a text saying so though.

As he was working on his chest and stomach muscles, he was only half conscious of people coming and going from the various different machines. When someone clapped a hand on his shoulder and a breathless voice spoke his name, he came out of his daze and looked up into a pair of familiar, cloudy blue eyes.

"I thought it was you," Cordiline said with a smile. "Haven't seen you down here before."

Jake was just as surprised to see him. "I usually come in late in the day when no one's here," he said. "You work out in the middle of the day? How do you get the time?"

"Split shifts," Cordiline explained. "If I just go home and sleep, I'm sluggish in the evening. Makes more sense to do something physical and sleep at the end of the night. Plus, I get to work off a few excess pounds."

It seemed to do the trick too. In a suit the detective was still a trimmer figure than most of the men of his rank, but in a tank and shorts Jake was able to appreciate that there was hard muscle under the well-cut linen, not a body gone soft from years of desk work.

"So, what are you doing down here? I thought you were back at work this week?"

"I am. I was. Professor Newberry decided four hours was enough for my delicate constitution to handle my first day back." Jake rolled his eyes. "I'm not going to complain though." He didn't feel the need to mention that he'd also been so distracted he wasn't getting anything done anyway.

"So, you thought you'd come over and push yourself at the gym instead. Well, I can't say it's not paying off." Cordiline looked him over. "I'm sure your pretty boyfriend would agree."

Jake's lips twitched into a small grin but he was not about to discuss the fact that Mari didn't even want to talk to him at the moment, much less appreciate his muscle tone.

"Mind if I join you?" The DI slid down on the bench beside his and adjusted the weights. He worked the press with practiced ease, not looking at Jake, though a couple of guys that Jake recognized from his evening sessions were watching Cordiline from the rowing machines.

Jake didn't answer him one way or the other since it didn't seem to matter anyway. He set the free weights back in the rack and added another twenty to either side of the bar he'd been pressing earlier. He lay down and wrapped his hands around it, taking a few slow breaths before lifting it off and bringing it down to his chest, drawing air in then blowing out again as he extended his arms. *Oh yeah, that burned.*

Cordiline waited until he had the bar on the hooks before he asked, "Whose fist did you put your face in front of this time?"

Jake glanced over at him. He didn't like to lie. He'd never been very good at it. "Bumped into the wall at night when it was dark." Jake grunted as he lifted the bar again. Down, and up.

"Yeah, right. I never heard that explanation before," Cordiline uttered a humorless laugh then adjusted his weights up by another ten each side and settled down on the bench. "You ever boxed, Jake?" he grunted as he hefted the bar, lowering it in a slow, measured maneuver before pushing smoothly up and onto the rest.

"A little," Jake answered. "It wasn't really my thing." A lot of his fellow students at the academy had liked boxing, but Jake didn't like hitting other people, at least, not on a regular basis. He fought if he had to, but he'd seen too much violence to enjoy it as a sport.

"Your drill master didn't teach you to block," Cordiline said, adding another pair of fives to the bar and lying down again. "He's got a bit of temper, your boy. I can imagine why you don't want to hit him back, but you shouldn't let him take his frustration out on you, Chivis."

Jake didn't want to tell him it had only been the first one Mari landed, by surprise, and he'd blocked the rest, because that just made it seem far worse than it was and Cordiline already had a low opinion of Mari. Instead he said, "He was provoked. He doesn't really have a bad temper. And yes, I'm aware of what that sounds like."

His companion grunted and hefted the bar again, bringing it down faster than before and pushing up slow and hard. Like Jake he was long and lean from the midriff down, his thighs hard-muscled and dusted sparingly with dark hair, his torso and upper body more packed and less hirsute. When he relaxed and returned the bar to the rest, he didn't look bulky but the lift showed off what simmered beneath the skin.

"You're looking out for him. It's understandable," he said, turning his head to look at Jake without sitting up. "If he's as hot with his clothes off as he is fully dressed, I can't fault you for it. But you wanna teach him not to treat you that way, Jake. I've been around boys like him, and believe me, if you let them get away with it a few times they think they can do anything."

Jake laughed softly. "He's not a Labrador. I'm not training him. We had an argument, that's all. And what do you mean, 'boys like him', anyway?"

A wan smile pulled at Cordiline's mouth and he murmured, "You and me, we're men's men, you know what I mean? We can fit in, with the straight crowd. We don't ruffle any feathers. But that one, he's never really learned any boundaries. He does his own thing. And that's good, don't get me wrong, Jake." He held up a finger when Jake opened his mouth to say something. "It's great. He's got a lot of spirit, but he's got no brakes. He thinks if he makes a fuss about things then he'll get his own way, and life doesn't work like that. I hope he made it up to you in bed, that's all."

"That's none of your business," Jake said, just a little snappier than he intended. He knew it was a mistake as soon as it was out of his mouth.

"Ah, right." Cordiline sighed and adjusted the weights. "Trouble in paradise, huh? I'm sorry, mate."

Jake wanted very much to deny that but he knew any protest to the contrary would only make it seem like he didn't want to face reality. Instead he pressed the weights a few more times, pushing himself hard. He was not at the limit of what he could lift but after ten reps his arms were burning and his muscles were twitching as he forced his arms to get the bar back up on the rest. Sitting up, he grabbed his towel from the end of the bench and wiped his face off.

"He found another fucking video," Jake muttered under his breath. "I've got the address of where it was uploaded for you."

Cordiline stopped and looked at Jake, his eyebrows raised and eyes round. Jake could practically see him putting this info together with Jake's bad mood and drawing up the conclusions.

"He can't leave this alone, can he? Is that what you were fighting about?" He sat up, swinging his legs to the side of the bench so he could face Jake. "He doesn't want to play those kinda games with you, I hope."

"You know, this is why detectives don't have friends," Jake told him for that astute observation. He shouldn't talk about his relationship with Cordiline, he knew that. It was not just a bad idea, it was a terrible idea. If Mari ever found out it would make last night's fireworks seem like a mild spat. But who did he have to talk to? Other than Mari, he hadn't made any close friends here, and he had cut ties with just about everyone he knew back home. "I don't understand what you mean by playing games."

Cordiline laughed softly. "Oh, yes you do, Chivis. And you're terrified that one day he'll go too far." He pushed himself to his feet and looked down at Jake with a rueful smile. "And you're wrong, by the way.

Detectives can have friends, just the friends they do have are the rocks in the river of life. They're the ones that can't be budged by stupid talk or a chance mistake. I could be a good friend, if you'd let me, Jake. The best kind."

He patted Jake's shoulder again and turned toward the showers.

Jake wasn't stupid. He knew exactly what he was offering, and it was more than just friendship. The thing was, John Cordiline was not an unattractive man, even if he was ten years Jake's senior. In fact, that kinda made him more attractive. If Jake hadn't met Mari he might have followed him and corralled him in the steam room. He wasn't a cheater though. He couldn't do that to Mari. Not even if he wouldn't answer his damn phone. He waited a good ten minutes then headed for the showers himself.

* * * *

Barnard was his usual oily self and Mari was thoroughly irritable by the time Mama's appointment with him concluded. The experiment he was pushing did sound like something worth trying, though. It was not drugs, more a form of reiki type healing, but the practitioner had good results. Barnard was not bloody minded enough to stand in the way of anything that improved Mama's health, so they agreed on a date to commence the treatment and he made an appointment for her with the healer. They took the relatively short walk home instead of getting a cab, since it was a fine, bright day.

"Call him," Anni instructed, once they were outside. "He likes you, Mari. What are you doing? You don't want to wind up old and alone like your mother, surely."

"Since when have you ever wanted for company?" he chided her. "He'll be working, Mama."

He did check the voicemail message though. Then checked the time on his phone and frowned. It was past lunchtime and if he wanted to save face he ought to get back to Trafalgar House. He swore under his breath. Now Jake was going to wonder if he'd been stood up and wasn't that going to be another difficult conversation?

"I'll call him later, Mama. I promise," he told her, kissing her on the cheek as they reached the front door. "I have to get back. Will you be okay?"

"I'm fine, Ilmari. Just worried about my baby, that's all." She pouted.

"Stop it. I am perfectly all right, Mama." He gave her an irritable half smile.

"You look tired, darling. Don't work too hard. You've not been well since you both got caught in that bar fire. I worry about you. Both you and Jake," she said.

"Go and get some rest. I'll see you later," Mari told her more firmly. He saw no point in arguing her last point since it was true. He was tired but his current malaise had less to do with smoke inhalation than with his repeated immersion in the Web. She had no idea about that, though, and he had no intention of enlightening her.

Mari worked late that night, and it was gone nine in the evening when he got home and checked his calls. Jake had rung again, asking if he was okay, and he sent a short text message back this time, just saying yes but he was working and not to worry. He considered getting a takeaway since Mama had eaten already, but he wasn't especially hungry and at last he just went to bed.

Sleep was elusive again though, and following an hour of restless tossing and turning he reached for his laptop and hunted down some music. Sometimes it helped to have something to listen to and he lay back again with his earbuds in and closed his eyes. His fingers would not stop tapping though and it was nothing to do with the music.

Finally, frustrated and needy, he propped himself in a pile of pillows and opened the search page on his browser again. When he had located the webpage he needed, he touched his fingers to the screen and satisfied the itch inside.

Chapter Fourteen

Jake knew Mari was pissed at him but the refusal to answer the phone and curt text still was hurt. He preferred the yelling, even the hitting. Those were things he understood. He'd lived with explosive anger in one form or another most of his life. This cold shoulder business was something he was far less adept at dealing with. Alex had liked to sulk and give him the silent treatment on occasion, but it was all an act with him. Jake had been aware of what he was doing, had known it was all manipulation, and in hindsight he knew it hadn't worked for Alex because Jake hadn't much cared.

The ugly thought crossed his mind that now Mari had achieved the goal of being fucked by him, he'd used this excuse to dump him. He didn't want to believe Mari could be that kind of person, so he pushed the thought away. They hadn't been dating very long, but the time they'd spent together had already been the happiest few months of Jake's life. He didn't want to lose that joy. He didn't want to lose Mari.

After a sleepless night contemplating the ceiling and how much colder his bed seemed without Mari in it, he came up with a plan. If Mari wouldn't answer his phone he would go over there. If Mari told him to fuck off and shut the door in his face at least he would know where things stood. Jake hoped that he could coax him out for a run though, and that maybe they could, at least, agree to talk about what had happened.

Usually he just threw on sweats and hit the streets, not giving a second thought to how scruffy he might look before a shower and shave. This morning he took the time to run a brush through his hair and instead of his usual baggy yet functional attire, he pulled on a snug tee and track-pants that were not half as tight as Mari's leggings but certainly showed off more of his ass and legs than his comfy sweats.

He felt ever so slightly ridiculous dressing in running gear with a mind toward seduction but maybe he could distract Mari long enough to get him to listen. He was willing to try anything at this point.

He left his apartment early enough so they'd have at least an hour to run, if he could get Mari to come out.

When he knocked at the door, though, it was Anni who answered. Even in a housecoat, with her hair piled loose on top of her head and held with a simple tie, she had a curious elegance that seemed transmitted to her son by osmosis.

"Hello, Jake, darling. So lovely to see you," she said in a tone of pleasure that could not have been feigned. As if to emphasize it, Tonka barreled down the hallway and launched himself at Jake's knees, his tail wagging furiously. "I was worried that you were avoiding us. Come and have some breakfast."

Jake stepped inside and brushed a kiss on her cheek. She was not an overly demonstrative woman but they had developed this ritual greeting over the last couple weeks. Jake genuinely liked Mari's mother. She was nothing at all like his own mother, and although she looked nothing like his grandmother either, she reminded him of her in some way. Anni had a poise and strength that were hard to define, and that was exactly how his grandmother had been. He gave Tonka's head and jowls a good rub. "How's the little mukwa, huh? You behaving yourself?" Jake glanced toward the kitchen. "Is Mari making breakfast?"

She heaved a sigh and shook her head. "He's still upstairs. He came home at some ridiculous hour last night, said he'd eaten at work and went straight up there. What's happened between you two? And don't tell me *nothing*. That's what he said but I know my son, and this is not him. Is it work? Or did you argue? He's been in such a strange mood for days now."

Jake glanced at the stairway and down at Tonka to avoid looking at her worried gaze. If it was a terrible idea to talk to Cordiline about his relationship with Mari it was far, far worse to talk to his mother about their troubles. Mari might forgive him for calling him out on his addiction, and he might get past his frustration with Jake's 'overprotectiveness', but if he told Mari's mother what was going on with him, he might as well turn around and keep walking.

"We had a disagreement," he said. "I'm hoping it's something we can work out."

"Take him up some coffee and a pastry. I'm sure he hasn't eaten since yesterday morning," she said with a grave frown. "I tried knocking but he didn't respond. Maybe you'll have more luck."

Jake followed her into the kitchen and took the offered plate and mugs and brought both up the stairs. There was a small side table in the hall and he set the food and coffee down there before knocking softly on the door with one knuckle. He got no response from inside and after a moment he gave the door another rap. "Mari, it's Jake. Can I come in?"

He waited. Nothing. That was odd. Surely he'd knocked loud enough that even if he was sleeping he'd hear it. Mari wasn't childish enough to just ignore him and hope he went away. If he really didn't want to see him he could get up and tell him to his face.

Jake hesitated, but it wasn't in his nature to just give up. He reached down and turned the handle, easing the door open and hoping he wasn't about to have his head taken off for barging in.

What he saw stopped him cold. Mari was slumped in his chair at the computer desk, his desktop and laptop screens still running, his fingers touching both. His head was resting on one arm, as though he'd only meant to put it down and stop for a moment, but his eyes were open, glassy, reflecting the data scrolling on the screens. The fine hairs on the nape of Jake's neck stood on end.

"Mari? Mari?" Jake called his name as he moved toward him. "Jesus, Mari!" He touched Mari's shoulder and he could feel his muscles rock hard under his fingertips, but he didn't move or respond at all. "Oh fucking— Mari! Mari!" Jake drew him back into a sitting position, breaking his touch with the screens, then reached under the desk and yanked out the plug on the computer. He pushed and held the power button on the laptop until both screens went black and dead. Mari almost fell out of the chair and Jake scooped him up, carrying him over to the bed.

At last he made a sound and Jake's heart was beating so fast and hard in his chest he wasn't sure if it was a good sound or not. He laid him down and sat on the edge beside him, patting his cheek gently. "Mari, can you hear me?"

Mari was sickly pale, his sunlight-colored hair lank and tangled as if he'd snarled it continually around his fingers, and his shuttered eyes were dark-ringed, sunk in shadow. His body convulsed, fingers twitching and restless as if they were possessed. He moaned, struggling to get his tongue around words and failing to make coherent sounds. When his eyes opened, they were red-rimmed and Jake was stunned by the intensity of his translucent blue-green irises. That incredible gaze had been one of the first things to strike him about this curious young man, but right now his eyes were not quite sane.

"Wh-what?" Mari managed to stutter at last. "What-the-fuck-did-you-do?"

"What did I — ? Mari, you were fucking catatonic! Are you okay?"

Mari looked toward the desk and he uttered a small, apoplectic noise.

"You — did you? What-the-fuck?" he squeaked furiously, trying to lift a finger. "So — I was *this* close! How — dare you?"

"Mari, you were *this* close to frying your fucking brain! How long have you been plugged in? All night? Jesus, you can hardly move. You think that's fucking normal? You are going to fucking kill yourself!"

Mari was huffing and he squeezed his eyes shut again, as if he was trying to trap something behind his eyelids. His long fingers clenched for a moment then released and fluttered like ragged pennons.

"I...know," he said hoarsely, trying to swallow. He had to try twice.

"You know? What the fuck do you mean? *Are* you trying to kill yourself?"

Mari opened his eyes again and stared at Jake. "I *know* who the other guy was. I *know* how they found him."

He enunciated each word with painful precision, as if he was trying them out for the first time.

"I can *find* them."

Jake stared at him. What he was saying slowly sank in, and once it did his temper spiked swift and hot. He could feel it rise up and flush through him like a literal flame.

"Are you out of your fucking *mind*?" He actually yelled. He didn't mean to but he couldn't help it. "I don't fucking *care*! Don't you get it? You are way more important than solving some fucking case. Fucking Christ, Mari! They can find the bastard without you fucking killing yourself to do it!"

Jake stood up. He was shaking. He couldn't seem to make himself stop. He was so angry with Mari, so utterly pissed that he'd risked himself like that. He was hot in more than just temper, he could feel it burning in him. "I have to get out of here," he muttered, quieter. The last thing he wanted to do was leave him like this but he was afraid of what might happen if he didn't get a hold of his temper, and fast.

Mari blinked at him and one hand twitched toward Jake, trying to catch his fingers perhaps, but still too uncoordinated. He swallowed again, a small, perfect frown line between his eyebrows, struggling for some elusive words.

"He still loves…still wants you," he said cryptically. His gaze moved toward the desk and there was something hopeless in his eyes.

Jake had no idea what he was talking about, but that look of longing cast toward his computers twisted a knot in his belly. He stalked away from Mari, out into the hall. Anni was just reaching the top of the stairs, probably to tell him to stop yelling at her son, or maybe just to find out what the hell was going on. He gave her an apologetic look but kept moving.

"Call a doctor to him. Don't listen to him when he tells you he doesn't need one. I have to go, I'm sorry, Anni." He didn't even wait for her to argue or ask questions and he felt terrible leaving her to deal with it on her own. He shot down the stairs and out the front door, closing it harder than necessary and taking off at a dead run as soon as he hit the bottom step. Fear was starting to creep in over the anger, but that was good. If he was afraid maybe there would be no room left for the rage inside and maybe he could get himself under control. For now, he just ran, no pace, no stride, just ran flat out as fast as he could.

Chapter Fifteen

The morning passed by like a nightmare for Mari. For the first time in his living memory he and Mama fought. Not physically — he was not capable of raising a hand to her and she never would return it, no matter how much she might believe he deserved it, but their war of words was no less violent. She wanted him to see a doctor as Jake had counseled, but he was adamant that there was nothing worth wasting a medic's time on and that he would be fine if he could just be left alone to get some rest.

After their slanging match there was no point in telling her there wasn't a problem between himself and Jake so he didn't bother to lie.

"Mama, it's over. It was over before it started," he told her angrily when she wouldn't stop berating him about it. "He was always too good for me. And his ex wants him back. I expect he'll get what he wants, because if Jake can't use his psychometry anymore he thinks he'll lose his job. Which means they'll send him home. There is absolutely no point in us pretending things can be more than they are."

"Ilmarinen Wesley Arthur Gale, I love you. You are my only child. But sometimes I want to strangle you," she fumed at him. "Jake came around here for you. He wanted desperately to see you, Mari. Why are you pushing him away? Why does he think you're ill? Are you taking drugs?"

"Mama, I'm not taking drugs," he protested, incredulous that she could even think it of him. "I barely even drink. Why would I need drugs?"

"Ilmari, you can barely walk. You're slurring. You can't focus on me. What am I supposed to think?" She was shouting and he flinched from her anger, sitting down hard on the bed as if his legs had been kicked from under him.

"I'm exhausted. I'm working on a project. I can't sleep. That's all."

"You're lying, Ilmari," she flashed back at once, no trace of tenderness in that accusation. "I don't understand why, but I can see it in your eyes. You are lying to me. In my own house."

"It's *my* house, Mama," he reminded her with quiet dignity. "Angela *gave* it to me."

She shook her head at him, disappointment evident in her gaze.

"That's a low blow, Ilmarinen. Even for you. Suit yourself. You destroy yourself in *your* thrice damned house, if that's what you want. I'm not your keeper any more. I don't think I ever was—but I never saw a day coming when you would cut yourself off from the people who love you. Whatever it is, I hope to hell it's worth it to you ultimately."

And with that she walked out and slammed the door. His teeth vibrated from the impact and he slumped down on the bed after she had gone, trying to remember what he had been doing before Jake had ripped him out of the Web. His memory was in tatters, fluttering in ragged strands that interfered with one another and made no sense.

One strand was clear though. Once he had pushed as far as he could humanly stand into the activities of the snuff production line, he had made a less caustic detour into the surprisingly small Internet footprint that surrounded Jake Chivis.

His gentle, infuriating knight had virtually no social media presence at all, which could be seen as a good thing in some respects, but it gave Mari precious little to work with when it came down to snooping. Jake's ex-boyfriend, Alex, on the other hand, had an online persona that more than compensated for his lover's reticence.

Alex was a surprisingly flamboyant character, given what he knew about Jake's tastes before they had started dating. Unlike Jake, Alex was not averse to sharing, so it hadn't taken Mari very long to trick out links to pictures of the two of them, together and individually, tall tales of Jake's prowess in bed, snarky comments on the subject of their rocky road to break up and a lot of speculation on what might have been if Jake had been trendier, pushier, queerer.

Mari huffed through his nostrils at the memory of that remark. Jake was, in his opinion, plenty queer enough, but that hadn't been enough for Alex.

The kid was cute though, and there was no denying he and Jake looked good, and even quite happy together in the pictures. One thing was bugging him, and that was the discovery that Alex knew Jake was in London, and had deliberated more than once about the possibility of coming after him.

It was fairly plain to Mari that whatever Jake's feelings were for Alex, his ex had not given up on the idea of him and Jake as a couple.

That, more than anything, was enough to put him into a tailspin of pure depression. He crawled under the bedclothes and stayed there for the rest of the morning, ignoring all his calls.

* * * *

Sprinting was not the same as running. Jake could not keep the pace up indefinitely, for one thing. Also, running like Satan himself was on his heels garnered more attention than just loping through the park, even briskly. Not that Jake had any attention to spare for anyone that happened to stare as he flew past. He was down the street, into the park and halfway through it before he was forced to slow down. His sides were heaving and he was soaked in sweat but he thought his terror had achieved the goal of driving out the blind rage.

He stumbled his way to a bench and put a hand on the back and one on the seat, bending over as he gasped for air. Closing his eyes conjured an image of Mari slumped in his seat, glazed over and blank faced. He had thought for one sickening moment that Mari was dead. The shock of that alone had been enough to drive him half out of his mind. The gut-tightening realization that Mari wasn't dead but might still be a vegetable had only spiked his adrenaline further.

Then he'd just left, ran out on him and left him lying there twitching and furious. Jake crumpled down onto the bench and put his head in his hands. His chest was heavy with more than just the frantic run. His heart contracted as if there was a great big hand around it, squeezing, forcing the pressure up into his throat in a big lump. He hadn't given in to tears in ages and he hadn't felt this close to falling to pieces since his grandmother had died. He had gotten through yesterday by holding on to the hope that he could still fix things between him and Mari, but today he was sure he'd destroyed any chance of that.

On top of his misery, he was still scared to death that Mari was going to hurt himself. That he would plug himself back in and just waste away. He couldn't let that happen. Even if Mari never spoke to him again, even if he hated him later, he couldn't just turn away and do nothing.

Jake took a shuddering breath and rubbed his hands down his face so that he could pretend no moisture had leaked from his eyes. Still trembling with a combination of shock and sorrow, he stood up straight. His legs felt hot and shaky but he pushed himself into an easier run. He needed to get home, get showered and changed and go to work.

If Mari would not listen to him, if he couldn't stop himself, there was at least one person that Jake knew who might have an idea of how to help him. And if he was going to expose Mari's dark secret, he could not in good conscience be hypocritical enough to keep hiding his own. Professor Weston had spent the better part of his life studying Elementals. He had been and still was involved with countless research projects. If there was anyone who knew how to help Mari, or himself, Weston would be the one.

Barely two hours later Jake was seated in front of Professor Weston. His office was still cluttered with teetering piles of books and stacks of papers and folders in danger of avalanche. The professor was sitting across the desk from him, leaning back in his chair with his hands steepled over his chest, staring at Jake with a grave expression.

Jake had laid it all out. His recent inability to pick up any memories from objects, how he seemed to be much more easily provoked of late, and the scary way his temperature spiked when it happened. He told the professor about Mari's confession, that he could no longer resist the lure of hooking himself into the net, and how he had found him that morning, and how very worried he was. He told him everything, then sat back in the chair and waited, too relieved to have told someone, and too drained from unburdening, to be discomfited by the fact that Weston was silent and staring for nearly two full minutes.

"I'm screwed, aren't I? They'll send me back to Detroit?" he said, still numb from the shock of this morning's discovery. If they sacked him, and Weston couldn't help, Mari was going to die. Jake fought the sick feeling that thought set off in his gut again.

"Jake, we're not that mercenary. If something has prevented you from opening to psychometric memories, it's in our best interests to find out what and why," Weston said in a level tone. "This change in your abilities is down to the drug they gave you, isn't it?"

Jake nodded. "Possibly. I can't think of any other reason, and it seems too coincidental." He'd never thought he would feel so bad about losing the ability that had sometimes felt like a curse. But that curse had brought Mari into his life and it might be the only link between them that was still left open to him.

"In that case, we will need to investigate in more detail," the professor said logically. "The University is not going to dismiss you out of hand because of a change in your symptoms. You are still doing a job for them. Dr. Gale is a concern, though. There have been studies done on Interfaces in the past but they are rare and the chance to observe them in action is limited. It's not the first time I've heard it suggested that Mari's ability might be compulsive."

Jake looked up at him. He ignored the part about the consequences of what Mari was doing for the moment and asked, "So in these studies, did they figure out a way to break the addiction before their brains melted?"

Weston huffed and leaned back in his chair. "He needs to stay away from technology, for a start. There's no easy fix. Like any addiction, the cure has to come from within. Given his current job, I think that's going to be a big ask."

Jake's jaw muscles went tight. "He's not going to stay away from tech. He doesn't even think he has a problem, not really." This was hopeless. How was he supposed to help Mari break out of his habit when it was literally a part of his job?

"If his employers thought there was an issue, it would be in their best interest to look in to it, don't you think?" Weston quirked a half-smile. "I'm sure that something could be insinuated, on the quiet."

"Right. Like if anyone suggests to him he should lay off plugging in, he's not going to realize exactly who tipped them off. Not only am I violating his privacy, I'm supposed to jeopardize his job? Oh, he'll fucking love that. Right now, he's just pissed off. I was really hoping to avoid making him hate me."

Again, that not-quite smile, this time gentler. Weston mused, "I had wondered about you two. So, it has gone further than just friends and colleagues. In that case, it's even more important for you to stop him at all costs, wouldn't you think? Can his family not help?"

Jake sighed. "Short of physically locking him in a room with no tech I don't see how anyone can really help him."

Weston shook his head. "Maybe that's what they need to do then. The skill runs in his family. They understand it as well as any. You, on the other hand, are an unknown quantity. We've not had the opportunity to study Fire Elementals with your gift before. Did other members of your family back home have a talent for seeing, as you do?"

Jake's gaze wandered toward a stack of dusty books then he brought his eyes back to Weston with a quirk of his lips.

"Both my grandparents could do it. I never met my grandfather but my grandmother told me he spent a lot of time 'in the spirit realm', which was her way of saying, in a self-induced trance state. He would come back and tell her about things that he'd seen, things that hadn't happened yet. I have no idea how accurate he might have been but she seemed to think he was. They're both gone though, and I don't know of other Fire Elementals that have any ability."

"And neither of them spoke of the gift waxing and waning, I presume? Still, like any ability, there must be factors that influence it," Weston told him, looking thoughtful. "If, as you seem to believe, the drug you were administered caused this to happen then perhaps there is a cure. We just don't understand what that might be yet. It was a substance manufactured by scientists working for the Secret Service, though. So, their talents might aid us. If we can discover precisely what it was that they gave you – "

Jake snorted cynically. "It's classified. It's not like they are just going to hand out the recipe on how to mix up a batch of chemicals with the potential to turn people into human flame throwers or walking time bombs."

"Not just to anyone, no," Weston soothed. "But the drug is in your system. It is in their interest as much as yours to study you."

Jake gave him a hard stare. "I'm not all that keen to hand myself over to your government so they can 'study' me. You might think they'll be benign about the methods they'll use but I don't believe I'm being paranoid to imagine it would be a whole lot easier for them to just eliminate any potential problems I might raise for them."

"You may be right to be paranoid, Jake. But don't you understand that you are more beneficial to them alive and able to do what you do than dead or locked away somewhere?" Weston shrugged. "The decision ultimately is yours, but that would be my solution. Alternatively, we find scientists of our own and conduct our own experiments. Would you trust us any better than MI5?"

Jake blew out his breath and slumped back in the chair. Honestly, he didn't trust anyone. "I don't know," he said, which was more diplomatic than the truth. "I don't think there is a way to undo what was done." He should be more bitter about that, but his mind was in a million different places and he was more worried about

Mari than himself. "You've spent most of your life studying Elementals — haven't you ever come across something like this? I was hoping you might have some other ideas before we summon the men in white coats and break out the needles and probes."

A short nod was his only initial response, but Weston finally said, "Jake, I would advise you, based on my experience working with Elementals, to be patient. There are things you can take to control your emotions in the meantime, if you would be willing, but I would say that if this is pharmaceutically created then it will gradually diminish. The odds are already in your favor. You are still alive, you haven't met the fate of your predecessors, which would seem to indicate that your response to the dose is favorable. If that is the case then sooner or later, the abilities will return."

Jake stared at him incredulously. "That's your advice? Wait and see if it comes back?"

"You could push yourself, but do you want to take the risk that it will have adverse consequences?" Weston asked, looking very serious.

"I couldn't push myself, even if I wanted to. It doesn't work like that. I can't control when I'm going to pick up an impression from something, or stop it from happening." Jake closed his mouth at the subtle change in Weston's expression. It was nothing dramatic but the professor's face smoothed into a sudden blankness. Most people wouldn't even have thought twice about it, but Jake had been trained in body language and expression for the purpose of detecting lies, and he had a natural instinct for it as well. Weston was avoiding something.

"You've heard of Fire Elementals that were able to control their psychometry?"

"I thought that most of you could, to a degree," Weston responded. "Fire Elementals are pretty rare out here so I've not had the chance to study too many of you. But yes, I believe that it's within your grasp to 'push it'."

Jake drummed his fingers on the arm of his chair and Weston added, "Although, as I've just said, I'd advise against forcing your ability for the present time, at least until you wait and see if the trouble you're having with anger and body temperature regulation can be brought under control, or fades with the effect of the drug you were given."

"How exactly did they control their ability?" Jake asked.

Weston sighed. "You aren't listening to me, are you?"

"I am. I just want the truth. Also, why haven't you ever said anything about this before?"

"I've written about it," Weston said, as if this counted. "I'm just the moderator here, Jake. It's not really my place to interfere with the natural order of things."

Jake laughed. "What, you think you're Jane Goodall? We're not some subspecies of primate. It's not interference to pass on knowledge. So, how did they do it?"

Weston spread his hands in a helpless gesture. "The precise mechanism is undocumented. It seemed to be a combination of focus, along with use of trance, in some cases."

Jake mulled that over for a moment before he rose to his feet. "All right, thanks."

"So, what are you thinking?" Weston rose with him, suddenly concerned again.

"I'm thinking I need to get back to work, and that I might do some research later. I also need to figure out where I can securely lock Mari up for a week or so."

Weston's expression turned shocked and Jake quirked a half smile. "I'm joking."

"Take care, Jake," the professor said, more earnestly, as they shook hands. "Don't worry that you have to go through this alone. You can get hold of me, if you need to?"

"Yeah, and thank you for the info," Jake said. He might not have given him all the answers, or even the answers that he wanted, but it hadn't been a total waste of his time.

Part of his work did involve research and it wasn't particularly structured, so he could feel justified in spending the next few days hunting down clues to both Mari's problem and his own. The only guilt he felt at the moment was that if he could just have asked Mari for help, he might have found all the answers they needed in a fraction of the time. However, the way Mari would go about it was likely to defeat the purpose.

At lunchtime, he called Mari's number and, as expected, got no answer. He left a brief message asking him to ring back, and when he still hadn't done so by that evening Jake called again, with much the same result. His concern for Mari warred with the knowledge that treading on his toes any more would only result in forcing them further and further apart. Jake had to know if he was at least okay, though, so he called Anni.

"Hi there," she said, her voice soft so he knew right away that she wasn't alone in the house. "Just wait a moment, I'll take this through to the other room."

"How is he?" Jake asked her as she was making her way through to a more private part of the house.

She was quiet for a moment and he thought he heard a click as she closed the door, then she breathed. "Jake, I am worried about him. He's restless. He hasn't eaten. He either sits and stares at the wall, or he sleeps. What is he taking? Has he told you? Is that what you argued about?"

Jake closed his eyes. He wasn't sure what hurt more, the pain and worry he could hear in her voice or the mental image of Mari pale and listless, battling his inner demons.

"He's not taking drugs, Anni," Jake told her. "Although I'm not sure what he is doing is any better. It's—it's his ability. He admitted to me that he can't stop. The lure of interfacing has its hooks in him, and I don't know how to help him."

She was silent for a moment. When she spoke, her voice was more serious.

"I wondered if that was it. My grandmother—she was very odd toward the end of her life, so the family said. Like she was just fading away from us all. Such a bright woman, so clever, but it was like she slowly turned down the contrast on herself. I don't want to watch my son do that, Jake. We need to stop him. Will you help me?"

Jake gave a short bark of laughter that held not a drop of real humor. "I've been trying, Anni. I talked to him, argued with him, pleaded with him, told him I would help him any way he needed, and it has gotten us nowhere. I would do anything for him but...I just don't see what else I can do."

"You can keep him from walking away from me, Jake. I'll do the rest," she said more firmly. "I'm not about to see my baby throw everything away because he's too proud to take advice. But I'm not strong enough to physically make him behave any more. I can't just put him over my lap like I did when he was small, more's the pity."

Jake opened his mouth to tell her he'd already tried that. If the situation were any less serious he might have anyway. Instead he cleared his throat. "Uh, you want me to—what, exactly? Hold him down while you yell at him?" He was trying to envision that scenario and what the fallout might be, but his brain refused to see it.

"If he can't use his toys responsibly, then someone will have to take them off him," she said with the same brutal logic that Mari was so capable of.

Jake put one hand over his eyes. He could hardly believe he had reached a point where he was considering what she suggested, and worse, he was trying to staunchly crush the small flare of hope that her confidence wanted to bring him. He might not have worked vice but he was still a cop and had been on many a patrol—he had seen addiction destroy enough lives, including his own father's. If Mari was resistant, and he most certainly would be, this plan was doomed to failure. Still, he could not outright tell her that, not when he heard the fear underlying her own determination.

"He's not a child, Anni, and as much as I would like to take all his electronics away from him, it is kind of illegal to lock him up away from all his stuff."

"It's for his own good, Jake," she said. "I'm not saying that we imprison him, just that we keep him away from his thrice-damned devices until he can see sense. The alternative is that I sit here and watch him fade in front of my eyes. I can't do that. I love him, for all that he can be as insufferable as his father sometimes."

Jake rubbed his eyes hard enough to see flashes of red behind his lids. As plans went, there were too many ways this one would fail, but he didn't have any better ideas.

"I will come over and help you, but he's not going to be happy to see me, and he's not going to thank either of us," he told her.

Chapter Sixteen

Mari had spent the day being ingenious. Or so he told himself.

He had convinced his office that his mother was sick and needed him at home but promised he would work on a couple of projects there and mail things in if he needed clarification. This seemed to fly, much to his satisfaction. The situation at home was less comfortable.

Mama was tiptoeing around him and trying to pretend that she wasn't. To keep her happy, he took Tonka for a brisk walk, but he was not in the frame of mind to run. Even the stroll to Regent's Park and back left him feeling short of breath and he went upstairs to lie down as soon as he got back. The walk had given him some space to reorder his thoughts and memories of last night's online activity. He sat down with the laptop and composed an email to Jake summarizing what he had managed to find out. Then he remembered that Jake wasn't talking to him and saved the email as a draft, tapping his finger against the side of the machine for a full minute before electing not to send it right away.

Mama came up to spy on him under the pretense of bringing him a cup of tea, which he was grateful for, and a couple of slices of toast which he ignored. Rehydrated by the tea and relaxed by the caffeine hit, he resisted the urge to pick his laptop up again and look at what Alex, Jake's ridiculous ex, was up to.

Instead, to placate his mother, he went downstairs and sat in the lounge while she read the newspaper and Tonka snored quietly in his dog basket. He brought his tablet with him but put it down when she gave him pointed looks every time he attempted to switch it on. Finally, in a fit of frustration and screaming boredom, he snatched up the device and returned to his room with it, where he sat on the bed biting his lips until they were raw, willing himself just to be able to log on and do a normal email check and switch off again. It was a nightmare denying himself when it had become second nature to him to rely on technology for all his information and entertainment. Maybe he did have a problem.

But doesn't everyone, if that's the case?

The final straw fell when he came down for supper. The phone rang while Mama was eating and he was moving items of food around on his plate and looking for reasons not to put them in his mouth. She jumped to her feet like she was on elastic and refused to let him answer it, even though it made more sense. He wasn't hungry. He was nearer. She was talking in that tone of voice that was designed to imply everything in the garden was rosy. At the same time, she went through to the front parlor, which they never used because it was cold and got less light than the dayroom, and closed the door.

Mari went out into the garden, where nothing was remotely rosy, and slammed the French doors behind him, not quite hard enough to break the glass. Then he paced around in the fading light, kicking pots over and swearing under his breath. At last, he let himself back in, went up to his room and sent Jake the email, having added a terse note to the bottom of it.

My mother is treating me like a convict. I hope you're pleased with yourself.

Then he curled up on the bed and tried to sleep.

He had been lying on top of the duvet failing to fall asleep for just over half an hour when he heard the soft chime of the front doorbell and grabbed a pillow, burrowing his head under it. Most probably it was just one of Mama's friends dropping by, but he had a sinking feeling that it wasn't. That it heralded more unwelcome interference in the quiet of their lives.

"Leave us alone!" he grumbled, irritably. "For fuck's sake!"

He seemed to have gotten his wish, at least for a few minutes. He couldn't hear anything from downstairs anyway. Only very faintly did he think he detected the sound of Tonka running down the hallway, but there was no accompanying barking. That could only mean one thing and Mari pressed the pillow over his head tighter. Tonka barked at everyone, except Jake.

There was no avoiding it. Unless he wanted to jump out of the window or hide in the closet, he was going to have to face him. According to Jake's ex, he probably wouldn't mind hiding in the closet with him. That was what he complained about the most on his social media.

Before he could get up and lock his bedroom door there was a knock, and Jake's soft, apologetic voice. "Mari, it's me. Can I come in?"

"Will it make any difference if I say no?" he asked, rolling out from under the pillow and pushing himself up so that he was at least sitting and not sprawled across the bed. He caught a glimpse of himself in the mirror on the bedroom door and winced at the sight. *Okay, so maybe I do look rough.*

The door opened and there was Jake, looking considerably less rumpled than he did. He had either come straight from work or hadn't changed before coming over. The jacket and tie were gone but he was still wearing a nice button-down shirt and dark tailored trousers. Jake's usual smile upon seeing him was replaced with a worried scowl and his eyes flitted from Mari on the bed over to the corner where his monitor sat dark.

Jake took a couple of steps into the room but stopped short of sitting down on the bed next to him. "Can we talk?"

Mari wanted to laugh. He wanted to shout at this anxious, foolish, beautiful man, to tell him that he was being stupid about nothing. Why was it that the men he fell for always seemed to either think he was a soft touch or believe he needed saving from something?

"I don't think I'm that far gone, Chivis," he answered curtly instead. "And yes, before you ask, I've been behaving myself. I sent you some information because I thought your friend Cordiline might be interested in it, but otherwise I haven't touched a button or even paddled in the tiniest cyber wave. Happy?"

Jake's mouth twisted into a hard line. "Yeah, I'm thrilled, let me tell you." He took a breath. "I am more concerned about you than Cordiline's case, Mari."

"Oh good, because that makes two of you. Thanks to you overreacting, Mama's been on my bloody case all day." Mari tried hard not to snap but he could feel himself start to shake every time he forced himself to remain calm and dispassionate. This was not how it was supposed to be when he was with Jake. For a short while after they had first met, he had blissfully allowed himself to think that he might at last have found a soulmate. It hurt to be angry with him but he couldn't help it. "I'm twenty-eight years old. I am not a child. So, if I sometimes overdo things, that's my business. Okay? I'm fine. Absolutely fine. And I'm glad you came over because there is so much I need to tell you about. Important information, not stupid fussing about me staying up all night, okay."

He realized he was talking too much, getting carried away again, but he couldn't help it.

You never do know when to shut the fuck up, do you?

Jake crossed his arms and leaned against the bedpost. Those dark golden-brown eyes were locked on him, intensely focused. "It isn't about you staying up all night and you know it, Mari." He held up a hand when Mari opened his mouth and he closed it again with a little huff of impatience. "Just listen to me for a second, please. I believe you're a good person, Mari, I couldn't love you like I do if you weren't. I can see that you care about other people, and you want to do everything you can to stop people from getting hurt. I get it, believe me. I wouldn't have become a cop if I didn't feel the same way. But you can't help other people if you get yourself killed. What you do might not be as dangerous as facing a gunman, or walking into an unknown and possibly lethal situation, but it *is* dangerous. It's just killing you more slowly than using a bullet. I'm not telling you this because I think you're some fragile flower that needs protecting. If you and I were on the force and you were my partner I'd tell you the exact same thing."

Mari bridled at first, but when Jake talked about loving him a lump began to grow in his throat, and when he spoke about him in terms of a partnership, he ached inside for something that he couldn't quite reach or understand. His shoulders slumped and he folded his hands in his lap, trying to concentrate on the mundane reality of his clammy fingers as he said, "It isn't as easy as just stopping, Jake. It's what I—damn it, if I say it's what I do, you're just going to lay into me again, aren't you? I know I need to regulate it, Chivis. I understand too what it's capable of doing to me. My great-grandmother died ahead of her time. It wasn't an accident. She wasn't ill. The ability in her burned her out and there was nothing she could do to stop it. She was stronger than me. Better than me, in every way." He looked up at Jake, studying that solemn, handsome, anxious face again, committing it to his memory, half afraid of a time coming when he would not recognize the man he was slowly beginning to fall in love with. "I don't want to die, Jake."

Jake closed the distance between them. He reached out and touched Mari's face, tracing his fingers over his cheek. Mari thought he was going to lean down and kiss him but he didn't and that made him sad.

"I don't want you to, either." Jake took a deep breath and let it out slowly, as if bracing himself. "It's part of who you are, it's even part of your job. You can't escape it and it would be both cruel and a waste for you to never use it again, but, you have to get a handle on it, so you are using the ability, instead of the other way around. The only way you can do that is to go cold turkey, until the craving stops."

Mari's heart lurched and he turned his most wide-eyed and appealing look on Jake, hating himself for doing that but terrified all the same of what would happen to him if he was not able to reach out, to escape into the places where only he could go.

"I *can't*, Jake. What if…what if I stop, then discover I can't do it anymore? The more you interact with it, the smoother, the easier it gets. It's like diving into silk. It just feels perfect. I'm practically at peak performance. I can't just *stop*."

He closed his mouth, hearing himself, hearing how that sounded like a dull, sick echo in his skull. What had Jake called him? *Junkie. Oh fuck*!

"Yes, you can, Mari. You can. You are strong enough to control it." He paused. "And you have no choice. I'm not passing any more information you give me to Cordiline, and he won't accept any from you."

"What?" Mari exploded, the incredulity rushing his system like a flood. He was on his feet instantly, and had to force himself not to grab Jake and shake him hard. "Don't be ridiculous. Look, have you even checked your mail? I sent you something really important. There is no point in me knowing this and no one else. I would have told you this morning but you just went off in my face and didn't give me a chance to get my head together. And—Jake, I found another one. No, listen," he added at once, seeing the darkening of Jake's eyes and the way his eyebrows dipped into a scowl. "It was last night. I swear I haven't done anything else today. I swear to you. The police need to hear about it because they've already looked at the case and they think it was a suicide. They're wrong."

"You've been in the police database again?" Jake asked.

Mari uttered an exasperated huff of laughter, born more of frustration than humor.

"It would serve them right if I had. I told them the first time that their security was woefully inadequate but I doubt they've done much about it." He touched his fingers to Jake's lips when he opened them to argue. "Shhh. No, I didn't need to go into their database because I knew they were investigating it. *You* told me. The guy that lived across the hall, remember him?"

"You're telling me they made a film in my building? They broke pattern and left a body?"

"Yes, if you had looked at your email – "

"Okay. I will give Cordiline what you've already sent me, but that is all. That's the last of it, Mari. You are off the case."

"Who died and made you Chief-Super?" Mari chuckled darkly. "There's something else. Your neighbor was on a suicide watch list. He was on medication because he told his doctor he was having suicidal thoughts."

Jake pinched the bridge of his nose. "You didn't get that information off of Google."

"No, I didn't but we'd still be here in years to come if we had to wait for the regular cops to find that nugget," Mari told him, combing a hand through his tangled hair, self-conscious about his bedraggled and borderline hysterical appearance. "He was registered on a handful of chat-sites dedicated to people who feel that way. Some of them are genuinely suicidal, some are just a bit unhinged. But there are sites that cater for their fascination with ending everything. And our enterprising mobile snuff team have been capitalizing on them, using them to chat up vulnerable young guys online and lure them in. Offering their services, if you like."

Jake frowned again and Mari could tell he was doing his own version of luring him in. Jake's nature was just as curious and determined as his own and Mari knew he would not be able to resist the information he had gathered for long.

"What? Some kinda twisted version of assisted suicide?"

Mari nodded agreement. "Precisely that. The guys in those movies probably knew what was going to happen to them. Just not exactly how. Creepy, huh?"

Jake made an affirmative noise, but he wasn't all that easily distracted from his course. "I'll let Cordiline in on your theory as well, but I am serious, Mari. If you go digging for any more I won't use it. I don't care if you find out the royal family is somehow involved, I'm not using any more information you find. You have to stop."

Mari pouted. He had been riding a wave of euphoria up to that moment, happy that Jake was interested enough in what he'd found to briefly not be mad at him. But they were back to square one again.

"We're so close," he protested softening his approach, letting one hand come to rest on Jake's arm and gently stroking up and down, never letting his eyes leave that melting caramel gaze. "We can pin them down with this. Just one more connection and we will have them. I can possibly even do it without interfacing. Then I'll stop. Completely. I promise."

"Yeah, like you promised before. And before that." Jake took his hand, the one that was still stroking his arm. "The cops will find them on their own. You've already put them way ahead on the right trail. That's good enough. If you decide to keep going and you contact Cordiline with more information, he will tell me about it. If that happens, I'm going to tell Karden you're in trouble. He'll speak with your new boss about making sure your duties don't include any interfacing until you can prove you've conquered the addiction."

Mari opened his mouth, then closed it again. His teeth clicked together audibly, though for a moment he was unable to process another coherent sound.

"You can't do that. Jake, please! You will ruin me," he implored at last, a cold trickle of fear running through his core at the seriousness of Jake's threat. "I need the money, for Mama, not for me, you understand. For her treatment. Please, Jake, don't say anything to Emmanuel. If I lose this job, we're done. Everything is just—" He held his hands out wide. "Am I supposed to beg, is that what you want? I will beg you, Jake. I will go down on my knees and beg you like the miserable fucking sinner that I am. Don't tell anyone. *Please*."

Jake lifted the hand he was holding and pressed it to his cheek. "You're wrong, Mari. I can do it. I don't want to, it's the last thing I want to do. So, you have to listen to me. No more interfacing. Leave it alone, leave the case alone. Do you understand?"

He did, that was the worst thing. He understood completely and that understanding filled him with horror. A void opened up before him, an emptiness that had been packed with all the nonstop communication that he took so much for granted. The buzz that gave him was his world, and Jake wanted him to walk away from it.

"How am I supposed to keep a promise like that?" he asked in a smaller voice, because his voice was threatening to shake. Terror lurked just beneath the surface of his calm veneer. "Everything I touch is potentially a gateway for me. Phones, any computerized device, hand-held pagers, satnav equipment, the fucking burglar alarm in the hallway. Jake, are you going to handcuff me to the bed and spoon feed me until you're satisfied I'm cured?"

"If I have to, yes. If you need me to. This would be so much easier if you actually wanted to get control of it, but you don't really, do you?" he said. "You think you can just keep going on the way you are, that it won't get any worse, that you won't spend more and more time with your brain plugged into a database. That you won't cause yourself some kind of aneurysm, or a stroke. It can't happen to you, right? Mari, for god's sake, if you won't do it for me, if you won't even do it for yourself, at least do it for your mother. She needs you."

The chill that had been gripping his heart flushed with a sudden shameful heat as he processed those words, that flat accusation. He pulled away, briefly angry again.

"Why the hell do you think I've been doing all this? Why sell myself to the highest bidder? It's all for her. You think I don't know how much?" He stopped, unable to speak for a moment. Throughout the years following his disastrous break-up with Tomas, only the love he had for—and received from—Mama had kept him sane and somehow dragged him back from the dark undertow he was struggling through in its wake. "If I lose her, I am dead, Jake. I might as well be dead."

He knew it was the wrong thing to say as soon as the words were out of his mouth but they could not be unsaid. Mari sat down heavily on the bed and slapped his forehead hard.

Idiot! Idiot! What are you doing?

"You'd better go and find some handcuffs then," he said angrily. Angry with himself as much as anyone else.

Jake sat down next to him, putting an arm around his shoulders. That in itself was a surprise. He had thought that Jake would pull away, seeing his declaration as a rebuttal. If the shoe had been on the other foot, he knew he would have been hurt by it.

"Does that mean you're going to try, or do you literally want me to handcuff you to the bed?"

Mari shuddered and leaned into the warmth of him, pathetically grateful for that unexpected tenderness after all that he'd flung in Jake's face, but still embarrassed by his own weakness at the same time. The thought of being handcuffed by his handsome lover was impossible to deal with. It made him want things he wasn't sure Jake was in the mood to give.

"I have to try, don't I? You give me no choice. I will need help though. I have no clue how long it will take, and I don't even know, should I actually manage to break the craving, if it won't start again the minute I go back to it. Promise me that you will make sure the police catch those bastards, Jake. Promise me that."

Jake leaned into him and placed a soft kiss on the nape of his neck. "One step at a time. First, we work to break the addiction. Then we work to get you to a point where you have control of it. If it turns out that isn't possible, then you will have a decision to make. You'll either have to give it up entirely, or find an external way to control your usage. I promise I will help you with this, Mari. You don't have to do it on your own. And I will do everything I can to make sure the people involved with making those videos are caught."

Mari shivered with need at the touch of his lips and silently cursed his dwindling willpower. When Jake spoke of him having to give up his gift, he brought his head up so fast that he practically cracked Jake's chin with it. He didn't argue, though. After the events of the last few days he felt emotionally bruised and physically exhausted.

"Right now, all I want to do is sleep," he said, and it was for once not far from the truth.

Jake stroked a hand over the back of his head, smoothing his hair. "Do you want me to stay with you?"

Mari wanted far more than that—weary and dejected as he was, the comfort of his lover's powerful body was almost as great a need as the hunger for losing himself in the Web. That comparison pulled him up short. When had the desire to interface become more important to him than pure physical gratification? He touched his fingers to the sides of Jake's solemn face, not missing the hopefulness in those lovely dark eyes. It hurt like a knife in his chest. He tilted his head and brushed a soft kiss across Jake's waiting lips.

"I think you should go," he said, and the words were like strangling vines around his throat. "I need to be able to do this on my own, don't I?"

Jake's expression didn't exactly crumble, but he wasn't able to completely hide the hurt in his eyes before he looked away. He nodded once.

"Give me your phone, and your tablet, and anything else in here you can interface with. I'll give them to Anni, just to remove temptation for a while."

Some steel returned to the set of Jake's lower jaw in response to whatever he saw in his answering glare. He was the one who averted his eyes first.

"You've thought this through, haven't you? Fair enough, take what you want." He waved a hand toward his desk and retreated to the head of the bed, where he hugged his knees to his chest as he watched Jake investigating everything with a lead or a power pack attached.

It took Jake three trips to remove everything. When he came back in, he kissed Mari gently and left, looking about as miserable as Mari felt. There were no promises to call, or text, or get in touch with him later.

Chapter Seventeen

After he left Mari, Jake forwarded the email Mari had sent him to Cordiline, with all the information he'd gathered. Half an hour later Cordiline called, skeptical that the drowning case was related to the snuff films case, but he told Jake he was willing to revisit the scene in the morning and invited him to join him and see if he could use his psychometry to find any evidence.

Jake stared at the hairline cracks in the plaster of his bedroom ceiling, his stomach sour and churning. He wanted to call Mari, but of course, Anni had his phone and every other communication device he owned. Thinking about the issue with his psychometry wasn't helping him get any sleep either. He had never *tried* to use his ability before. When he'd worked cases in the past, he had simply touched random objects and hoped he might pick something up. That was not quite the same as actively trying to get an impression. *Or was it?*

He'd always thought of it as passive acceptance of the memories he picked up, but there *was* a certain amount of mental preparation going on. A switch in mindset from hoping he didn't stumble into someone's past argument when he was out in public, to opening himself up to the possibility of receiving an impression when he was working a crime scene.

Ever since he had noticed that he wasn't getting any memories at all, from anything, he hadn't made any active attempt to receive them either. But was that resistance blocking his ability to see into the past? Whether it was as simple as that, he wasn't sure, but without any further information about his gift or instruction on how to use it, it was the best he had to go on.

When at last Jake gave up on sleep he got out of bed and made coffee, waited for the sun to rise and Cordiline to knock on his door. It wasn't until he was standing in his dead neighbor's apartment that he wondered if having the added pressure of Cordiline watching and, in a way, testing him, would help or hinder the process. All he could do was try.

"Certain objects hold on to memories better than others," Jake told him. He didn't have to explain, but talking sometimes helped him calm his nerves and get in the zone. Funny how he'd never thought of even having 'a zone' before, but he supposed it was true. He had a better chance of getting an impression from an object if he was relaxed, if he was focused.

Cordiline didn't respond. He stayed where he was, observing. Jake lightly glided his fingers over items in the room. The fact that he had still gotten nothing was stressing him, but at the same time there was no way for him to be certain if it was just that the object hadn't retained any memories, or if he had permanently lost his ability. He took a couple of deep breaths.

"I've been meaning to tell you that they've set a trial date for Aled Mustatti," Cordiline said at last, when nothing seemed to be happening.

Jake's fingers twitched on the piece of junk mail he'd picked up. "Yeah? Good." He didn't know what else he was expected to say.

"They've charged him with a whole shopping list of items, including treason and espionage. Really threw the bag at him."

Jake raised an eyebrow. "Those are some serious charges."

"I imagine MI5 are a wee bit pissed off that he was unleashing their experiment without their say so," Cordiline said dryly. "Guess what he *isn't* being charged with?"

Jake glanced over at him and those slate-blue eyes regarded him solemnly.

"He's not being charged with sexual assault."

Jake's gaze didn't even flicker, he made sure of it. "I'm sure, if they lock him up for treason and espionage, his sentence will be long enough."

"Granted. Still, you understand how prosecutors like to be thorough."

"What makes you think anything like that happened anyway?" Jake demanded, angrier than he meant to sound.

"Your boyfriend isn't the only one who knows how to snoop around."

"It's not even your case."

"No, but as I was on the case initially, I was able to request some of the transcripts to close out my files." Cordiline leaned against the doorframe, still watching him, his hands pushed down deep into the pockets of his long, dark-blue wool overcoat. "There were 'biological samples' found at the scene. That's the only thing it says in the official report, but I'm pretty tight with some of the guys that work in evidence."

Jake clenched his jaw. "Is there a point here?"

"Why didn't you tell them what happened in your statement?"

Jake laughed bitterly. "Are you serious? If you had been drugged and tied to a bed would *you* tell anyone about how being jerked off against your will can actually happen? Why would I tell anyone about that? He's already going down for the other shit, I don't need any vindication for him being a dirty bastard on top of it. You know how it would go. Those cops would snicker behind their hands and figure I probably wanted it anyway, just because I'm gay. It's not worth the aggravation."

Cordiline shrugged. "If that's the way you feel, that it's okay for him to get away with that," he said keeping his tone casual.

"Oh, fuck off. You can take that reverse psychology bullshit and shove it up your ass." Jake put his hand on a jar that was sitting on the table and a jolt went up his arm like he'd touched a live wire. Cordiline disappeared and the room darkened.

Jake turned around and looked over at the two men sitting on the sofa.

"So, do you want something to drink first?" The voice coming from his mouth belonged to Jim Sullivan, his former neighbor.

The man he spoke to was small and fair-haired, totally unassuming. His smile was languid, knowing. Like he was humoring him about something. "Sure, do you have black tea?"

The man sitting next to the blond guy on the sofa snorted. He had sharp, dark eyes, reddish hair and a pinched look to his mouth that made it seem like he was permanently sneering. He also had a small tattoo on his arm. This was the man that had strangled Wade in the snuff film Mari found, he was sure of it. The guy in the mask. And now that he got a good look at him, Jake also realized he knew him.

As Jake tried to place him, he was slammed back into the present and he let the jar go with a gasp. Strong, warm hands were on his upper arms, and he let himself be maneuvered into a nearby chair as the fallen jar rolled across the wooden floor toward the kitchen units and thunked to a solid halt.

"Are you all right, Chivis?" Cordiline crouched in front him, his brows drawn down and his gaze intent.

"Yeah, yeah, I'm okay," he got out. His voice quavered and he cleared his throat. For all that it had been a short vision, it was one of the most vivid he'd ever had. It had felt incredibly real and he was still trying to sift details before he forgot them. "I think I've seen him before, John."

Coraline went still. "You saw someone here, saw their face?"

Jake nodded toward the couch only feet away in the living room. "I saw them both, the guy wearing the mask in the videos, *and* the one I'm assuming was behind the camera, through Jim's eyes. The guy shooting the videos I've never seen before, as far as I know. But I recognized the tat on the other guy. And I recognized *him*. I've seen him somewhere, recently. I just—" Jake stopped talking for a second, thinking, then said, "I think I've seen him downstairs, at the bar."

"They're local then." Cordiline mulled this over. "Do you think you could help our photographic people do an e-fit of him?"

Jake shrugged. "Possibly. I'd recognize him if I saw him again anyway. If we don't get a hit on him, though, there is always the possibility that he'll show up once the bar re-opens this weekend."

"Okay." Cordiline nodded slowly. "We can try that, Jake. But we'll get an image in circulation as well. Even if they aren't connected to his death, if we can talk to them they might be able to tell us something. You're sure about the tattoo? It's the same one you saw, just now?"

"Yes, it was pretty distinctive. Like a SIM card, or a microchip maybe."

"Well, that's something to go on, at least. Do you get a sense of the time period they were here, or is it just —?" He waved a hand vaguely. "Could it have been any time, I guess is what I'm saying?"

"I can't tell you when they were here, it doesn't work like...that." Jake stopped talking. He was often frustrated by not knowing how old a memory was, unable to pinpoint a time until there was something very specific in the memory to tell him. However, he had a vague feeling now that he did somehow have a sense of how old this memory was.

"I think it was recent." He stopped again, frowning, replaying the memory frame by frame in his head. He looked down at the table and picked up the envelope he'd been touching earlier. The postmark was just over a week old. "This was on the table in the memory, so it must have been not long after it was delivered, and you've established when he died, so I'd say they were probably here the night Jim was killed."

Cordiline rose to his feet and patted him on the shoulder. "Well deduced. A good detective never loses his instincts. We'll get you booked in to talk to the e-fit guys and circulate a description."

Jake smiled. Now that the initial violent shock of being thrown into and out of the memory was wearing off — along with the realization that he'd actually seen the killer outside of his building before — he was excited. They were getting closer. If he could get a positive ID it would only be a matter of time before they brought him in, and Jake would have kept his promise to Mari.

Of course, thinking of Mari damped down his sudden elation. He had no idea where they stood now. Mari had seemed accepting that he needed to make a change in his habits, and he'd made promises, but that didn't mean everything was patched up between them or that they would go on as they had before.

"You can tell that pretty boy of yours to stop fraying his wits at both ends then," Cordiline said, as if reading his mind. "We've got his bad men for him. I'm sure that will astonish him."

Jake managed a cynical smile. "I'm sure it will. For the moment, I don't even know if he's talking to me." He rolled his shoulders to ease the tightness there and stood.

"Your on-again, off-again relationship with the good doctor is becoming something of a pattern," Cordiline murmured. "What's biting his backside this week?"

They walked out into the hallway and Cordiline locked up behind them. Jake waited until the detective followed him inside his own apartment before answering, "Let's just say he did not take it well when

I told him I wasn't giving you any more info from him, and you wouldn't accept it either."

"You really think that will stop him? He's headstrong, Jake. Nothing short of a straitjacket will hold him."

"No, I'm not that naïve," Jake told him. "He's got other reasons to stop, though, and that's the best I can do for him. Other than that, it's up to Mari. Until he gets his head around it, I'm as good a target as any for his anger. I'm just hoping he doesn't hate me too much when it's over."

Or even that he's still alive and sane when it's over.

"So, you really are serious about him?" Cordiline flopped down on the sofa, looking up at him with genuine sympathy. "What is it with him? I'd not have said he was your type at all. But what do I know, huh?"

Not too long ago, Jake would have brushed him off and told him to mind his own business, but he'd warmed up to the pertinacious detective and managed a dry chuckle. "If you have to ask, you need to get your eyes checked, Detective."

"It's just his pretty face and his nice arse then?" Cordiline laughed. "Not sure whether to be jealous or disappointed."

Jake shook his head. "That was it initially, yeah. Isn't it always? But Mari is a good person, he cares. A lot of people, all they give a shit about is making bank, or getting laid, or gossiping about who's fucking who. Mari is interesting to talk to, he has a good brain between his ears, and I like that."

"Well, I hope he sees sense and stops jerking your chain, Chivis." Cordiline leaned forward, clasping his hands between his knees. "You deserve better than that, mate. I'm gonna have to talk to him about what he's seen, you understand that. I'll try to be nice."

"Yeah, I know. And I'm sure he's gonna want to turn the other videos he found over to you." Jake hesitated. He knew he was walking a line here between his personal feelings and Cordiline's case. "I'd really appreciate it if you stuck to what he's already collected in the email I forwarded to you and not ask him if he can find anything else."

Those shrewd blue eyes narrowed inquisitively. "Dr. Gale isn't employed by the Met, Jake. I'd be acting outside my jurisdiction if I encouraged interference. I don't have to tell you that," Cordiline said, his voice professionally neutral for once. "And if he volunteers? Presumably you want me to tell him as much?"

Jake nodded. "If you'd tell him you don't need his help, *if* he offers, I'd be grateful." Although at the moment he felt like a heel for asking. He knew Mari's expertise could be invaluable to solving the case. Also, he understood how badly Mari wanted to help.

"And I suppose it's a given that I don't mention your assistance this afternoon?" Cordiline said pointedly.

Jake rubbed the back of his neck. "I'd rather you didn't. You could just tell him you're looking at suspects already."

Cordiline rose to his feet and held out his hand.

"Thanks for the advice, Detective. I could indeed," he said and Jake couldn't quite tell if he was being sarcastic or not. "I'll be on my way then, if you're not gonna offer me a brew, or anything?"

Jake tried to push the guilty feelings aside. It was bad enough he was talking about relationship stuff with Cordiline, he didn't also want to lead him on in any way. "Sorry, some other time maybe. I need to get into work." Which was true enough, since he'd only told them he'd be in a few minutes late.

Chapter Eighteen

Mari slept surprisingly well that night. For a while after Jake had departed, taking his equipment stash with him, he'd remained huddled up against the bedpost with his chin on his knees, determined that he was not going to get hysterical about the situation. He was angry and also slightly hurt that Jake hadn't pushed harder to stay. But then he figured he probably didn't deserve that much kindness.

"Oh, Gran Amelia, why couldn't you have gifted me a nice, tame, manageable talent?" he exhaled at last and wriggled under the duvet, trying to sleep.

With his arms around the pillow, he imagined holding Jake's warm body close and that helped. Soon, in spite of all his frustration and his fears that Jake would never want to speak to him again, he let his eyes fall closed and at last dreams overtook him.

He woke early the next morning and took Tonka for a run, though he still ached everywhere when he tried to push himself as hard as normal. Back home he went through his usual daily routines, minus the itchy habit of checking his phone, checking his mail, checking the news online, posting the curious sights from the park like the one-legged man doing his tai chi exercises and the chubby hangover from some office party sleeping off the beer under a bush, clad in a pink bikini, with a balloon hovering above him, its string tied somewhere between his legs.

He set out the breakfast things for Mama but didn't take her tea up as it was still early, and the temptation to search her room for contraband IT would be too great. Besides, like every evil genius, he had a plan B.

The office on the fourth floor of Trafalgar House was quiet at this time of the morning, and he was grateful that Jake hadn't seen fit to confiscate his security pass and door tags last night. Embarrassing enough to have missed most of his first proper day at work, and the day after that, not being able to get in the building would have sealed his mortification. He settled into his cubicle and laced his fingers, cracking the knuckles in anticipation, then fired up his desk PC and monitor with a wicked smile.

You're a clever boy, Chivis, but you can't watch me all the time.

He let the system warm up, then logged in to his mailbox and set a notification with a bell alarm for quarter to eight. That gave him half an hour, give or take a few minutes, which was more than enough time for what he needed to do, and surely a short enough span that he could come out of it without taxing his mental resources too badly.

That done, he went back to the main office door and touched the tag scanner, reaching into the system and interfacing with it briefly to jam the unlocking mechanism. A satisfied smile quirked his lips and he returned to the privacy of his cube and opened an online mapping application. Touching his fingers to the three areas he knew were already murder locations, he closed his eyes and jumped in.

Eighteen minutes and thirty-seven seconds later, he jolted out of the Web, disturbed by a noise that he couldn't readily identify at first. The alarm he had set went off seconds later, making him jump but bringing him to his senses. He traced the initial disturbance to the glass doors leading out into the corridor. Someone was trying to get in. Mari shut down the mapping app and went to the door with his own tag key. He feigned an expression of bewilderment that the door wasn't working, then tapped his tag to it. At the same time, he touched a finger to the pad and pressed a tendril of his own will through into the locking system, unjamming it.

"Mine works fine," he said when his co-worker came blustering in, expressing disgust at the uselessness of their security system. "Maybe your tag's compromised. I'd get it checked out."

He returned to the desk and opened the maps again, checking coordinates and scribbling notes on the pad by his side. That felt odd after almost a decade of recording everything on his phone. His handwriting was scratchy and disjointed, like someone had dipped a dying crane fly in ink and dragged it across the page.

True what they say about doctors' handwriting then.

He composed an email to Jake, summarizing the notes he had made on potential locations for their killers and hit send, then locked his PC and went in search of coffee.

* * * *

When he got home from the office late that evening, a familiar, tall, dark figure was waiting near the three steps up to the front door, and his heart sank when he realized right away that it wasn't Jake. Cordiline spotted him straight off and headed along the pavement to intercept him before he reached the house.

"Good evening, Inspector," Mari said cordially. "What a surprise. How can I help you?"

"Good evening, Dr. Gale. I hope you don't mind my stopping by unannounced. I looked into the information you provided Jake with, and wanted to discuss a few items with you."

"Always happy to help the boys in blue," Mari said with a theatrical smile. "I suppose you'd better come in, the neighbors do like to gossip."

As he opened the front door, Tonka came pounding down the hallway to meet them, took one look at Cordiline and set up a clamorous howling until Mari dragged him to the kitchen, admonishing him with less severity than usual. Privately he was quite pleased. Even Tonk disliked the man. Though right now Tonk disliked just about everyone that wasn't Jake.

"What on earth is going on out there?" Mama asked, looking up from a heavy textbook in her lap as he poked his head around the door into the day room.

"Just a visitor. Keep Tonka in here, will you. We'll use the crypt. Won't be long." He backed out and shut the door before she could ask anything else, then ushered Cordiline into the front parlor. "It's more private in here."

Cordiline went in and Mari flicked the light on. It wasn't dark outside just yet, but it was going to rain soon and the clouds made the evening sky even grayer.

"Jake tells me you stumbled across the first video by accident. I don't suppose these others you claim to have found were an accident as well?" he asked Mari.

"You don't suppose correctly, Inspector," Mari told him, pacing to the window as he shrugged off his raincoat and tossed it over the back of the nearest armchair. He turned to face him, steeling himself. Cordiline didn't like him much, he knew, and the feeling was mutual, but they could at least be polite. They were trying to reach the same end. "I went back in deliberately to see if they'd made more than one. Sadly, I was right. They seem to have developed a taste for the game."

"And you have copies of those as well, I presume?"

"Naturally," Mari said, reaching for the messenger bag he had discarded with his overcoat. Jake had taken the hardware but he still had his trusty flash drives. "I even made copies of the copies for insurance, you'll be pleased to hear. I expect you would like to see them."

"Yes, if you wouldn't mind turning them over I will bring them in for forensics to look at as well. We appreciate your cooperation, Dr. Gale," Cordiline told him, with only the faintest hint of condescension.

Mari had retrieved a ziplock A5 wallet from his bag and he opened it up, like a surgeon revealing his scalpel set, ran a fingertip over the array of plug in drives arranged neatly within, and selected one. It was pink and had a Hello Kitty logo on it.

"There you go, Inspector. She's all yours," he said, handing it over solemnly. "Excuse the design, it was all I could get at short notice. There was something else—

the victims were all undergoing counselling for suicide prevention. There were referrals from their GPs in two cases and the other was talking to the Samaritans. They were all members of an online forum for young men with severe mental health issues. I've made notes on that and they're on the memory stick too."

He zipped up the wallet and returned it to one of the side pockets of his dark leather bag, then sat down on the arm of the chair, looking seriously at Cordiline.

Cordiline slipped the Hello Kitty flash drive into his pocket with hardly a glance. He met Mari's intent gaze and said, "If that's all you have, I will take my leave, Dr. Gale."

Mari combed the fingers of his left hand through his hair, nervous and excited in equal measure.

"I think I've worked out where the killers are, Inspector. I've followed communications between them and their three known victims, via that forum I mentioned, and they all triangulate here, or near as damn it, to the King's Cross area. They're clever, they never communicate or set up meetings from home. The message arranging to meet Wade was sent from an internet cafe on Judd Street, the communications with the victim in St. Albans came from a public access terminal in Pancras Square library and victim number three lived just around the corner from here, practically. He's perplexing me — I haven't established how they contacted him, but he was a member of the forum, though he didn't speak to either of the killers on there. They could have walked to the apartment though. The other two were both on rail services out of Kings Cross. I'd stake good money that's how they traveled to meet their victims, you should be able to pick them up on CCTV at the station on the days we know the men were killed."

He closed his mouth with an innocent smile because Cordiline was getting that glazed look that told him he'd been talking too long without breathing again.

Instead of a smile, or any comment on the information Mari had just given him, Cordiline looked down at him, his eyes nearly hooded by the drooping lids. "Is there a reason you didn't include this new intelligence with the email that you sent Chivis?"

Mari shrugged. "I wasn't sure until this morning, Inspector. I needed to check on a couple of things first, and I was — I was having connection issues. Once I'd sat down and mapped the pattern of their communications, it was obvious."

"Uh-huh." Cordiline looked at him without blinking. "Well, that was thoughtful of you, but maybe unnecessary. We have a positive ID on one of the suspects."

Mari's eyes opened wider. He felt his pulse quicken and wondered if this was how it felt to be a hunter, sensing prey, ready to spring.

"You know who he is? Have you arrested him yet?"

"I can't divulge that information." Cordiline paused, still pinning Mari with that unblinking gaze. "Jake Chivis ID-ed the suspect, just a few hours ago. Thought you might like to be in the loop. Maybe if you'd had more faith in him from the start, he might not have looked like someone had just shot his puppy when I met with him this morning."

That hit him like a Taser bolt to the chest. Mari narrowed his eyes. He wasn't sure if he was angrier that Cordiline had been sniffing around Jake like a dog round a bitch in heat again, or that Jake hadn't bothered to tell him that he'd managed to identify one of the killers.

"I *do* have faith in him. What has he been saying? Did he tell you that?" he demanded. "If anything, it's the other way around, he has no faith in me."

Cordiline's lips curled in a cold smile that came nowhere near his eyes. "I don't really see that he has a reason to put any faith in you, Dr. Gale. He seemed to be under the impression that – for 'personal reasons' – you wouldn't be able to use your rather unique talents to assist on this case in the future. Yet you had no problem doing just that, as soon as his back was turned. Maybe you should go and ask him what he's had to say, although I'd be just as happy if you left him alone."

Mari's lower jaw sagged briefly and for a second or two he wasn't sure whether to punch Cordiline or laugh at him. In his head, he heard Li Chao murmur, '*Count to three, Master Ilmari.*' And he did.

One.

I am going to see you eat your badge you bastard!

Two.

Either that or shove it up your arse for you, myself.

Three.

Cool. Calm. Game face on.

"I'm absolutely sure that you'd love that, Detective Inspector," he replied, in a voice that might have iced the Serpentine over. "Although, even if I promised I would never look at him again, *you'd* still stand less chance with him than you would of marrying the Prince of Fucking Wales! Why don't you just do your job and stop speculating about the private lives of people that have fuck all to do with you? And, here's another thing to chew on, if you'd asked him more about my 'personal reasons' for not checking up on this sooner, he might or might not have told you, bearing in mind that it's none of your fucking business, that I didn't do it sooner because *he* had taken my fucking computer equipment. I suggest that you leave, Inspector. I don't think we've got anything else to say to one another."

His voice had dropped to barely more than a soft hiss between his teeth by this last remark

Cordiline shook his head. "You talk enough for three people, do you know that? I wonder why it was he had to take all your computer equipment away in the first place, huh? Not that it did any good, did it. I've seen boys like you treat plenty of men like shite. When he gets tired of your tantrums and games, don't be surprised if someone else is ready to snatch him up and treat him well, that's all I'm saying. Good evening, Dr. Gale. I'll show myself out."

Mari uttered a huff of incredulous laughter. He wasn't sure if he was amused or offended, but he was not going to let Cordiline have the last word.

"I'm not a boy! I'm twenty-fucking-eight, as a matter of fact. And whoever gets him will be lucky. He's a catch all right, don't think I don't realize that. But it won't be you, old man!" he pitched his voice louder as he heard the Inspector head for the front door. "Go and solve some crime!"

Mari could hear the faint sound of a cheery whistle as the door closed behind Cordiline. It was enough to make him want to throw something.

"Smug bastard!" he muttered under his breath. "I hope you choke on your false teeth!"

"What is going on out here?" his mother asked from behind him.

Only as he turned around did he realize that his cheeks were wet. The faint draft from the hallway brushed the saline tracks and chilled them before he dashed them away on the back of his hand.

"Nothing. Just making a contribution to Help the Aged, Mama. It's fine, go back to your book."

"Don't you patronize me, Ilmari," Anni told him. "Here." She handed him his cell phone. "In case you need to phone someone."

He almost didn't close his fingers around it in time and even when he did it was with a faint sense of relief and incredulity. The sense of comfort he got from it almost overrode the double meaning behind her last remark.

"He doesn't want to speak to me, Mama." The words caught in his throat and he stood there staring at the slender rectangle of plastic and chrome in his right hand as if it was an insult, not a gift.

"Oh, Ilmari." She came closer and put her cool, fond hand on his cheek. "How could I have raised you to be so brilliant and yet so dumb. Of course he wants to speak to you. He wouldn't have come here last night and promised you the things he did if he didn't want to speak to you again."

Mari sat down then, because his legs wouldn't support him anymore. He put the phone down carefully on the sofa, at arm's length.

"I made him go away. Last night, I told him to go. Not in an angry way or anything. I was tired. I felt ill. But he just looked so...so hurt. And I thought he didn't want to be with me, but now I'm not sure." He put his elbows on his knees and his head in his hands, digging his fingers hard into his scalp. "Inspector Gadget's right. Jake could have his pick. He could have anyone. Why would he want me?"

"I don't think the why matters as much as the fact that he *does* want you. You are being silly, Mari. I am not wrong about this. I've seen it every time he looks at you. He adores you as much as that silly dog of mine adores him. Speaking of which, why don't you take Tonka over there, before he pines away?"

Mari lifted his head. "This is all a clever ruse of yours to get me to walk your bloody dog, isn't it?"

He managed a weak laugh though, pushing down the groundswell of emotion that had briefly threatened to overwhelm him. In truth, it was not a bad idea. If he called or just went round there on his own, Jake could easily ignore him or shut the door in his face. But he would never do that to Tonka. As evil genius plans went, it was a pretty solid one.

"I love you, Mama," he said, and meant it.

"I love you too, my darling boy. Go and take Tonka for that walk, and make it up with your man," she told him firmly.

He picked up the phone and saluted her with it. "Yes, ma'am."

Chapter Nineteen

Jake went for a run after he got off work, since he'd missed going in the morning. He was about to hop in the shower, and thinking about whether he should try calling Mari or just drop by unannounced, when someone knocked on his door. His heart rate picked up. The only occasions when anyone knocked directly on his apartment door rather than use the buzzer downstairs, it was either Mari, or the cops or even — one time — MI5.

It proved to be the former, this morning, and the relief that swept through Jake as he opened the door to see those anxious, wide blue eyes looking at him pushed away all his other concerns about what Mari might be doing here, just for the moment.

"Come in," Jake said, sweeping one gentle arm around Mari's back and giving Tonka a pat and a scratch behind his ears with the other hand. "I just got in from a run."

Mari sniffed him lightly and murmured, "I can tell. Fortunately, this stupid dog has just dragged me around the park twice, chasing a squirrel, so I can't really complain." He hesitated, stopping short of just planting a kiss on him the way Jake so wanted him to. "Your dog has been missing you, pack-leader."

Jake smiled down at Tonka. "He's my dog, is he? I think your mother might have something to say about that." When he lifted his head, those eyes he could fall into and drown in were watching him intently. "I missed you too."

"You did, huh? Good. So you should have." Mari looked stubborn, his chin lifted an inch or so, but his lips quirked into a little grin.

It was so strange. Just a few days ago Jake wouldn't have hesitated for even a moment to wrap his arms around him and kiss him hard, but after all the arguing they had done, after the ultimatums he'd given and how Mari hadn't wanted him to stay, Jake wasn't sure if Mari was here because he wanted to be, or if he was here to break it off with him in person.

"Mari—" Jake wanted to ask if he was okay, if he was still furious with him, why he was here, a dozen other questions. Instead he ran his fingers over Mari's cheek and kissed him anyway.

To his relief, Mari didn't push him away this time. Some of Jake's tension eased as he stroked his other hand slowly up Mari's back. For a few moments that was all there was, just himself and Mari, joined at the lips, bare inches inside the front door.

"Well, that was nice," Mari exhaled softly when their lips finally parted. His eyes were a glittering shade of cobalt, much darker than before. "You should miss me more often."

"I'm so tired of arguing with you, Mari. I just want you to be happy again." Jake kissed him again, just a brief touch of the lips this time.

"Hmmm, that's funny," Mari mused, eyeing him with a thoughtful look on his face. "Not what your friend said this evening, at all. He seemed to think that you'd be a lot better off if I just left you alone."

Jake brought both hands to Mari's shoulders. "What? Who the fuck said that?"

Though he had some idea.

"I'll give you three clues, shall I? Let me see, he's grumpy, he hates me and he asks a lot of really stupid questions. I did try very hard to be polite to him seeing as how he's getting on in years, and he's a lonely, bitter old stick, but he didn't help himself much, in all fairness."

Jake sucked in a breath and took a moment to think before he spoke. He very nearly made the mistake of asking Mari if that was word-for-word what Cordiline had said, but he was stunned, not stupid. "I can't believe he told you that. I would *not* be better off if you left me, Mari. I really hope you didn't come here to break it off with me."

"Why would I want to do that?" Mari asked. "I thought that, if anyone was going to dump anyone else, then it would be you showing me the door, especially after the way I spoke to you the other night." He hesitated then, more tentatively, added, "I'm so sorry, Jake. Really, I am."

That smallness in his voice tugged at Jake's heart, even as the relief that Mari wasn't planning on dumping him threatened to take him out at the knees. He pulled Mari into his arms, squeezing him tight and burrowing his face into the crook of his neck. That warm, familiar, woodsy scent of him filled his nostrils and calmed his nerves.

"Stay with me. Can you stay tonight?"

He felt Mari nod, awkwardly given the way they were pulled together.

"Yes. Okay," he whispered, his breath warm against Jake's ear.

Jake eased up at long last, loosening his grip enough to lean back and brush another kiss over Mari's lips.

"I used psychometry today. I think I can turn it on and off at will. I saw the men that killed Jim Sullivan."

"I love your dirty talk," Mari teased him, hooking a finger in the neckline of his running T-shirt and walking backward the four steps to the sofa where he flopped onto the cushions and pulled Jake down with him. "So that's what your stalker meant when he said the police already had a positive ID on the killer. Clever you. We know what they look like and we have a good idea where they live. The net is closing in."

"Yes. I promised you that we would get them. It's only a matter of time. They won't go unpunished, Mari."

"Of course not." Mari caught a lock of Jake's hair between his finger and thumb and used it to tow his mouth down onto his again. When Mari's tongue slipped out of his mouth he murmured, "I told you it would come back, didn't I? You should trust me, Chivis. I know these things."

Jake figured he should just leave it at that and continue kissing him, but the words poked at him.

"I do trust you. There's something I need to tell you." He saw the flicker of doubt and concern in Mari's eyes and hurried on before he changed his mind about coming clean. "I kept something from you. I'm still not sure I have a handle on it. Don't look at me like that, it's not as bad as you're thinking. My temper hasn't been the only thing that been hot lately. I literally have been spiking a fever when I get angry. That's why I left so fast the other morning. I was so mad I had to run it off before, well, before anything bad happened."

Mari opened his mouth to say something but for a few seconds nothing came out. Those huge, luminous blue eyes stared at him, comprehension dawning in them.

"You mean, you might not— The drug they gave you?" Mari stopped and swallowed hard. "You think that you might still…burn? Why the fuck didn't you say anything?" He didn't raise his voice but there was an edge of anxiety there.

"I didn't want to worry you. I don't know what might happen. No one does, Mari. It could go away on its own. It might not. I— I've no idea."

"Oh, well, that's okay then." Mari's voice cracked on the last word. "Jake, you let me get you riled like that, when it might have— Oh fuck! You *idiot*!"

He snaked his arms around Jake's neck and towed him down again, kissing him more hungrily, as if he was scared it might be his last chance.

"I'm sorry," Jake murmured between kisses. "I wasn't thinking about myself." And he didn't really want to think about it now either, given the way Mari kept kissing him between each word. He gave in and pressed Mari down on the sofa. A rush of heat of a different sort ran through him as Mari sank his fingers into his hair and he spread his knees so Jake could fit between.

"Uhhh, fuck, Mari, I missed you," he murmured.

"I've missed you too," Mari crooned against his cheek. The hand that wasn't clutching his hair raked down his back, then crept beneath his T-shirt, pushing the hemline higher before Mari peeled it roughly off him.

Jake lay down again, holding himself up on his elbows as Mari caressed him. Desire made Mari's mouth softer and his eyes darker. Just an hour ago he'd wondered if Mari would ever want to see him again, but he was here and touching him and Jake could hardly believe it was real.

He was already more than half hard, the outline of his cock tenting the track pants he wore. Mari stroked lower with one caressing hand, finding and encouraging the growing stiffness, rubbing him through the clinging material. With his other hand, he tugged down the zipper on his hoodie. Under it he was nude, a sheen of sweat already forming between his candy-pink nipples. His tongue flickered between his lips and he pumped Jake harder, then eased his hand inside his pants and into his boxer briefs, wrapping his fingers around Jake's cock.

"You are so hard," he breathed, a tendril of mischief twisting through his words. "That's good."

"Mmhhh, yeahhh," Jake exhaled as Mari pumped him slowly up and down. He had a normal healthy sex drive and the last few days of fighting, worrying and stress hadn't been particularly conducive to thinking about sex but, the second Mari touched him, his body reminded him that it had been a while. "That feels so much better than good, babe."

Mari pulled him down, his free hand hooked around the back of Jake's neck, and kissed him again. The slow, rhythmic stroke of his fingers and thumb glided up and down his swollen length from root to tip.

"He's a big boy tonight. Have you been neglecting him, Chivis?" Mari teased.

"He's been missing you," Jake chuckled. He bent his head and kissed Mari's collarbone, the center of his chest, and sucked one pink nipple into his mouth. He eased a hand between them and over Mari's crotch, rubbing him in return, and he swore his own cock got harder yet at the way Mari arched and moaned.

"Let me get you out of these." Jake fumbled with the tie on Mari's pants and pulled them down his hips. "That's much better." He wrapped his own hand around Mari's dick, mirroring his strokes and scraping the edge of his teeth over one small, hard nipple.

His slender lover arched his back, his body making a long, lean curve, that pushed up against Jake's hips and belly as he tormented Mari's sensitive nipples. He gasped and bucked in Jake's hand, pumping Jake's shaft faster in response.

"Ohhh, fuck! So sweet!" Mari thrust himself in the tunnel of Jake's fingers. "I'm so hot for you right now."

Jake gave a soft growl in response, sucking harder on the tender pink bud in his mouth. He didn't want to move, didn't want to rearrange his limbs or do anything else. He didn't think it was going to take all that much more to get off anyway and it felt so damn good just to have Mari's mouth and hands on him, to have him writhing in response to his own touch. He tightened his grip around Mari's shaft, aware of just what it did to him when he treated him rough. He teased the tip of Mari's nipple with his teeth, pulling it away from his chest.

"Uuuhhhh, uuhhhh, fuck, yeah. Fuck, yeah!" Mari panted over and over, his voice growing huskier and more ragged. His soft, warm hand ghosted over Jake's chest and he pinched one of his nipples, twisting it and tugging on it. "Mmmhhh, Jake. I'm gonna come, gonna come soon if you keep, uh, ohhhh!"

His body contorted and thrashed sinuously as he kept that promise.

"Oh, god, Mari, my beautiful, beautiful Mari," Jake panted as he jerked him off, his own climax building. He held off long enough to fully enjoy the way his lover moved and spurted in his hand, then it was too much to hold back any longer.

The clench just behind his pelvic wall released the moment before his balls tightened and he unloaded in a warm gush of white over the muscles of Mari's flexing stomach.

"Mmmhhhhh, so wonderful. You needed that." Mari grinned, still gently stroking Jake's twitching cock. He drew a finger through the thick, salty semen on his undulating belly and put it in his mouth, making small, happy noises.

Jake chuckled weakly, resting his forehead against Mari's shoulder. "I don't think I'm the only one that needed that," he murmured, bringing his sticky hand up so he could caress Mari's bottom lip with his thumb. "How about a shower, and we can start over, hmm?"

"Sounds perfect to me," Mari agreed.

Jake found some kibble and a little bowl of water for Tonka, who had been most respectful of his young masters' need for playtime, though he was watching them with interest when they untangled and rose from the settee. Mari made a warm nest for him out of a blanket and one of the seat cushions from the sofa, and once the little dog was happily curled up there, they retired to the bedroom and spent the rest of the evening making up for the time they'd been apart. Their lovemaking had a peculiar intensity, powered by the relief of being in each other's arms again, of knowing that they had survived the storm and were still together. Jake steeled himself for the moment when Mari decided he needed to go home, but to his relief that moment didn't come. Just before midnight, Mari fell asleep in his arms and stayed there until morning.

Chapter Twenty

When Jake woke, there was a warm, comforting presence beside him on the bed. As he scrubbed the sleep from his eyes, he was greeted by a rough tongue licking his face. He fended off the over-friendly mukwa, and Tonka hopped off the bed when he got up and trotted after him into the lounge, tail wagging. His young master hadn't gone far. Mari was curled up on the couch, wrapped in a checkered woolen throw that Jake usually tossed over the leather sofa cushions for additional warmth. He had Jake's laptop on his knees and was studying something, with a bemused expression on his face, though Jake was grateful to see that he was just browsing like a normal person and not zoned out on the settee at the first available excuse.

Mari lifted his face for a kiss as Jake leaned over him to find out what he was doing. There were three or four windows open on the screen and he was flicking back and forth between them, bringing up different chatrooms and forums.

"I've set up a profile on a couple of these," he explained. "The killers have been monitoring a handful of chatrooms, mostly on this one site. I figured I could see if they want to talk to me. I just need your phone so I can take a selfie. Your laptop won't talk to my cell phone, for some reason."

"Should I even ask how you managed to log on to my machine?" Jake said drily. He'd encrypted the password system on it himself. Mari just gave him a look that said *duh!* and he waved it off. "Whatever. I can't keep you out of trouble for five minutes, can I?"

"I'm not in trouble, I'm just ta-a-alking." Mari stretched out the word, a response that made him sound about ten years younger. "And you kept me out of trouble for quite a long time last night, as I recall. I ache in all the right places." He held one hand out. "Phone. Please?"

Those big blue eyes turned up toward him again, wide and imploring. Jake huffed and stomped into the bedroom for his phone, trying to ignore the way his cock twitched at the reminder of last night.

His convenience store mobile wasn't as technologically advanced as Mari's—which, coupled with its owner's elemental abilities, was in all likelihood capable of piloting a space shuttle—but it did have a camera. He returned with it and dropped it into Mari's hand.

"*Merci*," his boyfriend said, with an easy grin. "I made coffee."

"Thanks." Jake crossed to the kitchenette to pour them both a mug.

Mari pulled up the hood on his track top and tugged a few wayward streamers of pale hair down over his face. The early sunlight creeping through the blinds glinted off the twenty-four-hour golden stubble on his chin and made his long, tawny lashes half-translucent as he held out the phone at different angles, taking snaps of himself and surveying them critically one at a time.

"What happened to 'letting the police do their job'?" Jake asked, coming to sit facing him at the other end of the sofa and sipping his coffee, grateful for the caffeine rush.

"I'm not stopping them, am I?" Mari said, a grimace twisting his lips as he waited for the images to upload to Jake's machine. "There's no law against a guy joining a few online groups and making new friends. Though some of them are a bit OTT, even if I do say so myself. They're supposed to be 'Mens' Health' forums but quite a few of them are basically online meat-lockers. No wonder young guys feel under so much pressure!"

His fingers flicked over the keys, barely making a sound above a gentle scuffle, as he added images to his new social media persona. The laptop pinged at him and he uttered a small, incredulous laugh.

"The power of the image. I upload two photos and already I have a guy wanting to show me his dick. Classy. Not!"

He tapped a short, rapid message and hit send.

The laptop pinged, then pinged again. Mari tilted his head and wrinkled his pretty nose, then looked across at Jake, still sprawled comfortably naked on the other throw, facing him. "Not as big as yours. Or as hot," he assured him.

"What the fuck is this site?" Jake demanded. "Grindr for the suicidally inclined?"

He pushed himself to his feet again and wriggled in behind Mari, rearranging the soft, woven blanket around them both so he could snuggle up against his lover's bare backside and peer over his shoulder. Beneath the blanket, Mari was enticingly nude from the waist down.

"Ruff Me Up," he read from the header of Mari's new profile page. "What sort of a name is that?"

Mari turned his head and touched his lips to Jake's, letting the kiss linger there.

"The sort that attracts heavy-handed playmates, I hope," he murmured.

"Uh-huh. And what do you plan to do with them once you've got 'em in your web, Mr. Ruff?" Jake asked.

Mari touched noses with him and gazed imperiously into his eyes. "Why, drug them and eat them, of course."

Jake arched one eyebrow at him and examined the screen and the number of messages he was already collecting. He also took a look at the pics he'd uploaded.

"Jesus! Bunch of pervs! How did you even do that? You look thirteen in those pics."

Mari snorted. "Fuck off! I do not! I look *Emo*."

"Is that still even a thing? You don't look legal." Jake pulled a sour face. "Thank god you don't look like that normally."

Mari squinted at the shots. "It's just me, as far as I can see. I even have a shadow." He rubbed his chin thoughtfully. "It wasn't what I was aiming for but if it works, it works."

It was working. One of the guys that had latched onto him pinged a message back asking to see him nude.

Mari chuckled. "Cheeky!"

"Give me that, I'll tell him what to do with his dick pics," Jake grumbled. He reached for the laptop but Mari scooted it out of the way.

"That's not the image I want to portray either, Chivis. I'm supposed to be slutty but vulnerable, don't you know?"

Jake sighed. "Mari, even if you do manage to attract the attention of the snuff tag-team, what then?"

"I talk to them. I feed them some sob story and get them to PM me, maybe confess how I feel like my life's going nowhere, like I want to end it but I'm not sure if I'm brave enough to kill myself. I tell them I'm desperate to have one last big blast of a night with a couple of hung guys, offer to be a real pain whore for them and see if they're willing to help me in return," Mari explained in a sweetly rational tone. "I've figured, from the chat logs for the existing victims, that they practically interviewed the guys they chose before meeting them. It was pretty intense, dark stuff. I don't have to physically meet them, so long as we can get them to make me an offer to help me die. That'll stand as evidence, surely? Perfectly safe, you see."

"It sounds ridiculous. They'll never fall for it." Actually, they might, but Jake hated the idea of Mari anywhere near them, even if it was just online. His precious Ilmari might not think he was vulnerable, but Jake did, even if he wouldn't ever say as much to his face. Mari's hard shell might fool most people, but Jake was not 'most people' and he saw through the firewall to the more sensitive man sheltering behind it.

"We don't know that. And until we find out exactly where to look, we're going around in circles. Let me try, at least?" Mari soothed.

"You are impossible," Jake told him. "I swear you have a self-destruct button."

"You must like that, since you can't leave me alone," Mari chuckled, twisting around in his arms to press a longer, slower kiss on his mouth this time. "It's making me very horny."

He pushed the blanket down and reached for Jake's phone, taking a couple more pictures and letting them upload to the laptop before posting them to the guy who'd asked for nude pics. They only showed his body from shoulders to knees, but also revealed Jake's hard cock between his legs. Predictably, the forum went wild—it was like watching a feeding frenzy in a piranha tank with messages pinging every second as guys made him offers and begged to see more and sent him pictures of themselves 'hard and ready'.

"What the fuck are you doing?" Jake made a grab for the phone but Mari held it away.

"Calm down, you said yourself that it doesn't look like me. And they can't see my face in the nude shot," Mari drawled, leaning back in his arms and tapping two and three-word responses to some of the messages that made him laugh.

The original guy sent him a PM begging him to put his webcam on and let him watch them fucking. Another offered money if they would go to a private cam chat with him and give him his own personal show.

"Mmhhh, do you like being watched?" Mari teased, wriggling in his lap as Jake stared open-mouthed at the rapidly filling message screen.

Is he your step-dad?

Mari typed, *No. Pervert!*

Is he your REAL dad?

That made him laugh out loud and he typed, *My dad isn't THAT hung.*

One message got Jake's back up properly though.

U need to get raped. If I see u london boi i will tie u nd rape you 48 hrs nonstop.

"Right, that's enough. Sick fuck!" he snarled, reaching for the laptop.

"Jake, no! He's an idiot. Ignore him. He's horny and frustrated. What can he do? He has no idea who I am." Mari moved the machine out of his reach again and crawled into his arms, smothering him in kisses. "Seriously? Forty-eight hours? I'll be amazed if any of these tossers last forty-eight seconds."

Jake looked hard at him. "You sound like you're talking from bitter experience."

"Well, what do you expect?" Mari scrambled into his lap and sat astride him, kissing him again. As their lips wetly parted he breathed, "I was alone for nearly three years before you came along, Chivis. A boy needs to have some fun, even if it's just through the medium of a camera lens."

"You are a bad boy," Jake growled, kissing the side of his throat and giving his ass a swat. "Do I need to punish you for showing off in front of complete strangers?"

"Now wouldn't that be a show?" Mari giggled at him. "Don't you think?"

"I think you are a born exhibitionist, but I'm not fucking you on camera for a bunch of horny perverts," Jake told him, more seriously. "I'm going to take little mukwa out for a walk. And then, we both have to go to work."

Tonka's ears pricked and he jumped to his feet, tail wagging enthusiastically, having waited with uncharacteristic patience for his moment in the sun, while Jake and his young master were play-fighting like puppies on the sofa. Mari sighed and nodded, his eyes flickering to the clock at the bottom of the screen.

"I suppose we do," he conceded and turned off the browser screen. "Bye, boys!"

Jake gave Mari another kiss, then pried himself reluctantly off the couch to throw some clothes on and take Tonka out. They had slept in, so he didn't have time for a run this morning or to take him for a longer walk. As he rounded the corner of his building, his phone chirped at him from his pocket and he pulled it out thinking it must be Mari with a question, but the number on the display wasn't his. The caller ID read George Seligman. His former partner before he quit the force and moved to London.

He considered letting it go to voicemail. He didn't have a great deal of time to catch up with old friends this morning, but George hadn't called him in several months, so it might be something important.

"Jake! How are you, man?" George greeted him when he answered and Jake felt some of his tension ease. If something terrible had happened, George wouldn't sound so happy to hear him.

"You know, life is being life. Things are good. Just on my way to work," he lied. "How about you? Pam and the kiddos doing okay?"

"Yeah, they're fine. Listen, I figure it's early there, I just got off the night shift and I wanted to give you the heads-up, just in case no one else did. The parole board granted your old man his release yesterday. He'll be out in a few days."

Jake stopped walking as Tonka sniffed around and found a good spot to do his business. Jake bit down on a laugh. He supposed that was a fitting tribute to the news.

"Thanks for telling me. I hadn't heard." Jake pushed the words out of his mouth because he didn't know how else to react.

"No problem, figured it's the least I could do. So, you planning on staying over there a while then? You know, I understand, what went down here was shitty, but if you ever did decide to come back, the lieutenant would rehire you in a heartbeat. You can have your spot back anytime you want it."

"Yeah, thanks. I kinda like it here. But it's nice to be wanted. Listen, thanks for calling and telling me about my dad, really, George."

"Eh, no problem. Give me a ring sometime, when you don't have to head off to work. It'd be nice to catch up."

Jake told him he would and hung up. By then, Tonka was done and it was time for the plastic bag. Also a fitting tribute when it came to anything involving his family.

Mari had showered and dressed when he got back but was perched on the sofa with the laptop again, talking to one of the guys on the forum. Or rather the guy was trying to letch him and Mari was palming him off with casual put-downs. Whatever was going on, he didn't try to hide it from Jake, so his conscience must have been clear on that point. He shut down once Jake sat beside him.

"What's wrong? You look like someone stole your milk?"

"Got a phone call from home. My dad — um, he's kinda — well, he's been in prison and he had his parole hearing. They're releasing him," Jake said, matter of fact.

Mari's eyes widened for a second, then he slid closer, putting a protective arm around Jake's shoulders. "That explains why you don't talk about him, I guess. Um, is that a good thing? The parole stuff? Or not?"

"I don't know. Neither? I don't talk to him. Don't have anything to do with him. I'm sure, once he's out, he'll try and look me up. He's got no one else that will talk to him anymore, and nowhere to go, probably." Jake stopped that line of thought. He didn't care if his dad didn't have anywhere to go. It wasn't his problem.

"Well, I doubt they will let him come here," Mari said rationally. "Not with such a recent record anyway. So, you're safe, for the time being. I just wondered if, maybe — " He broke off, and Jake guessed he wasn't sure what to say.

He gave Mari a crooked smile. "You thought maybe, what? That I'd want to talk to him? See him? That perhaps he's changed? He's been in prison twelve years, Mari, I don't think it's done him any good. Even if it has, he can't undo what he did. Not to the people he killed in the accident, and not to me or my mom. I'm not exactly *worried* about him getting my number and calling, I just don't want to deal with it."

"Maybe he found God, or something, when he was away, and he just wants to open a flower stall and bring love and peace to all mankind," Mari mused, toying with a strand of his hair. "Though personally, I can't think of anything worse!" He leaned in and planted a tender kiss on Jake's lips.

"He could be an internet pervert with a thing for young boys, though I can't imagine it personally," Jake said, looking darkly at the laptop.

"Oh hush!" Mari hit the power button and shut it down, clicking his tongue. "I can handle those freaks. Now gimme the dawg. I gotta git gone!"

He kissed Jake's nose with a playful smirk and retrieved Tonka's lead from under the sofa, heading out again as if nothing could possibly go wrong.

Chapter Twenty-One

Work distracted Mari for the next couple of days as he made up for the time he had already lost. He quite liked Ashcroft, the department head, and his unit supervisor, Ghislaine Macq, was surprisingly down to earth. She had grown up in Paris and spoke three languages by the age of four, could dismantle and rebuild a computer by the age of six and had been writing complex construction programs by the time she started senior school. His talent, the primary reason for his being headhunted to her department, fascinated her. Never able to resist the temptation to show it off, he set aside the fact that he was supposed to be abstaining and gave her a short demonstration of why her much-vaunted information security system was flawed, if targeted by an interface.

He came out of the test with a slight visual aura, but a croissant and a cup of strong Italian coffee sorted that out soon enough, then he and Ghislaine spent the rest of the day trying to construct a patch that would shield against a determined interface invasion. Mari was in his element on work like this — he had written his PhD thesis on a similar theme, and spent three years developing security systems very much like this.

When he finally left work, at a quarter past nine in the evening, it was too late to head to the nearest IT store, which had been his plan, so he went straight home and did normal things — eating, showering, sleeping, being a good boy so that Mama and Jake didn't have anything to give him grief about.

The next day, at lunchtime, Mari went to C-Zone and bought himself a very nice tablet with a detachable wireless keyboard. Jake might think he was clever, taking away Mari's tech, but he'd neglected to take his credit cards.

Ten points away from Team Chivis!

Having run through the second stage of security-patch testing with Ghislaine in the afternoon, he clocked off early, at four-thirty, and went to the British Library. Finding himself a quiet study booth to work in, he ran through the setup of his new toy, using their Wi-Fi, then logged in at WellManUK and skimmed his messages, of which there were many. Approximately ninety-seven percent of them he ignored, deleted outright or treated to single syllable replies.

He posted a short blog complaining about the fact that his life was a waste of time, his job was rubbish and his parents didn't understand his complex — and kinky — needs, and despairing, at length, of ever finding anyone that could see past his appearance, to care about him for who he was. The instant upshot of this was that fourteen men commented to him on the public chat feed, and three sent private messages, all —

with a weary predictability — offering him a good hard fuck, to help him find himself.

One of the earlier messages, from his photo posting spree the other day, was from a man who actually enclosed a picture of his face — as well as his quite nice, dark-furred torso and yes, his dick — but wrote at some length about how a cute guy like him shouldn't be so down on himself, and how he'd love to get to know him better, etc. etc. He wasn't pushy though, quite the opposite, in fact.

Mari tapped his fingernails on the shell of the keyboard and wondered if he ought to ignore it, or reply. His solution was to crop the upper part of the picture and email it to Jake, asking if it was one of the men he'd seen when he was in Jim's head.

This done, he signed out again, feeling grimy, even though he'd had no physical or even psychometric contact with the men. He stashed the tablet in his messenger bag and took his time walking home, his head buzzing with ideas.

* * * *

"Do you think the experiment is repeatable?" Professor Newberry asked. Jake had just finished telling her about his morning with DI Cordiline, at his neighbor's apartment.

"I'm not sure," Jake replied. "It's difficult to say if I have control over my psychometry, when I'm not actually aware if an object holds a memory or not."

"But you said you had not picked up on any memories at all, since you were captured by Birthright, until you opened yourself up and actively tried to see something," she pressed him.

"Yes, but it could also have been that I just didn't touch anything that held a memory up to that point."

"That seems unlikely."

"Very," Jake agreed. "I am going to tentatively log this as a new development, *possibly* due to the EQ-10, but I'm listing it as unpredictable, and unverifiable for the time being."

"Couldn't you simply pick up an object that you've already received a memory from?" she asked.

"I could, yes, but that still doesn't tell me for sure, because I've never been able to get the same memory, from the same object twice. I've always thought of it sort of like a static charge — once it zaps me, there is nothing left of it. Theoretically, it might work the other way as well. I could close myself off to receiving memories, and make a point of touching new objects, that are more susceptible to holding memories. If I open myself to the same objects I've got nothing from a second time, and I pick up a memory, then, it would tell me if I'd successfully blocked them the first time around, at least."

"That sounds like the most reasonable approach." Professor Newberry nodded and tipped her chin down to look over her glasses at him. "Talk to David next week and let him know what you need to test your theory. Congratulations on the breakthrough, Jake."

"Thanks." He smiled, and he swore she flushed before she turned and walked away.

When he got back to his desk to wind up his non-psychometric work for the night there was a message from Mari, with an attachment, in his mailbox. He opened it and blinked. Even before reading the email, he knew why it had been sent. The plain, unassuming man in the photo was so familiar that his blood ran cold. He had been at Jim's flat, been in his building, just a few days ago, a short while before Jim Sullivan had been found dead in his bathtub. This was not the guy they had watched fucking Wade in the first clip so, presumably, he was the cameraman. Jake got chills looking at him — so relaxed, an eager smile on his face. Mari's message read, *Do you know him?*

If he replied in the affirmative, that this was one of the killers, there was no telling what Mari would do next.

How did you get this?

* * * *

Mari was lying on the bed in his room, reading an online article about Missing Persons' procedure, when Jake's email landed in his inbox. He scanned the single line enquiry and a humorless smile twitched his lips.

Jake didn't want to confirm or deny that the man in the photo was one of the killers but his evasive response was answer enough and Mari ignored the question. Instead he opened up the WellManUK webpage again and navigated to the private message box. He clicked on the message from the guy calling himself 'Here2Help' and sent him a response.

You look nice. Can we meet somewhere? If I like you maybe we could…

He left the suggestion open and hit send.

He waited all of ten seconds, pouted a bit when he got no immediate reply and minimized the window to work on a couple of less intriguing projects. It was not until he was settling down to go to sleep, much later on, that his tablet pinged softly again.

Can I cum to u? 'Here2Help' asked.

Mari typed, *I live with my parents *sadface** and tapped send.

Again, there was a pause, and he worried that this would be the last he heard. A few minutes later his tablet pinged again.

Do you know a bar called Just Dessert, on Great Marlborough Street?

He sent back a short message in the affirmative. The wait this time was considerably shorter.

Meet me there at half nine. How old r u btw?

Mari exhaled a short huff of incredulous laughter. He'd asked for naked pictures straight off but only now did he worry if his target was legal.

I'm 28. U want me 2 b younger?

That's good then. See u soon. Wear loose jeans, no undies.

Why? Mari sent, raising an eyebrow.

Why u think? I wanna fuck u sexxi. Ur webname turns me on. Do u seriously like it ruff?

Yes. Mari hit send and tapped his front teeth with a fingernail. *Do you?*

i love it. The guy sent back at once. *I wanna tie u tight n fuck ur throat n til u gag n fuck n fist ur ass hard til u cum. u want that?*

Mari sighed as his brain deciphered this linguistic mess.

Sounds hardcore, he typed back.

dirty slut. ;)) u r making me cum.

Me too.

let me see

He hesitated, deliberating over his response.

I have to go. I'll miss the bus, see u soon, he typed at last and shut down the screen.

* * * *

Jake lay awake, his hands folded behind his head, staring up at the fine spider-webbing of cracks on his bedroom ceiling. Mari had not responded to his email, or called or even sent a text. Since he had last left in a happy mood and was not pissed off at him as far as he knew, that could only mean he was up to something. Jake had pretty good idea what. Mari didn't seem to have any qualms, or sense, when it came to baiting a bunch of perverts. He didn't doubt he was chatting with half a dozen right at this moment. Or was he? Mari might lack common sense when it came to seeing the danger he was putting himself in, but that didn't mean he was stupid.

Jake groaned. No, Mari wasn't the stupid one. He was.

Of course, Mari knew as soon as Jake had replied to his email without answering yes or no, that the answer had to be yes, and what would Mari do with that information? He would try to find the guy.

Jake rolled out of bed and hastily got dressed. If he found Mari half comatose over a computer, trying to track the bastard, he had no plan for how to stop him.

As he took long strides up the street, Jake debated calling ahead. If he called and Mari was plugged into the dark recesses of the internet, it would give him a warning. If he didn't, then it felt like he was trying to catch him in the act. Neither option was appealing. He wanted to trust Mari, but he knew how addiction worked. Jake had no doubt that Mari would waste precious little time replacing the tools that enabled his fix.

He was so caught up in his dithering that he nearly didn't see Mari's front door open. Instinctively Jake stepped behind a tree, and wondered at once what the hell he was doing. He was not spying on his boyfriend. He was not seriously thinking of tailing him. *Was he?*

Jake looked around the tree. Mari's tall, lean frame was silhouetted by the street lamps, heading back the way Jake had just come, on the opposite side of the road. He didn't have Tonka with him, so he wasn't taking the dog out for a last walk before bed. Jake watched as Mari went around the corner. He should turn around and go home. At least he knew Mari wasn't interfacing tonight. But what *was* he doing? Intuition had brought Jake this far, and intuition told him that despite all his maneuvering and ranting and beseeching, Mari had not given up on trying to find the men who had made those snuff videos.

What if he's already found them?

The snide voice in his ear made his stomach drop and his heart beat harder. If he'd already gotten a pic of the guy and had been chatting with him, it was within the realm of possibility that Mari would go and meet him. Although Mari could just as easily be coming around to see him. Jake slipped out from behind the tree and followed at a distance. If Mari headed for his flat, he could catch up with him at the door and pretend he'd popped out for something. If not, well, he would have to cross that bridge when they got there.

Chapter Twenty-Two

Just Dessert was a popular supper club that had sprung up during the last six months on the corner of Great Marlborough Street and Poland Street. By day it traded as a sandwich bar, but after dark it was popular with patrons of the Old Compton Street area of Soho, and a start and end point for the night's clubbing revelries. By nine-thirty-seven p.m., it was still quite crowded, with a primarily male clientele in the twenties to forties age bracket, and Mari figured he fitted in just fine in his pale blue, ripped jeans and skin-hugging, midnight blue velvet jacket with the nipped waist. Three big silver buttons fastened it at his midriff. His pale hair was casually disheveled and he had lined his eyes in dark blue kohl and silvery powder which made them look even larger.

The venue was popular because of the range of delicious sweets it sold, along with its cocktail menu. He ordered a tiramisu and a brandy alexander and perched on a stool by the bar, sipping the creamy concoction through a short gold straw, between mouthfuls of marsala-soaked sponge cake and coffee-flavored cream. He kept at least one eye on the door though, in search of a familiar face.

He didn't have too long to wait. The man who had sent him the photo came into the bar only a few minutes later, although if Mari hadn't been keeping watch he would have missed him. He was not a particularly remarkable fellow, dressed down in jeans and a faded band T-shirt, under a large, padded jacket. His hair was the color of wet sand, and cropped short, perhaps in an effort to conceal the fact that he was losing most of it early. He was also not as tall as he'd seemed in the photos, probably a good five or six inches shorter than Mari, although to be fair it was hard to tell his height given the way he slouched. The only thing that stood out about him at all were his eyes. They were large and blue-gray, half hooded, which made his expression look sleepy. Without the benefit of hindsight, Mari would never have pegged this thoroughly unremarkable man as a killer, or guessed that he filmed murder for kicks.

He spotted Mari after those half-closed, dreamy-looking eyes had scanned the place. The smile that spread across his face held such warmth it made it hard to believe this was the same man that had just spouted off what filthy things he wanted to do to him.

He wove through the crowd toward Mari.

"You're even more fit in person," the killer greeted him. His voice was very warm and soothing and Mari wondered if he practiced talking like that or if it came naturally.

"Thanks," he said, playing it coy for the time being. He was in character and the character he was playing wouldn't have held the older man's eyes for long, so he toyed with the drinking straw in his wide bowl glass for a moment, letting the guy think he was shy.

Leaning in closer, the fellow placed his hand on Mari's back, which felt intrusive, even given the circumstances.

"What's your name? Or do I just call you Mr. Ruff?" he teased, and a shiver ran down Mari's spine, all the way to his tailbone.

"Y-you could," he managed to stammer, catching the tip of the straw between his teeth and mauling it until he had recovered his composure. How weird was that? With the exception of Tomas, he never fluttered around men, even when he found them attractive. Mari glanced at *Here2Help* through his eyelashes, then looked away while he lied to the man. "I'm Mackenzie. Or just Mac will do. What should I call you?"

"Ed." He held out his right hand for Mari to shake then tilted his head to one side, looking him over. "So, how can I help you, Mac?"

Mari pushed his empty dessert bowl aside and slid down from the stool, his cocktail glass still caught in the fingers of his left hand. He nodded over toward a booth that was more private, and thought that he caught a glint of eagerness in Ed's eyes, that was very promising, as he followed. When Ed was not crowding him he felt as if he could think more clearly. Once they sat down again, across a small, round table from one another, Mari leaned in close and made his eyes as wide and appealing as possible.

"I don't know what to do, Ed. I can't carry on the way I am. That's why I joined the group. I just feel like I'm a useless adult. I'm in the way. I'm gonna be stuck with my stupid parents forever. I haven't got a decent job and that's a proper disappointment to them. I haven't got a life. I can't tell them I like men, they'd just go mental, so I can't even bring a date home. I feel so fed up all the time. I joined groups online for someone to talk to but they were mostly pick-up sites. When I found WellMan, I got talking to a few guys that were different, that said…said there were people who would be able to help me. Help me to" — he lowered his voice — "to make it stop. I tried stuff before, pills and things. Cutting myself." He toyed with the deliberate wristbands that decked his forearms and chewed on his lips. "None of it worked. I'm crap at suicide too, it turns out. I can't even kill myself properly."

He bent his head and rubbed his eyes with his finger and thumb, managing to shed a crocodile tear or two, much to his delight.

Ed reached across the table and took his other hand, holding it gently. Through the shimmer in his eyes Mari could see that curious look cross his face again. His hands were warm and soft — a clerical worker maybe, or a teacher even. He was not a laborer — the only heavy duty those hands had seen was in the work of dispatching unfortunates to the hereafter. The touch was comforting on his skin though. His racing pulse slowed but he shivered again.

"You know what some of those people were suggesting is illegal, don't you?" Ed told him, in his kindly tone. "As unfair as it may seem, you can't simply kill someone and claim it was suicide."

Mari squeezed the warm fingers around his own harder, surprised by this. He'd expected some zealous talk about the compassion of assisted suicide but Ed seemed to be trying to persuade him to stay alive. The way Ed looked at him, it almost felt insulting to insist that he wanted to die. Mari swallowed and reached for his drink.

"Yes." His answer was barely audible and he had to clear his throat, then take a sip of the creamy concoction in order to speak. "I get that. But what they were saying, apparently, you can make it look like an accident, you know. When you said you wanted to help, I just…" He pulled his hand away and forced a frown. "Never mind. I'm stupid, aren't I? No one is gonna risk prison just to help me out. Not even if they do think I'll let them fuck me first."

"I don't think you're stupid, Mac," Ed said. "Confused, maybe." He sat back in his own seat and regarded Mari through eyes that were nearly closed. "You don't really want to die, do you?"

"What else can I do?" Mari pressed a little whiny note into his voice, though it annoyed him more than Ed, he thought. His head was clearer now though. Some of the fuzziness he'd experienced on first meeting Ed was subsiding. "Are you going to help me, or what? I thought you were *Here2Help*. If you're not, I can go talk to someone else."

"Perhaps you should, a therapist maybe. You may be troubled, but you're not so far gone as to be hopeless. I can tell."

Mari blinked at him. He hadn't factored in the idea that the guy might not be interested. That kind of screwed with the plan.

"Oh fuck off!" he huffed, opting to stay in character for the time being. If he wasn't going to get anywhere with Ed then it wouldn't hurt to vent his spleen. The bastard might just lose his cool and try to throttle him for it, and someone in the bar would call the police. As plan Bs went it was not the greatest but it was all he had. "You don't know shit about me. What are you talking about?"

Instead of taking offence, Ed smiled at him. For just a moment, Mari figured the guy had somehow worked out what he'd come here to do. His heart stuttered against his ribs.

"I know more about you than you realize. Do you understand what an aura is, Mac?"

Mari made a rude noise in the back of his throat. Inside though, he felt the warning bells go off. "Isn't that something out of Harry Potter?"

Ed just sighed, his expression patient and kind, like a schoolteacher or a priest. Maybe he *was*. What an unnerving thought. His next comment did nothing to alleviate that concern.

"Ever see old paintings of angels? How so many of them have a glow around them? Some people believe the artists were painting the aura they saw around people. Only most people don't have pure white or golden auras. There are all kinds of colors in them, and the color and intensity tells those that can see them things about that person. Like, for instance, the greenish-gray color around your head denotes anxiety. There are also some clouds of sharper blue that tell me you have a keen intellect. Now, I do see some darkness, handprints almost, marks on your aura that tell me you've been treated violently in the past. There is red deep in those shadows, possibly sexual hurt. I don't want you to take this the wrong way or get angry, but I think you were lying to me when we chatted online."

Mari's heart jumped for a moment. Was the guy on to him? Did he really see the things he was claiming to be able to see?

"I-I don't know what you mean."

205

"You know exactly what I mean, Mackenzie. You like to get fucked. You're no more a virgin than I am." Ed grinned at him.

He looked down to hide the momentary awkwardness that must have crossed his features. Ed stroked his hand though and his anxiety gradually subsided.

"I-I'm sorry."

"Don't be." Ed folded both hands around his own and smiled at him. *Definitely a priest. Too tactile for a schoolteacher.* "I think that perhaps someone in your past went too far with you. They did something that you didn't want them to. And though you've tried to push that incident into the background, you still feel the echoes of it. That is what the dark shadows on your body aura tell me. What I don't see is a total shroud of black and gray, that means someone is truly wishing to escape their emotional pain."

Mari managed a slow blink but behind his eyes frantic thought processes were kicking in. *Is this guy serious? Does he genuinely believe that he can see a person's emotional pain? And if that's the case, is he using that as some kind of justification for his video crusade?*

Ed had hit far too close to home there for Mari's comfort. He should not have come here. The excitement of playing secret agent was crushed beneath the weight of questions this man's revelation provoked. *How could he know something like that just from looking at me?*

"Maybe you're not looking in the right places," he suggested, keeping his tone just on the right side of cynical. Given his own abilities it seemed rude to cast aspersions on someone else's claims but, he reminded himself, he was playing a part. "Yes, I'm anxious, you're right, but then what I'm asking you for isn't easy. So, if you could see black round me you'd do it?"

Ed shook his head. "I didn't say that. What I am saying is that you aren't ready to take that step. You have a lot of issues to deal with, Mackenzie. The help that I offer takes many forms but I'm not a qualified therapist."

"You're saying I need therapy?" Mari glared at him, forgetting that he was in character for a moment. Ed just looked back at him with that calm, beatific smile though. He ran his fingers up and down Mari's forearm, above the wristbands.

"Probably, yes. You're angry. And you need to deal with that before you go out looking for extreme solutions. Your aura is also about this thin—" He held up his hand with his finger and thumb about a quarter of an inch apart. "That's not good. You need to learn how to relax. I could definitely help you with that," he said more suggestively.

Mari had to struggle to keep his eyes from widening. He shivered at his body's insistence that he take this offer seriously. He and Jake had things sorted. He didn't need anyone else's help. Ed was just being spooky and mysterious in the hope of luring him in.

"How—?" He had to clear his throat. "Um, like…how would you help me with that?"

"Why don't you come back to mine and find out?" Ed offered.

"Why don't you just tell me?" he said, leaning back to look Ed more squarely in the eye.

"Well what we talked about in the chatroom, for a start." Ed told him, his smile turning more sensual. "You do still want to get fucked hard, don't you?"

Mari's breath caught in his throat. He was beginning to understand how this man reeled in prospective victims. Ed did not move like a panther but he talked with the kind of confidence in himself that Mari would have killed for. If he wasn't already with someone he loved, it would be so easy to just go back to this man's flat and get laid. And while Ed was chilling in post-orgasmic bliss, perhaps he could even do a little bit of covert surfing through his tech.

He could not do that though. It would be betraying Jake, and cheating had never been a part of his plan.

"Okay," he conceded. "I thought you seemed to like it that I might not have, though."

"I do." Ed grinned at him and there was no longer anything saintly about that smile. "I've no problems if you want to carry on pretending. A little play-acting always gets me hot. What about you?"

Mari ground his teeth. Jake was right that a whiff of danger turned him on. He was shivering with excitement, for all that Ed was not remotely his type and he had no intentions of giving the man what he wanted. He nodded once, not trusting his voice. Ed took his hand again, pulling him forward as he moved in closer, leaning across the table and kissing him. Not a long kiss, but not just a friendly peck either.

"Let's go." He stood and pulled Mari up beside him.

His thoughts went into overdrive. This wasn't a game. It was real. If he did this he would have to live with the consequences. And if the consequences included losing Jake? That made up his mind for him. As his companion made to leave, Mari tugged back, holding his ground.

"Ed, I really want to. But I can't. Not tonight. I'm not ready," he protested, wishing he'd had time to think this through more. He had not expected the man to be so persuasive. That was a shock to his system.

Ed looked genuinely surprised when he said no, and Mari braced for the angry backlash, but even though this man got off on filming his partner fucking and killing people, he was more civilized than most of the men Mari had dated in the past. He didn't get frustrated or pissed off, at least he didn't let those emotions show.

"I understand. I've given you a lot to think about. Why don't you mull it over and come by tomorrow night instead?"

Mari managed not to do a complete double-take but he must have looked poleaxed by this because it made Ed smile, like he had a secret.

"It's not what you think," Mari told him, eager not to be misunderstood. "I'm not leading you on. I do want to. But I've never just hooked up with someone like this before. It's a big step for me," he protested in what he hoped was a smaller, more timorous voice.

"You didn't sound nearly so shy earlier," Ed said.

Mari did not have to fake the tremor as he drew a long breath and another, trying to keep his thoughts from scattering. He needed to know where the guy lived.

"Where should I come to?"

"Got your phone handy?" Ed asked, and when Mari pulled it out Ed gave him his phone number and address.

"See you tomorrow then, Mr. Ruff Stuff," Ed told him sardonically, as if wondering just how rough a guy who wouldn't even get his pants down could like it. Although, he did stop short of chuckling.

"See you tomorrow, and we'll find out how much you can help," Mari told him, unable to resist a dig back for that.

He lingered and finished the sweet, creamy drink, taking some comfort from the burn of the brandy on the way down. Then, when he was sure that Ed had gone, he too went on his way. Mari felt calmer and less bewildered, but he was still mulling over what Ed had told him, about being able to read a man's aura, as he made his way down the steps to the street. That little insight, into how transparent he might be was disturbing and he could not stop thinking about it. When someone stepped out in front of him, he was initially impatient, reaching up to shove the unfortunate out of his way, until he realized that the obstruction in his path was Jake.

"What on earth are you doing here?" he asked, which was rather rude, he knew, but the surprise had hotwired his brain.

Jake's expression was totally blank but Mari could see that his jaw was clenched so tight that the dusky skin was nearly white there.

"You sent me a picture of a guy that's been killing people, or at the very least setting them up to be killed, then you stop responding. Do you think I'm stupid, Mari? Or do you just keep forgetting that I was actually a detective? Are you out of your mind?"

"Of course you aren't stupid, Chivis," Mari said, forcing himself to stay calm. "I don't think that. And I don't want to argue with you over this but—damn it, Jake! He went *that* way." Mari pointed along the street. "A decent cop would be following him, not standing here bitching at me."

"You were going to follow him?" Jake snapped, utterly incredulous.

"No. I don't need to follow him. I have his address and his phone number," Mari said coolly, hoping his expression was not too smug. "Actually, I was coming to see you. You've saved me the trip. That was thoughtful of you."

Don't. Don't. Don't poke him, fuckwit! his conscience ragged him for that. Why in the world could he not just keep his mouth shut at times like these?

"Uh-huh, I'm sure you were." Jake's mouth twisted into a humorless line. Mari had seen Jake plenty angry before, seen him yell and bluster, even to the point of getting into a physical confrontation with a man, but he'd never seen him with quite this expression. Jake's temper tended to burn hot when it got the better of him, but the look in his eyes was cold and hard, his eyes so dark in the low light they looked nearly black. "Got you hot, did he? All that *acting* push your buttons for you? Were you going to *tell* me you met with the fucking guy, or just get your itch scratched?"

Mari felt his jaw drop and for a moment he wasn't sure if he wanted to laugh or get mad. "Are you jealous, Chivis? What the—? He has *killed* three guys. Or, if he didn't then he certainly didn't stop his friend from doing it while he filmed them. And you are jealous of him? No fucking wonder Alex had issues with you. Did you buttonhole him about every guy he talked to as well?"

As soon as the words were out of his mouth he wanted to swallow them. A cold, hard knot of anger and fear had lodged in his chest and he could not move it. For a moment, the surprise on Jake's face superseded the rage. Then his expression settled into confusion, before returning to an angry scowl.

"You looked up my ex? Why? What exactly did you find?"

Mari chewed his lips then looked away, uncharacteristically subdued. "I was curious. And you tell me nothing. Or you say something that tells me nothing. I suppose I wanted to get a handle on the kind of guy that you go for. He's cute. Brainless, but very cute."

And he still wants you.

Mari didn't say that last part out loud. It burned away at him inside though.

Jake wiped a hand over his face, his frustration obvious. "So, instead of asking me a question, you go and snoop around online. I'm sure you got a very good one-sided snapshot too. It's not like Alex to own up to a damn thing. Great! Then you figure, *I'm going to just go and meet up with a guy that gets off making snuff films*, and not so much a text to warn me."

That was a snipe too far. Mari exhaled a furious huff and laid into him.

"This is exactly what I mean. If I'd asked, you'd have told me nothing, Chivis. The one thing I did sympathize with your stupid ex over — and believe me, there wasn't much, because he strikes me as a selfish, manipulative little bitch, but he's right about this — you want to control everything, Jake Chivis. I'm not a child. I'm not some fainting flower that can't handle himself. Why the hell should I call anyone? It's not like I was arranging a threesome or something! I wanted to find out more about him, so I arranged to meet him, in a bar, in a public place. I took heed of all the sensible shit that sensible people say you should do when you meet a stranger. And it paid off. I know where he lives. Result! I think you just can't stand the fact that I don't actually need your help all the damned time. And I think you felt the same way about Alex. You need to get a fucking grip, Jake. You can't run someone else's life for them."

"Sometimes, I think you actually believe your own bullshit. You weren't meeting a fucking *stranger*, Mari, you were meeting with a murder suspect. Even seasoned cops don't do that without backup. But you don't need backup, you don't need me, huh? You're too smart for that. Only, the reason you didn't call me wasn't because you were afraid of any pushback on your hare-brained plan. You didn't call, or tell anyone, because you want to prove you're smarter than all of us. You can do it on your own." Jake took a short breath as they stared furiously at one another. "And fuck you, if you think I tried to *control* Alex. That is just about the opposite of what happened. Well, congratulations on solving your case, Mari. I'm sure Cordiline will be fucking thrilled."

Jake shouldered past him and started to walk away. Mari grabbed him though, swinging Jake around to face him, which was no small feat even given his slight height advantage. A flush of heat was rising to his face and he struggled to contain it.

"Don't just storm off and sulk like a child," he hissed, also conscious that they were attracting attention from the people milling on the street just outside the bar. "Why in the world did you come here, if you can't handle what I was doing? This wasn't about proving anything. It was about getting the job done. And maybe I *am* fucking smarter than you give me credit for! Did that ever occur to you? I'm not looking for anyone's approval, Jake. I met the guy in a bar that sells *cake*.

Fuck's sake, what do you think he was going to do to me? Drown me in the trifle?"

One second Mari was standing with his hand on Jake's biceps and the next he had his back up against the bricks and Jake's hands were around his upper arms like steel bands, the fingers digging in hard enough to bruise, and all before he'd done more than draw a breath.

"I came to make sure you didn't get hurt. I shouldn't have to fucking tell you that," Jake growled at him, so close Mari could feel the intense warmth of the softly spoken words on his face. "Being smart does not mean you know everything, it doesn't grant you training and experience just because you *think* you understand what you're doing." He punctuated the comment with a shake that made Mari feel like a ragdoll in his hands. It was a curiously exhilarating experience. He fought the urge to brush his lips against that hard, angry mouth. A moment later he wished he'd given in, when Jake snapped, "I give up, Mari. You do what you want to do. Hell, give Alex a call. You two can commiserate on how bad you've had it. He'd fucking love that."

Jake let him go and stepped away, turning his back on him again and striding off.

For a second or two Mari just leaned against the wall, shaking, but not with fear, or even anger, so much. He shut his eyes and let his head fall back against the wall behind him, thumping against the brickwork, once, twice. A part of him wanted to call Jake back, to tell him that it wasn't Alex he wanted to commiserate with. But he doubted that Jake was ready to hear that, or even believe it.

How could it be possible, he thought sadly, *to be madly in love with a man who drives me so crazy, sometimes, that I want to pummel him?* And if he ran after Jake, what the fuck would that look like? Mari had been there before chasing after Tomas, so blind that he didn't see how stupid that made him. He took a long breath, and another. At last, he pushed himself away from the wall, trying not to think about how it felt to have Jake's hands on him like that, shoving him up against the brickwork. Even done in anger, that sent a frisson of need through him that made him weak inside. That was why he was shivering. How could Jake not see that he was all Mari wanted?

"Oh, damn you, damn you, you silly man!" he breathed at last, not sure if the words were aimed at Jake or himself.

He did not have time to chase after Jake or wallow in self-pity for very long. He had an address, and he needed to make a phone call, since passing the information to Jake was currently out of the question.

Chapter Twenty-Three

Sweat trickled down Jake's back, although it could have as much to do with his pace as his simmering anger. He didn't have the focus for a run so he headed home, changed and went to the gym. Lifting weights was usually a good way to take the edge off but every time he came down a notch he'd see Mari kissing that guy and get pissed off all over again. He set the weights down and moved over to the heavy bag. His fist connected, a good, solid, satisfying release of energy. Better.

An hour later, when the anger finally started to ease off, he went home again, took a shower and sat on his couch brooding. Had he just broken up with Mari? He wasn't sure. He hadn't meant to. He doubted Mari would see it that way, though. He looked down at his hands. The knuckles were swollen and scuffed. They ached when he flexed them. Pummeling the sandbag until he was ready to drop had helped bleed off some of the anger, but he'd also known, somewhere in the back of his head, that the pain was self-punishment. He was still horrified that he'd grabbed Mari like that. He'd barely gotten a block away from him before the guilt had crashed around him like bricks falling.

He looked at his phone on the table. If he called, he doubted he would get an answer. He decided he would wait until morning. And if Mari didn't want to talk to him? He wasn't sure what to do then. The thought that this might be it, that they couldn't fix it this time, left a hollow ache in his chest. His mind insisted on pulling up the memory of seeing the man Mari had met with kissing him, the way he'd touched him. The hollowness twisted in his gut, sour bile rising in his throat.

Mari might not have been right about anything else, but he was right about that. He *was* jealous. Furiously so. It had taken every ounce of his will not to go busting into that bar and beat the guy's stupid head in. Jake leaned back, letting out a long breath and staring up at the ceiling. He would apologize for getting so angry, that was all he could do, and if it wasn't enough— He didn't want to think about that.

* * * *

Mari couldn't think straight for the rest of that night. He didn't want to go back online just in case Ed was in the chatrooms. The last thing he wanted was to talk to the man. Oddly kind and gentle he might have been, and his dirty talk pressed a lot of Mari's buttons, but the knowledge of what he was made him shiver every time he thought about contact with him. At the moment, the only contact he wanted was with Jake. Jake's mouth covering his, his tongue delving deep between his jaws. Jake writhing between his legs, taking him and filling him, Jake's strong hands on his body. He could still feel the pressure of those strong hands wrapped tightly around his upper arms. The memory of the way Jake had handled him outside the bar still made him tremble in an entirely different way.

Maybe he should just ring him and apologize for being…what, exactly? An apology would only indicate to Jake that he was right about everything, and he was far from that. Okay, it had been wrong of him to go snooping in Alex's personal life, he could admit that much. He should have just asked and been content with the answer, or lack of it, dissatisfying as it might be. But tonight's meeting with Ed had been well thought out, or so he considered. He was proud of what he'd achieved, given how dumb Jake seemed to think he was. No way that ox-brained stud-muffin would have played things so subtly. And if he'd hung around giving Jake time to provide back-up, Ed would have got suspicious. He was not a fool, that much Mari had figured out within minutes of meeting the man.

No, he had done the right thing. And in consequence, he had another delightful chat with Inspector Cordiline to look forward to. That one, he decided, could wait until the morning. If Ed was ready to invite him back for sex this evening, he figured, the guy didn't have anything else planned. So, potential victims were probably safe until the following day.

"Stupid, am I, Mr. Smart-arsed Detective?" he muttered to himself as he settled back down under the duvet and tried to think of nothing.

Sleep was a long time coming.

Chapter Twenty-Four

On Saturday morning, Mari sent DI Cordiline a brief email asking if they could meet. He was anxious about this, after their last conversation. If Cordiline hadn't had much time for him before, he most likely had even less by now. But to his surprise he got a message back right away, just a brief, polite communication asking him to drop by the station in half an hour. As said station was only a couple of hundred yards down the street, this was not unreasonable. Twenty-five minutes later, having first taken Mama tea and toast, he was standing in the reception area in smart jeans and a sweater, waiting for the inspector to see him.

As he was reading a poster about how to report vandalism in his neighborhood, a door opened to his left and Cordiline poked his head out, nodding to him, and waved him through.

"You've got some new information for me, Dr. Gale?" he queried as he closed the door behind him and pointed the way along the spartan, carpet-tiled hallway to his office. His workspace was right at the far end. Within lurked a desk strewn with paperwork in various stages of completion, a filing cabinet, an elderly computer with a much newer flat screen monitor, and two flimsy looking office chairs.

"I hadn't realized the Met was so high tech," Mari murmured sarcastically, taking the chair nearest the door as the detective flopped down on the one beyond the desk.

"Do you have information, or did you just come by to take the piss out of my I.T.?" Cordiline grunted. "I'm a busy man, Dr. Gale."

"It's about the guy Jake saw, when you took him into Sullivan's apartment," Mari said, coming to the point and noting that Cordiline's interest was piqued right away. "I have an address for him, if you're interested."

Cordiline regarded him with narrowed eyes. "How did you obtain this address?"

"I asked him nicely for it," Mari said with a humorless twitch of his lips. "You'd be amazed where good manners get you."

"You asked him, and he emailed it to you?" Cordiline asked.

"No," Mari said, drawing out the word. "I met him for a civilized drink and he *gave* it to me. I don't do everything online, no matter what Detective Chivis might tell you."

"You met him. In person?" Cordiline reiterated, his eyebrows lifting toward his hairline. "And did *Detective* Chivis verify that it was the same man he saw in Sullivan's flat?"

Mari allowed himself a more satisfied smile. "In a way, yes."

Cordiline sat back in his chair and it made a small squeak. He regarded Mari for a few moments, then his thin lips twisted. "He chewed you out, did he? I can't believe it was his idea for you to actually meet with the man, seeing as how you're here and he's not. More trouble in paradise? What's the address?" he asked, without waiting for an answer to his first question.

"You would love that to be true," Mari said with a shake of his head that belied just how annoying he found that remark. "It wasn't his idea. He doesn't have the monopoly on good ideas. And no, he wasn't happy about it, but the fact of the matter is that I have the bastard's address and you don't, and neither does Chivis. Do you want to know where he is or not?"

"I just asked for it, didn't I," Cordiline said coolly. He waited until Mari unlocked his phone and passed him the information, glancing down at the device and setting it aside.

"How'd he catch you?" Cordiline asked.

"I beg your pardon?" Mari frowned, wrong-footed by the question for a moment. "Who? What do you mean?"

"Jake. How'd he catch you meeting up with the perp? That is what happened, isn't it? You went off on your own, he caught you out, so you're here in person instead of relaying the message through him. C'mon then, how'd he catch you at it?"

"That's nothing to do with you, Inspector." Mari laughed, running a nervous hand through his hair. *What the hell is it with these detectives? They are always trying to over-analyze everything.* "He's not my messenger. Your remit is catching criminals, isn't it? I've done the leg work. All you need to do is catch this one in the act."

Cordiline gave a low chuckle. "Do you boss Jake around like that as well? Bet that's the icing on his cake, innit. How pissed off is he?"

Mari opened his mouth then closed it again a moment later. He tilted his head while he was trying to decide how to respond to that. "Okay, since you fail to understand the concept of personal privacy, I will say this in words of one syllable. Jake does not like this. But on a scale of one to ten, what he likes or not is — I want to say irrelevant but that's more than one syllable. Is this or is it not a murder inquiry?"

Cordiline's humor this time was edging toward a delighted cackle. "You've got your head so far up your own arse, I'll bet you don't even realize why he's pissed off with you. You certainly wouldn't have cut him out of the loop if you had any idea what made him tick."

"Woah, woah, woah!" Mari leaned forward, his hands on the edge of the cluttered desk as if he would clear it in one swipe. "Excuse me! I'm not stupid enough to misunderstand why you're so delighted by the idea of him walking out on me, but that's no excuse for blatant smugness, Inspector. And personal insults? Really? I do hope this conversation is being recorded for training purposes!"

Cordiline put one elbow on his desk and cupped his chin, looking at Mari with complete disregard for his outburst. "You seem to be under some misguided impression that I'd like to see you and Chivis split up. Why would I keep trying to help you if that were the case?"

Mari frowned. He glanced around the room, half expecting Jake to step out of a cupboard and tell him he had just been edged into some kind of gameshow scenario.

"I wasn't remotely aware that you were helping, Inspector," he said at last, directing a less than cordial glare at Cordiline. "Quite the opposite, actually. You have been hitting on my man from the get go, and don't think I haven't noticed it. I wouldn't be surprised to find out you've been feeding him some of this bullshit about him keeping me on a leash. I am not his dog. If I want something, I get it for myself."

Cordiline ran a hand over his short hair and grimaced. "Did you tell him that too? Give him the whole 'don't try and control me' speech? Probably told him you didn't need him." He sighed and pinched the bridge of his nose wearily. "For someone supposedly so smart, you are awfully dumb. Or maybe you're just so wrapped up in yourself you don't give a flying one, hard to tell really. Jake is a copper, Dr. Gale. He might not be working under a badge, but once a cop always a cop, it never goes away. He thinks like a cop, he works like a cop, and you...well, you just told him the most important thing about him is useless."

"I did not!" Mari was halfway to his feet. "Are the police always this bloody blunt? I don't think he's useless. I would never — I just — I'm not used to being kept on a chain, Inspector. And you say that he's the way he is because it's a cop thing, well, I'm not a bloody copper, I never will be, you made your point. I'm a fucking research scientist, that is what I am and what I do. I find solutions to things. But I'm trying to fucking help here and the pair of you are driving me crazy." He turned away for a moment, conscious that his heart was beating too fast. There was something going on here that felt just out of reach. He couldn't get a grip on it. Pushing both hands into his hair, he turned back and stared at Cordiline, aghast. "Does he really think that? That I think he's useless?"

Cordiline gave him a cynical smile. "Do you have any idea how hard it is to make Detective before you're thirty? You have to bust your balls every day. You deal with the worst pieces of shit society has to offer and you slog through with worse than no thanks for it. It's not a job you do unless you love it. Unless it's part of who you are. You swear to protect the people, no matter what. So, when your own lover doesn't trust you enough to protect them, what kind of message do you think that sends? You slope off playing undercover cop, and you didn't even want him for a partner on the job."

For the second time in as many days, Mari was rendered speechless. It wasn't something that happened to him often and he sat down heavily, unable to look away. Cordiline's cloudy blue gaze remained fixed on him and he was painfully conscious of the sense of disappointment in that look. His father had looked at him that way sometimes when he was a child and he'd done something they both knew was wrong.

"I don't— It's not that I don't trust him," he faltered, shaking his head. "I'd trust him above just about anyone. And I don't trust easily, Inspector, believe me. That's not what this was about." His voice dropped to hardly more than a whisper.

"It *is* about trust. In his eyes. I guarantee that he thinks you don't trust him. If you trusted him not to yank your leash back, as you seem to think that's what he wants to do, then you would have laid out the plan and worked on it together. But you cut him out. So, if he needs you, how is he supposed to trust you?"

Mari's dropped his head into his hands and for a moment he just sat like that, bowed over, silent and despairing. When he came upright again he had to blink a few times to get rid of the pressure of tears.

"I didn't tell him because I knew he would try to stop me," he said in a softer voice. "And yes, I didn't want to be stopped. Oh, sod it. How do I fix this? All my life men have looked at me and thought the same damned things. 'Ah bless! Little geek boy, he can't do anything without a computer. He needs a firm hand. He needs taking care of.' It's bullshit. I'm a man, an adult. I don't need any of that, but I seriously didn't do this to hurt him, I did it because I *could*. That's all." He stopped for a moment, because Cordiline was giving him that bored look that said he was rambling again. "I-I think I'm— I *love* him, Inspector. I never felt this way about a man before. And I've broken that, haven't I? I've hurt him." Mari drew a shaky breath and lowered his head dejectedly. "I never meant to."

"Most people don't *mean* to." Cordiline sounded irritable. "It just works out like that. We trample all over the ones we love the most. So, you're the research scientist. Do some research. I'm sure you can figure out a way to wiggle back into his good graces, if that's what you want. In the meantime, seeing as how you've already shown a willingness to work undercover on your own, how would you like to learn to do it properly?"

Mari's head jerked up and he stared at Cordiline.

"You mean you'd be willing to have me along for the ride on this?" He knew the surprise must have showed on his face, because it provoked a grin from his opposite number at last.

"Be back here at five p.m., sharp. Dress for a date. Text your suspect and tell the bastard that you want to see him. We'll see how good a cop you can be, Dr. Gale."

Chapter Twenty-Five

Jake woke early Saturday morning despite having tossed and turned most of the night away. He went for a long run and tried to convince himself that he was neither surprised nor disappointed that he didn't find Mari in the park. By lunchtime he'd made up his mind that Mari would only show him the door if he went over to talk to him, and ignored the internal voice telling him he was being a coward.

He had just about worked up the nerve to ring anyway, and had the phone in his hand, when he got a call from Cordiline.

"I've had an interesting morning," the detective told him. "Thought you might appreciate the heads-up. Dr. Gale was in today with some information regarding the case."

"Uh-huh. I kinda figured he would be." Jake tried not to sound sour about it, but he was.

"We expect he'll have more for us soon. Tonight, in fact," Cordiline said, and Jake sensed he was choosing his words carefully.

His fingers tightened on the phone and he had to take a deep breath. He knew what Cordiline was saying, without hearing the words.

"You had better make sure he doesn't get hurt."

"We're professionals, Jake. We'll mic him up. There will be a team from SCO19 on call, since we don't know if these men are armed. He'll be fine."

Jake disconnected, and it was all he could do not to throw the damn phone at the wall. The fact that undercover ops procedures were at their most stringent when a civvy was involved did nothing to reassure him. Mari was putting himself in danger and he couldn't even be there. Mari was probably over the moon that he'd be able to work with the police to snag their killer, and Jake guessed he was the last person Mari wanted to talk to right now. He set his mobile down on the table instead of throwing it across the room, and forced himself to take another couple of deep breaths. Mari would be fine.

His phone rang again and this time the caller ID read *George Seligman*.

"Two calls in one week? I'm starting to think you miss me or something," Jake answered.

George laughed. "Yeah, well, I felt bad calling just to drop bad news on you."

"Eh, it's okay. I'm glad you got in touch anyway."

Jake sat and they spent a few minutes catching up, George telling him about his wife getting a new job, and the kids getting a puppy and how his daughter wanted to be an exchange student next year.

"So, what have you been doing with yourself. You seeing anyone?" George asked.

Jake paused. George had been one of the few people that had not batted an eye when Alex had splattered their messy break up all over the department. He had told Jake it didn't matter to him who he was sleeping with and that had meant more to Jake than he cared to admit. In the weeks after Alex had outed him at work, George had been more than a friend and a partner — he'd stood up to some of the uniforms that had given Jake shit, and gone to the Captain when the hazing had started to cross into dangerous territory.

"I have been, yeah," Jake said, at last. "We've, uh, kinda hit a rough patch."

"Sorry, man, didn't mean to stick my nose where it don't belong."

"No, it's okay. He's a great guy. I hope we can work it out, it's just, well, you know how it goes."

"Yeah. Relationships are tough. You deserve to find someone that makes you happy though, not jerk you around like that dickweed in dispatch."

The 'dickweed in dispatch' was Alex. When they'd been in the midst of breaking up, the strategic position he'd occupied in the division meant it had been child's play for Alex to let it out to practically the whole unit that Detective Jake Chivis was not the straight arrow everyone thought he was.

"No, Mari isn't anything like Alex. He's a lot smarter for one thing, and he's got a good heart. He's funny and independent, he can take care of himself. Total opposite of Alex that way, not high maintenance at all," Jake said.

"Sounds like a great guy. So, what's the problem then?"

Jake sighed. "Probably me. He thinks I'm smothering him, or something. It's kind of complicated."

"Give him some space then, see if you can make it work."

At the moment, Jake didn't have much choice but to give Mari his space. Even so, it was still hard advice to take.

* * * *

Mari spent the afternoon trying to behave like everything was normal, as much for Mama's sake as anything else. He didn't want to worry her by admitting that he was working with the police to bring a killer to justice. That was one more concern than she needed under the circumstances. And he didn't have the first idea how to start telling her what was going on between himself and Jake. Sometimes he thought that she would be unhappier that Jake wasn't going to be around than she would have been if it was him. Tonka certainly missed Jake more.

He went out and got his hair cut, then went shopping to distract himself. In the late afternoon he returned to the station, as Cordiline had instructed, dressed for a date, in his new purchases, a shimmer of silver lipgloss on his mouth and some metallic blue kohl around his eyes. He'd texted Ed to make sure he was still expected and received an enthusiastic reply, tempered with a lot of Ed's expectations for the evening ahead.

"I can't sleep with him," he said as Cordiline's tech guys were wiring him. The tracking device was much subtler than he had expected. A colorful wristband, of the kind popular with teenagers and charities, with the bugging device implanted into the rubber — it was quite ingenious and fitted in discreetly with his own collection of beads and bands. "I hope you're not expecting me to."

"Of course not," Cordiline assured him. "Your job is to get him talking. Get him to talk about the videos, if possible. Get him to show you his equipment."

The detective smirked. Mari flipped him the bird.

"You don't have to enjoy this so much, you know."

"Where would the fun be in that?" Cordiline pulled a faux-sulk then resumed his business-face. "You have the code words, right? You know what to say if he shows you some of his handiwork, or if you think you are in danger?"

"I have the script in my pocket," Mari assured him, patting the appropriate part of his jacket with one hand.

"Memorize it. Don't take that in with you." Cordiline frowned.

"I'm not an imbecile," Mari told him coolly. "So, do I hit the deck when you kick his door down, or just look surprised?"

"Hopefully neither. Unless you feel threatened, try not to call us in. If you do find something incriminating, just tell him 'I need to think it over' and make your excuses. If he turns heavy, get out as quickly as possible or use the safe words, we'll take it from there." Cordiline paused. "Did you tell Jake about your plans for this evening?" For once, the detective didn't sound like he was trying to bait him.

"No. Did you?" Mari asked, and didn't wait for a reply. "You did tell him, didn't you? I mean, you like to keep him in the loop if you think I'm doing something he'll disapprove of."

"You're undercover. I couldn't tell him, even if I wanted to." Cordiline's face gave nothing away. "What makes you think he'd disapprove? You're not going in alone."

"This is Jake we're talking about. He won't like it." Mari sighed, toying with the wristband until one of the Met technicians told him to leave it alone in case the bug worked loose. "Even if this plan comes off and we get enough to arrest him, I doubt it will make Jake Chivis happy. Come on, let's catch a bad guy before I change my mind."

* * * *

Jake had almost forgotten about the reopening of the Vault, his friendly neighborhood bar, until he got a text from Manny, the affable licensee, asking if he was coming over. He considered half a dozen excuses but knew no matter which he chose, Manny wasn't going to believe any of them. He wasn't sure when it had happened, but somewhere along the way Manny had become a friend and Jake knew he would feel bad if he blew off the reopening party just because he would rather stay in and wallow in misery.

With a heavy sigh, he got up and changed into something more appropriate for a night out. His plan was to show his face, drink a beer or two, then slip back upstairs when no one was looking. As he made his way down to the street, it occurred to him that if he bumped into anyone he knew, which he was bound to, they would probably ask where Mari was. He prepared an excuse and felt lame.

The place was packed. It seemed like everyone who had ever dropped by the Vault had turned out for the reopening. It was elbow to elbow people, spilling out onto the street. They would be exceedingly lucky if someone didn't call the Met tonight.

Three bartenders were keeping up a nonstop flow of alcohol as cute twinks dressed in nothing but tiny briefs and boots carried trays laden with mugs and shots out to thirsty patrons.

Manny looked harried but happy. It took a while, but at long last Jake made his way up to the bar and Manny spotted him. He broke out a big grin. "Jake! You made it!" he shouted over the music. "Let me buy you a drink." He set a bottle in front of him and opened it. "Where's Mari?"

Even when he knew it was coming, Jake had to push himself not to drop into a mope. "He had something to do tonight."

"Flying solo! You better watch your arse then, mate." Manny chuckled.

Jake forced a grin to his lips and sipped his beer.

A young guy, shirtless, in an open leather jacket, his light-colored hair cropped close to his skull, wriggled into the gap at the bar right next to him. One of Manny's barmen took his shouted order and returned moments later with another beer, the match of Jake's. Blue-green eyes twinkled as he turned his head and saluted Jake with the bottle.

"Awright. I haven't seen you here before."

"I'm just doing my part to keep local business alive," Jake said. There was no way he was getting out of here without getting cruised tonight — it was what everyone here was doing — but he would try to keep it from getting too serious if he could.

"Business will spike if you make a habit of drinking here, mate." The lad clinked bottles with him. "I'm Mischa. You wanna dance?"

Jake looked around the standing-room-only bar and chuckled. "Where?"

Mischa set his bottle on the counter and moved in chest to chest with him. They were practically a match for height. His hands slid boldly to Jake's hips. "Here will do, I reckon," he chuckled, rolling his hips to grind against him. "You have got a fucking gorgeous body."

Jake was caught off guard by how wrong it felt to be pressed so close against another man, and right on the heels of that was a flicker of memory, not a flashback, just a moment's recall from last night when he'd watched through the window as someone else had kissed Mari. It was ridiculous, but at the same time it wasn't like he was going to fuck the guy. Why shouldn't he have some fun?

He took a drink and set his beer down. "I'm not looking to get laid tonight, just so you don't waste your time."

Mischa looked disappointed. He touched his own bottle to his lips and took a swallow. "I can suck your cock, though, right?" he teased. "Are you with someone?"

Jake grinned. "Yeah. Big bruiser. You don't wanna mess with him."

"Nah, cos I'd be chatting *him* up if I did." Mischa winked at him. "Well, if you don't wanna play, I guess I'll go find someone that does. But if you change your mind…" He leaned in and kissed Jake's cheek then was wriggling through the throng again.

Jake moved on too, more or less because the press at the bar was more than he wanted to deal with. He wove his way through the crowd, got drawn into a small clutch of guys dancing for a few minutes, then continued on toward the back.

The staircase leading into the cellar was repaired and repainted, not a hint of the fire that had caused the temporary closure. He hesitated there. He didn't need to go down, but he sort of had to. It would look different, and that was good. It would help to scrub the memories of what had happened there from his mind. That was, if he could even get past the stairs. It was no easy task, but at least people were moving here.

The music was more muted in the basement, where it was pretty much business as usual. He recognized a familiar face. Colm, the Dom whom Jake and Mari had rescued from the bar fire, was standing by his padded bench in tight leather shorts that looked sprayed on, and showed off the well-toned curves of his leg muscles and the hard V of his abs. He was talking and laughing with a couple of guys, showing them different floggers and straps. He looked up and was professional enough to hide whatever his true feelings were behind a smile.

Jake tipped the edge of his beer at him in acknowledgment but didn't interrupt his private fan club. He moved over toward the far wall, the one that had been scorched so badly that masons and a structural engineer had been employed to make sure the stonework was still sound. There was no trace of the fire here either, and Jake was glad of that.

He turned away, intending to make his way back upstairs now that he'd gotten his look around the new dungeon playroom. A well-built fellow in an open, sleeveless shirt and snug, dark blue jeans was bent over, examining a set of stocks and talking to the Dom who owned it. As he straightened and turned his head, Jake caught his profile and something nagged at his attention. He looked again and this time noticed the small, rectangular tattoo on his arm, in the design of a chip or a SIM card with a corner clipped off. He was handling a thick leather tawse and didn't see Jake staring at him.

Jake quickly weighed up his choices. He could hug the wall and try to tail the guy, see where he went. Or he could take a more direct approach. Given what he'd seen this man do on film, he wondered if the direct approach would gain him any ground. Would he look like too much of a challenge to the guy? The men he had killed in the videos tended toward a smaller build. Or would the thought of a struggle turn him on?

He was still debating this when the mark looked up and caught his eye. *Shit.* So much for keeping a low profile. He'd have to go with option two. He gave him what he hoped was an inviting smile.

A piercing, pale gray gaze raked him over, then the faintest of smiles ghosted across the man's broad, full-lipped mouth. He handed the strap back to its owner with a nod and a smirk and both men turned their heads in Jake's direction. The Dom patted the smiling killer on the shoulder and turned away to talk to someone else. Tattoo guy headed right for him, his unblinking stare sliding over him, measuring him up.

"Allo," he said in an amiable tone. "You look kinda lost. You want some company?"

Jake took a drink and licked his lips to give himself a second to think. This man had killed people. According to Mari's theory, he'd preyed on people when they were at their lowest point, when they had no hope left. He had killed Jim, who was quiet and gentle and maybe, if he'd been given a chance, might have decided life was worth living after all. This guy had taken away his options. Jake made up his mind what he was going to do.

He had to admit, his flirting skills were rusty. If he'd ever really had them to begin with. He tried to emulate the coy looks Alex had thrown his way, before they'd started to see each other.

"Just checking out the equipment," he said, letting his gaze flicker up and down the man's body.

"Like what you see?" he asked, his voice deep and mellow. From his body language and the look in his eyes, he certainly liked what he saw.

"Yeah, I do." Jake cast a glance back toward the padded benches and other restraints. Colm was smirking at him and Jake returned his attention to his target. "What's your name?"

"I'm Ben, but you can call me Daddy, if you like. You're a Yank?" he speculated, aloud. "I never fucked a Yank before."

"I'm Jake. And I seem to be a novelty tonight."

"You're hot, that's why," Ben told him without a hint of self-consciousness. "You show me a bloke in this place that doesn't want to bend you over and have you, and I'll show you a closet hetero."

Jake tipped his head toward the bondage gear. "You really into that stuff then?"

"I like strapping sexy young stud muffins into the stocks and giving their arses a good hard paddling before I shag them. Does that sound like something you could accommodate, Jake?"

Jake blinked. Okay, there was bold, then there was just plain cocky. Even when he'd only been interested in casual hook-ups he'd spent more than ten seconds talking to someone before asking if they wanted to get naked.

"Umm—" Jake stalled brilliantly. "I...uh—"

"Don't be shy, Jake. We're all brothers in bondage down here." Ben stroked a hand up and down his arm and slid in closer, dropping his voice, lips close to Jake's ear. "Maybe you prefer to go somewhere more private, huh? We could do that too. My place isn't far."

Perfect!

"Yeah, that sounds better," Jake said. He reached out and caressed Ben's hip encouragingly.

"Jake, fancy seeing you here," Colm called out, just over his shoulder.

Great. Could your timing suck a little more? Jake turned and gave him a tight smile, suppressing the urge to wipe that smug, gloating grin off his face.

"Thought I'd stop in for the reopening an' all."

"You know this fox?" Ben asked and Colm chuckled in response.

"Oh yeah, me and Jake are like fuckin' brothers, mate. Where's that cute blond twink you've been banging, tonight? Not stood you up, has he?"

Jake would cut his own tongue out before he admitted to this snarky shitweasel that he and Mari were having any troubles, but then his actions were kind of speaking for him. He tried not to groan, or throttle Colm.

"He's feeling under the weather tonight."

"Bad lad. Did you tell him you were going out, making eyes at leather guys while he's tucked up in bed all on his own?" Ben chuckled. "Never mind. His loss!"

Colm laughed too. He touched his fingers to his lips and blew Jake a kiss.

"He was way out of your league anyway, babe," he teased, and there was a glint in his eye that said he wasn't heartbroken about it.

Jake almost had to bite his tongue in half to keep from retaliating, but he didn't have time to deal with Colm's shit when he had work to do.

"Me and Jake are gonna take a walk," Ben told Colm, patting Jake's backside in a proprietary fashion.

Jake's arm twitched and he had to control the automatic impulse to knock his hand away. Instead, he let Ben lead the way out and pushed thoughts of retaliation against Colm to the back of his head. *Later.* He would make the cocky bastard eat his words. For now, he could only hope he got to Mari before Colm had the chance to call him, offering a comforting shoulder and a hard cock to help him forget all about his wandering boyfriend.

They made it through the throng of milling bodies, back out onto the street, and Jake focused on making sure he was open and receptive to any stray memories that might be clinging to Ben. He put his hand on Ben's back and was immediately sucked into the man's head.

He was looking down at a body cradled in his arms. Sticky matter and blood coated his hands and chest and half the face of the man he was looking at was ruined. The bullet entry was under the chin. The exit wound had taken the right half of his head off. He was sobbing and cursing at him in equal measure. "Why? Why? Why?"

Jake pulled out of the vision with a gasp, and stumbled.

"You all right, mate?" Ben asked, strong hands on his arms at once, steadying him. "A few too many sherbets in there, huh? Don't you worry. I've got you. Nearly there. Just down this street here and into the passage on the right. I'll have you feeling better in no time."

Jake didn't resist. He felt like he'd just been kicked in the chest. It was disturbing enough when he got a vision of something horrible but this had been so damn real, so vivid, he could smell the blood and gunpowder. Okay, so not only could he now close himself off to psychometry at will, but when he did open up to it, the memories he picked up were more tactile than ever.

By the time they reached the top of the stairway leading to Ben's apartment, he'd shaken off the rolling in his gut. He closed himself down, afraid he would get sucked into a memory for longer than a moment or two and the guy would think he was having a seizure or something. It was also disturbing to realize Ben lived only two blocks from his flat and one street over. That was too close for comfort.

"C'mon in. It ain't much, but it's home," Ben said.

The flat was warm and clean. Jake had entered the abodes of so many murder suspects over the years that he had lost count, and they fell into all kinds of categories. Some had been like scenes from a nightmare but many were just like this, neat and simple, nothing out of the ordinary, no bloodstains on the carpets or gory knives in the kitchen sink.

In one, he hadn't picked up traces of anything suspicious on a single object he'd touched, so it had been a major shock to open the guy's refrigerator and find a human skull, half stripped of flesh, staring back at him.

"Take a seat. Lemme get you a beer." Ben was even playing the perfect host.

Jake took a slow look around. The place was almost as small as his own and there wasn't much to look at, but one thing did catch his eye — the camera on a tripod in the corner. He sat down on the couch and wondered what he was going to do here if he couldn't use psychometry. What he really wanted to do was pop open the camera and steal the SD card, but Ben was already walking back out from the kitchen with two open bottles.

"There you go, that should settle you down," he said with a grin. He plopped down on the sofa next to him and took a long drink from his own bottle. "So…you wanna stay in here, or maybe go through to the bedroom? Get more comfortable?"

Jake took a drink and, instead of answering, he tipped the bottle neck toward the camera setup. "Amateur photographer?"

"You could say that." Ben grinned. "You interested in photography then?"

"Yeah, kinda, I took a class in college but I'm no good at it, so I sort of gave it up." That was stretching the truth to water taffy proportions. The class he'd taken had been on forensic photography and interpretation. "What do you take pictures of?"

"Whatever takes my fancy." Ben winked at him. "Portraits and anatomical studies mostly. I've worked all over the world though. Snapped some seriously dark shit for the broadsheet newspapers, done photo recording for the police, for NASA, you name it. These days, I prefer to stick to artistic nudes. You ever fancied getting in front of the camera?" he asked. "I bet you're photogenic as any model. You've got the bone structure."

Jake laughed at him. "Bet you say that to all the guys."

As he said it, his eyes fell on something else of interest. A laptop. Another thing he'd like to get a look at but wasn't likely to. Then he had a plan. More of an idea, but it might work. If he could stall Ben long enough.

Chapter Twenty-Six

Cordiline wanted one of his units to drop Mari off near to their target's apartment building but he told them he preferred to walk. It gave him time to think, although most of his thinking revolved around Jake and the conversation with the DI earlier in the day.

Could it really be true that Jake felt pushed out by his refusal to let him be his knight in shining armor? And if that was right, how were they to resolve the problem? He wasn't looking for a hero. He just wanted a man who would be his soulmate, someone he could — one day, maybe — trust with all his secrets, an equal partner in his devious and romantic enterprises. Was that too much to ask for?

Cordiline had said he thought Jake wanted to see him as a partner. As someone he trusted and who trusted him in return. Mari wasn't sure if he was ready to trust yet, much as he wanted to with his whole heart.

Damn you, Chivis. You know how I feel about you, surely? Isn't that enough?

He was still mulling the problem over when he reached the address Ed had given him, which was a basement flat in the middle of a long Victorian crescent. He stood at the wrought-iron gate at the top of the steps leading down to his door for so long that curtains twitched in the window of the house across the road.

"I don't think I can do this," he said, to no one in particular.

When a squad of undercover cops didn't instantly sweep around the corner and whisk him away in response to his announcement, he forced himself to open the gate, to go downstairs, to knock on the door and drag himself into character. He was Mackenzie Martyr, special agent. And he had a job to do.

Mari rang the bell and Ed answered the door in short order, inviting him inside. Again, Mari was struck by how plain and unassuming Ed seemed. His casual beige slacks and dark blue, shirt-neck tee were the epitome of ordinariness. The kindness in his eyes and his warm smile were the only things even marginally noteworthy about him.

The flat was small and smelled of aniseed and damp. A single lamp in the living room was on and that gave off only a dim light. Offsetting that were the myriad scented candles perched on just about every flat surface. Some soothing music, heavy on sax, was playing in the background. He supposed the effect was supposed to be romantic, but it came off more cheesy than sexy.

Mari put on his most long-suffering and patient face and asked, "Have you got any Placebo?"

Ed gave him a perplexed look. "Like sugar pills?"

Mari sighed and played with his hair. "Never mind. The trumpet stuff is really irritating though."

"Oh, sorry. Come in and sit down. I'll change it to something else. Do you want something to drink?" Ed waved him toward the lumpy leather sofa which, together with the lamp and a few boxes covered with tie-dyed throws, was practically all the furniture Ed seemed to possess.

"Sure, whatever you've got." Mari ignored the couch. He wandered around the small basement lounge looking at a series of compact, square, monochrome prints, hung almost at eye level, in straight lines, on three of the whitewashed walls. A window with a dusty, gunmetal-gray Venetian blind covering it took up most of the fourth wall. The photos were borderline homoerotic shots of young men. Or rather, close up, detailed studies of parts of the male body — the muscles of a thigh in one, a sharp shoulder blade in another. He paused in front of a male abdomen, skewed on the diagonal, a hand sliding down the V to cover his cock and balls.

"Where did you get these?" he asked, half turning to look over his shoulder at Ed.

"Mm?" Ed was fiddling with his laptop and the music changed to a pop channel, which was only fractionally less grating than the bad seventies porno music. "Oh, I'm a photographer. I keep my kit at a friend's place, though. It's too damp, and there's not much room here."

Mari's lips quirked. For once he could not disagree. The little basement apartment made Jake's flat look palatial.

"You know him?" he asked, stroking one fingertip down the belly of the faceless man in the photograph.

"I did." Ed's dreamy eyes lifted and he looked at Mari with a hungry gaze.

"He's got a gorgeous body." Mari returned his attention to the photograph, uncomfortable under that purposeful stare. He dropped his voice, making it softer and more ingenuous. "Were you with him? Like, an item or something?"

Ed chuckled. "No, not me. He was with my friend, Ben, the guy that's looking after my photography kit."

"Was? Did they break up?" Mari asked.

"He killed himself," Ed answered bluntly, pointing at the print in front of Mari. "The guy in the photo. Shot to the head."

Mari turned around so fast that he risked tripping over himself. His heartbeat thudded against his chest and he had to close his mouth so he wasn't gaping like a fish. He hoped that Cordiline was getting this.

"Isn't that a bit, um, tasteless, having a picture of your friend's dead boyfriend on your wall?"

"What else should I have done with it? Thrown it away? Put it in the back of a closet?" Ed shrugged, returning to the sofa. "He's dead. It's not like he cares where his picture is. At the end of the day, it's still nice to look at."

Mari shivered and didn't try to hide it. He couldn't deny that the model had had an amazing body, but that didn't make it any less a dead body. Even if he hadn't been dead when the picture was taken. And Ed's story was that he'd taken his own life, but given what he knew about the guy already, he was skeptical.

"What about the others?" he asked, waving a hand at the gallery on the wall. "I hope some of them are still alive."

Ed leaned back and regarded him with a solemn stare. "Why does it matter to you? You wouldn't care if I hadn't told you. And weren't you the one stalking suicide hotlines? I'd have thought death would be a turn on for you. Don't think I don't know your type, Mackenzie."

"Bullshit! You don't know anything about me." Mari came back over to sit on the arm of the sofa, looking at Ed with narrow eyes. "And what kind of creepy person volunteers to listen to suicidal people in his spare time, anyway? If anyone here is getting a hard-on for death, I'd say it was you."

"I'm interested in people." Ed's smile faded as he patted the seat next to him invitingly. "What can I say? I want to give something back. I love taking photographs but it's not an ethical job most of the time."

Mari rolled his eyes. Subtlety was not getting him anywhere so he opted for a blunter approach.

"So, do people ask you to help them die often?"

"That's not what I mean, and I think you know it." Ed patted the leather cushion again. "Come down here and let me kiss you. It's making my mouth water, watching you up there, out of arm's reach."

Mari hesitated for a moment, then slipped down to sit on the other half of the two-man sofa. It creaked under him and he tried not to think about how many other men Ed might have brought back here, to fuck or kill, or both. Leather wiped down easily. He shivered again.

"Are you cold?" Ed leaned forward to stroke the hair out of his eyes and ran the backs of his fingers down Mari's cheek.

He shook his head, then decided it seemed odd. "A bit."

"Let me warm you up." Ed pushed one hand into Mari's hair and curled his fingers around the back of his head, pulling him down into a kiss. He let it happen, mind whirling, trying to remember the notes on the crib sheet he'd dropped into a litter bin at the end of Ed's road. As Ed's tongue slipped out of his mouth, he sat back in one corner of the sofa and chewed on his lips.

"Is that okay? You seem a bit tense," Ed probed, and he struggled to find a reaction for a moment.

"I'm not really into kissing much," he lied, then kicked himself because Ed might just push things to the next level. And he *really* didn't want to go there. Before his host could take the initiative he said, "I kind of want to know more about you before we…you know?"

"Before I strip you and fuck your brains out?" Ed winked at him.

"Yeah, that." Mari tried for coyness, though he knew he wasn't the best actor in the world. "Have you been with a lot of guys?"

"Enough to know what I'm doing." Ed chuckled. "Enough to know what men like when they're naked and their legs are spread. I can't wait to get your clothes off. Don't worry, I'll use a rubber. Do you want me to turn the heating up a bit?"

"Um, I guess," Mari said, wondering if he was talking about the boiler or just being salacious. While Ed was in the hallway tweaking the thermostat, he leaned over the edge of the sofa and took a major risk. The laptop was sitting on one of the throw-shrouded boxes, still playing away to itself, and he brushed his fingers over the screen and closed his eyes.

The files on Ed's laptop were like a series of rooms on a long, creepy corridor. He peeked into each of them in turn, not lingering at any of the doorways, just taking a glimpse of what they contained. They all had innocuous names, randomly generated access numbers, like the videos he'd already tracked. He almost knew what would be in there

before he even touched them, but he had to look. Just a few
seconds, that was all he needed. He pushed open a door…and
found the room empty.

"What are you doing, Mackenzie?"

Ed's voice had a harder edge to it and he sat up fast,
even as he was pulling back from his short-lived
interface, blinking rapidly.

"Uh, I wondered if there were any better songs on
there," he improvised, touching his fingers to his nose.
They came away bloody. Sometimes that happened if
he didn't surface smoothly enough.

Ed was full of concern. "Are you okay? Your nose is
bleeding. Let me get you some tissues."

While he was out of the room, Mari put the wristband
to his mouth and whispered, "There have been videos
on his laptop. A lot of them. The file signatures look like
the ones on the website, but they aren't here anymore.
He must have moved them. I'm going to keep looking."

He didn't have an earphone link to Cordiline's team
so he hoped they could hear him. His host returned as
he sat back on the sofa, pinching the bridge of his nose.

"Here you go? Do you get nosebleeds often?" Ed
handed him a wad of tissues and he put them to his face
gratefully.

"Yeah. I'm delicate, my mama always says." His
words came out muffled.

"You're fucking sexy," Ed told him. "Even with blood
pouring out of your nose."

"It's only a little bit." Mari dabbed again and
examined the tissues. A small scarlet bloom told him
that he ought to be more careful when he was coming
up from a short, hard interface. "I'll be okay. Maybe I
should go home though. I need to put ice on this."

"That would be a shame." Ed pouted. "We haven't had any fun yet. Maybe some ice might help though. I'll get you some."

He vanished into the kitchen again and Mari could hear him crashing about in the freezer as he reached down with one hand and rummaged under the throw for any external devices that might house the videos. Coming up with nothing, he touched the screen again, even as he buried his face in the nest of bloody tissues.

There were about twenty of the numbered files in all, clustered around the same part of the IT corridor. Not everything on Ed's internal hard drive was snuff. Some of the files had actual names and were collections of photos, ranging from innocent pictures of family, with pets and kids, to screenshots of young guys with very little clothing on.

He tried a different pathway and this led to a sequence of doorways into Word documents, and data files. There were lists and telephone numbers. Names.

"Just tell me what you want to listen to. I'll find it. You put some ice on your nose."

Ed's voice pulled him back out of the interface again and he held out his hand for ice, cooling his face with a chunk as Ed squatted by his incriminating laptop and waited for instructions. Mari gave him the names of a few random indie bands and held the ice against his nose until the bleeding slowed and stopped. By then, the background music was half-way acceptable and he was feeling more in control of his reactions.

"This lot are about right for a kinky little emo bitch like you," Ed teased, coming to sit beside him again. He took the blood-stained tissues and set them aside before pulling Mari into a kiss again. A longer kiss this time, and considerably more touching than Mari was comfortable with. As their lips parted he added,

"You're not going to bleed all over my sheets when I bend you over and shag you, I hope?"

"I dunno." Mari shrugged.

"I'd better fuck you on your back then. I don't mind. I can watch that pretty face while you pretend you're taking it up the arse for the first time." Ed grinned at him. He nodded toward the laptop. "Is this shit getting you in the mood?"

"Um, not really," Mari admitted.

"Well that's not a surprise. No wonder you gothy kids struggle to get laid." Ed stroked Mari's chest and belly, teasing his fingers under the hem of his hooded sweat jacket. He caressed Mari's stomach then pushed his hand down into his loose yoga pants, stroking between his legs boldly. "You can't even follow simple instructions. No undies, I thought I said."

"It's a cold night out there," Mari huffed at him. His fingers itched to play with the wristband, which felt odd against his skin. He resisted the impulse for a moment then pulled the band off and shoved it into the pocket of his hoodie. Lying back, he twisted a strand of his hair around one finger instead. Cordiline and his team had got the information they needed and he had no desire for them to listen to any of this.

Ed moved up over him and kissed him again, shoving his hand into his briefs, tugging and stroking his cock as he explored Mari's mouth with his tongue, and Mari tried to think of a convincing way to get the hell out of this horrible little hovel.

"You're not getting hard," Ed commented in a lull between raids on his mouth. "Are you scared, Mac? I wasn't serious about your kecks, you know, kid."

"A bit, I s'pose," he mumbled. "And I know."

"What do you want me to do to you, baby?" Ed murmured against his ear.

Leave me the fuck alone!

"I dunno," he said instead. "You could tell me how you're gonna help me."

"Or we can stop pretending," Ed told him, and for a heart stopping moment Mari figured the guy somehow knew he was working with the police, but then he added, "You don't want to kill yourself, not really. You came here for something else." He winked at Mari suggestively.

"Do you try to get everyone you help into bed?" Mari asked him, but he reached up and curled his fingers around the back of Ed's head, pulling him closer so that he could kiss him. He didn't even know why.

The experience was not unpleasant, but Ed was not Jake and he got none of the thrill from locking lips with him that he did from kissing the infuriating Mr. Chivis. Ed seemed to like it though, because he put one hand down Mari's pants again and wriggled the other arm around him, deepening the kiss and trying to get back on top of him.

Mari got both hands between them and pushed at him with a shake of his head.

"I thought you wanted to fuck." Ed pouted at him again.

"You're like an octopus. That's not what I meant at all," Mari protested, with an attempt at a giggle that kind of died on its feet because he was feeling distinctly unwell. The combination of the candles that ate up all the air in the room, filling it with their sickly scent and the repeated attempts to interface which were bringing on a dull headache, all served to fog his brain and slow his reactions down.

"You seemed a lot more up for it when we were chatting online the other night," Ed reminded him. "You wanted to do a whole load of dirty stuff."

"It's easier to talk sometimes when you're online," Mari said, and that was sincere. He had made some lasting bonds with internet buddies, which was more than he could say for his track record with people he knew in the flesh. "I can be the person I'd like to be when I have a screen to talk for me. It's harder face to face. Don't you ever think that?"

Ed slid a hand back down between Mari's legs and gave the swell of his unresponsive cock a light squeeze. "What I think is you just need to get laid. You've got all kinds of lust, desire, confusion and hurt in your aura. You're full of dark secrets, Mackenzie. Plus, you need some dick. I can always tell."

Mari laughed and tried to displace the groping hand on his crotch. That comment about secrets had him worried again though. *Was* Ed on to him?

"You can tell all that just from some invisible halo around me, huh?" he asked, hoping that he sounded as nervous as he was feeling.

Ed looked down to where Mari was pushing his hand out of the way and said, "Yes. I can also tell you've had a bit of a problem in that department. You don't need to be shy, Mac. You've got a great body, even if you are a bit skinny, and a lovely cock. And I sense that some of your issues stem from that stem, pun intended. Whatever the problem is, I can help you out."

He was so serious that for a moment Mari was drawn in. His observations left him with a trickle of ice in his gut. If he and Jake had not already managed to have sex he would have been convinced that the guy actually knew what he was talking about. But the only problem he had right now, apart from being stuck in a basement apartment with a many-tentacled serial killer, was that the man he wanted to do all those kinky things with didn't even want to speak to him.

"How would you help me?" he asked.

Ed smiled at him and this time Mari noticed that all the warmth had leached from his soft-looking eyes. "You just need some loosening up. You like bondage games, don't you? Let me get you trussed up nice and tight and I'll do all those dirty things to you that you've only talked about online."

Mari bent his head, hiding behind his hair for a moment as he tried to catch his breath. He wasn't attracted to Ed in the slightest and he knew for a fact that he was not so accomplished an actor that he could make the man believe otherwise. If they got as far as the bedroom, his entire validation for being here would fall apart. So why did he want this so much?

"Let me get you in bed." Ed grinned, as if reading his thoughts. "I've got a set of heavy duty cuffs and a nice big dildo to stretch your tight little arse with. That should get you warmed up. Then we can have some real fun." Ed unzipped Mari's hooded top and eased a caressing hand under the sleeveless running vest he wore beneath it. His fingers played over the ridges of Mari's belly and ribs, moving higher until they brushed his nipples, sending little jolts of electricity down to his cock, that made it jump. "You like that idea, don't you?" Ed observed, giving one of his nipples a sharp pinch that pulled a gasp of scented air between his lips. "You are so sexy, Mackenzie. Too beautiful for a boy, really. How do you feel about being watched? Being *filmed*?"

"I— I don't know," Mari faltered, but he did. A part of him just wanted to shout the safe word and run for it. That felt cowardly but he could not stay here. He had found the file path to the videos, and Cordiline knew exactly where to start looking for them. He could just get up and go. Why was he still here? Why was he even deliberating? He shook his head, wondering if Ed had actually drugged him.

Ed suddenly sighed and sat back on his heels, blindsiding him.

"Well, make up your mind. Are you going to cheat on him or not?" he said impatiently.

Mari stared at him as the words clicked into place in his head. That wasn't possible, was it? Ed must have come back last night and seen him arguing with Jake outside the bar.

"Wh-what are you talking about?" he managed to stammer.

"Oh, get off it. Your aura is all guilty pink and dirty yellow and your body language is screaming 'no' at me, even though your dick is half-hard. The only reason a guy gets like that on me is when he's stepping out. So? What's the story? He not doing it for you in bed? Not giving you the rough stuff you want?"

"Stop doing that!" Mari snapped at him. "Stop telling me how I'm feeling when it's nothing to do with you."

"You're in my flat. Supposedly, so that I can shag the mouth and arse off you, *Mackenzie*. *If* that's even your name," Ed threw back at him, the first hint he'd shown of impatience. "You're a liar, Mac. I can see it, even if you can't. I see all your dirty secrets, kid. Either get your clothes off and bend the fuck over, or tell me what your fucking boyfriend problem is, so we can sort it out. But quit with the cock-teasing and lies. These mixed signals are fucking with my head."

"It's not his problem, it's mine." Mari stood up and his hands were shaking with a mixture of rage and fear as he fought the urge to just punch Ed on the nose and run for it. "I think I'm in love with him, but I don't even know if he still wants to be with me anymore. He was the best thing that ever happened to me and I fucking ruined it because I was proud and angry and…scared that he would find out who I really am, and want someone less screwed up than me. I need to impress the men in my life, Ed. I can't help it. I need to be exactly what they want, all the time. I need to know that they want me and I'll always be the most important thing there is for them. I'll do anything. I'll go to any lengths. And it's too much. I know it is. I'm *too* needy. I've either got no control, or *too much* control. I don't know how to please them. So, I frighten them away. Every. Fucking. Time." He closed his mouth because Ed was staring at him with a mixture of shock and fascination. The man's cock was tenting his slacks though. *Interesting. Is that his weakness? Scared, needy boys?*

"God! You're magnificent," Ed exhaled in a husky whisper. "So hot. Let me teach you how to please them. Let me make you come."

Mari pushed him away when he reached out again. He backed up and put some distance between them.

"I don't think so," he said. The words felt strange in his mouth. He knew what he wanted to tell Ed, yet somehow hearing it out loud felt wrong. As he searched for something else to say his phone chirped, a familiar cop-show theme that made him jump, it was so unexpected. He reached into his pocket for it, his hand on auto-pilot, and looked down at the notification that he had a text from Jake. "Sorry. I have to take this." And just like that the wrongness dropped away from him.

Chapter Twenty-Seven

Jake closed the bathroom door and locked it. There was a voice nagging at the back of his head, even as he composed a text, that what he was about to do was wrong, on many levels. Mari was struggling with an addiction, one they had nearly broken up over more than once. And here he was, about to ask him to indulge it again. But if he didn't, if he walked out of here with no evidence, Mari would continue to use his interface ability to hunt them anyway. If he did this now, maybe there was a chance for Mari to stop using it and get some control.

I am with the guy with the tattoo. In his flat. I need your help. If I can plug my phone into his laptop can you get into it? The laptop, I mean.

He looked down at the phone, his thumb hovering over the send button. He could still leave. Tell Cordiline where the suspect lived. Let the Met try and build a case — and Mari would be pissed at him, that he didn't even let him try.

He hit send.

For what felt like forever, but was probably less than a minute, nothing happened. He was just cursing his bad timing when he got a terse message back.

What? You have to do this right now? And what are you doing with him anyway?

Jake read the message and tapped his finger on the side of the phone. He was tempted to just tell him to forget it. It was not in his nature to give up without a fight, though.

The camera equipment is here. I'm sure there is evidence on his laptop. It's now or never.

Fuck! I'm locked in the bathroom. This will have to be quick. At least I can tell Ready Eddie that something's come up at home. His machine was once loaded with videos, by the way, but he's moved them. He has some shame at least.

Get out as fast as you can, Jake sent him, feeling his heart quicken at the idea of the killer finding out what Mari was really there for. *I'll need a few minutes to get the phone plugged in. Ring me when you have what you need. I'll stall him as long as possible. Give Cordiline my location in case anything happens,* he instructed as fast as he could, keying in Ben's address at the end.

* * * *

Mari sat down heavily on the toilet lid and drummed his fingers on his knee for a moment. Talk about 'saved by the bell'. By the time he'd got to the bathroom, bolted the door and unlocked his phone, his hands were shaking. Ed no doubt knew the text he had to take so suddenly was from his boyfriend.

Mari prioritized, once Jake's instructions were complete, forwarding the address of Mr. Tat on to Cordiline, and telling him to send people round there, though he knew the Inspector wouldn't thank him for the order. He contemplated interfacing from here, but who knew how long it would take Jake to get set up, and if Ed freaked out and broke down the bathroom door, he didn't relish being yanked out of yet another interface tonight.

His mind was clearer as he calculated what to do, and with the clarity came awareness of just how weird and confused he'd been since he'd walked into Ed's apartment. Maybe there was something in the candles that was messing with his ability to think, after all. Whatever the reason, being out of Ed's proximity allowed him to get back in control of his faculties.

He returned to the lounge and retrieved his coat, pulling it around him, glad of its warmth.

"I'm sorry. I have to go. It's my mother. She's…had a fall."

"Uh-huh. Right." Ed blew out a breath. "Whatever. I hope Mr. Stud is worth it," he added bitterly.

"You know, jealousy doesn't suit you," Mari told him in a cool tone.

A minute later he was striding back along the street toward the main road looking for somewhere quiet that he could work without being disturbed. He took deep cleansing breaths and the farther he walked the more the whole experience with Ed felt surreal. From the moment he'd entered that apartment, he had not felt in control of his senses. But now, out here, he had no such concerns. Then it hit him. The aura reading thing — maybe Ed *wasn't* just trying to scam him. If it was a real ability…

Aura reading was a Water Elemental ability.

* * * *

"Do you want to watch porn?" Jake asked, when he came back into the living room.

Ben grinned. "We can do that," he said, pulling his laptop over as Jake settled next to him on the couch again.

Ben lifted the lid and turned it on and, while they were waiting for it to boot up, Jake ventured, "I'm sorry, this is going to sound totally weird, but my phone is almost dead and I need to keep it charged because there is some work stuff going on that I kinda have to be available for. Do you think I could use your USB port to charge it?" he asked, then just to seal the deal, added, "I really don't want to have to run home."

"Sure," Ben said readily enough, then hunted around for a charge cord, which to his relief fit his model. "So, what do you do, mate? For a living?"

He was pretty sure he only froze for a nanosecond. "I'm…an alarm technician. If someone's alarm goes off, I have to go sort it out. I know, I could stay in and wait around, but this is more fun."

"Let's hope the burglars stay in and watch the footie tonight then." Ben chuckled, and hooked his cellphone up to the laptop for him. "All done."

Jake suppressed a sigh of relief when it was plugged in. That had gone far smoother than he could have even hoped for. Now he just needed to wait for Mari.

Ben opened his browser and pulled up a video of a guy fucking a girl doggy-style. It wasn't that Jake had never seen straight porn before, but he had a theory about gay guys that liked straight porn. They seemed to be the kinkiest bastards out there.

"You like this?" Ben asked him, leaning closer and looking from Jake to the screen and back. "You enjoy taking it like she does? I'd love to get the cameras running then fuck you that way, on cam."

I bet you would, Jake thought.

"Seeing as how I don't have a vagina, I can't 'take it like she does'," he told him instead, trying to keep his tone casual. "How about you find something with more cock?"

"How about you get that nice fat dick out and stroke it for me until I do," Ben said with a grin. "I love to see a guy stroking himself."

He tapped something into the search bar on his laptop and moments later another screen opened and Jake thought he would have a seizure. The blond actor on the screen looked so familiar that, at first, he thought he was watching Mari, kneeling between two half-naked men and unzipping their pants to wank and suck them both. Only when the camera closed on his blissfully slurping features did Jake relax. The young man in the clip was not as gorgeous as his Mari, and his hair was bleached, the roots showing dark.

Shit! Ben was waiting for him. He was the one who'd suggested porn, and he wasn't sure how he was going to stall. He looked over at the camera.

"You want to take some pics of me, huh?" Jake asked in a teasing tone. "Get your camera set up then."

* * * *

It would take too long to go home, so Mari ran as far as the public toilets near the park, drawing the eye of a couple of patrons as he burst in, sweating and out of breath. One of them sidled up to him and asked, sotto voce, if he wanted some company. Mari told him briskly and economically, in Suomi, to fuck off, then locked himself into a cubicle and hoisted himself up to sit on the boxed-in cistern with his Converse-clad feet on the toilet lid. He leaned back against the wall and shut out the sounds of random strangers using the urinals and traffic buzzing by outside, as he opened up his phone and tapped Jake's profile on his contacts list. Then he cradled the phone in both hands, touching the screen with his thumbs, and closed his eyes.

It was akin to flying. Or those moments when he rolled over in bed and thought he was falling. He dropped into the channel and let it pick him up like an eagle riding an air current. And just as if he were an airborne bird, he could see the many different options available to him, similar to streets set out below in a grid on a three-dimensional map. He found the input-output port easily enough and used it to slide from Jake's phone connection into the tattooed man's laptop.

A chuckle stirred in his throat as he registered that the machine was running a hardcore porn channel, tempted to eavesdrop on the film clip but not knowing how much or little time he had. Instead he diverted to Ben's recently accessed files and began to scroll through them, dismissing most of the very recent stuff as either work-based files or downloaded pornography.

One file caught his attention. It didn't have a name, just a random generated accession number. *Identical to the ghost files on Ed's machine.* He slid into the file like a seal into an underwater pipe and caught his breath.

Gold-dust!

The video was darker, harder stuff than Ben was watching, unaware of the spy in his system. Reminiscent of the boy in the online video, the subject was being used by two men, but unlike the clip that was playing, the star of this movie nasty was being choked to death with a thick, metal-studded leather belt, as his partners in crime thrust urgently in his mouth and arse.

Despite a sickening churn in his gut, he skimmed through the video to the part where the man being choked started to struggle. The guy with the tattoo held him down, still strangling him. The other pulled out suddenly.

"Stop. Ben, stop."

"What the fuck, don't use my name, idiot."

"Stop, he's not ready."

"Bit late for that!"

Mari's stomach dropped further as he recognized Ed's voice as the one saying they should stop. He watched as the other man pulled his cock out of the victim's mouth and horror filled him as he also recognized Jake's neighbor, Jim Sullivan. He slumped to the floor and Ed's face came into view as he knelt and put his fingertip to Jim's throat.

"He's still got a pulse. Faint, but there."

"Shut your fucking gob, you stupid shite." The tattooed guy growled. "Fuck. Fuck it. This one's ruined."

There was a pause where they both looked at each other, breathing hard.

"Fill the goddamn bathtub," the tattooed guy said, and the video ended.

Shaken, Mari pulled the file through to his phone and stored a copy in his cloud folder. He forwarded a second copy to DI Cordiline. This was unequivocal proof of who had killed Jim Sullivan, and now he knew why that video hadn't surfaced. For good measure, he pushed back through the wireless connection to Mr. Tat—Ben's—camera system and left a glitch in it that ought to fuck with any ideas he might be getting about filming himself with Jake. Then he was slipping back out, dropping into the real world again.

Except he kept falling and only stopped when his face hit the concrete of the cubicle floor. The world swung around like his head was caught in a spinning wheel and he crashed into the darkness.

* * * *

Jake heard the shutter click of the camera behind him.

"That is amazing, mate," Ben said as he snapped another picture of Jake's back. Jake was pretty sure he meant the tattoo and not his body.

"Thanks," Jake said. "It's always looked out for me."

"Why don't you take the jeans off too?" Ben suggested.

Jake hesitantly reached for the button on his fly and Ben began to unbuckle his wide leather belt. The triple rows of bright steel spikes glinted in the overhead lights as he pulled it clear of his belt loops and wound the end around his hand. Jake was mesmerized for a moment, reminded of his regular spanking sessions with Mari, so much so that his cock filled the crotch of his own jeans in response. Ben grinned, checking him out and misjudging the reason for his sudden semi. Just then, Jake's phone emitted a familiar jingle. He turned around quick and snatched it up.

"Shit," he muttered. "I have to go. Something's come up."

"You're telling me!" Ben had his fly undone and he was rock hard. "Aww, c'mon, mate, you can bring me off at least, can't you?"

Jake's phone buzzed again in his hand. When Jake looked down the message was from Cordiline.

Get the fuck out of there. Now.

"I'm sorry, this is an emergency," Jake said, grabbing his shirt. "Top client. Gotta run."

"Ah fuck, no. You can delay it a few minutes at least?" Ben moved closer, still with the belt wrapped around his hand, and Jake took a step toward the door.

Before he reached it, a shadow fell over the glass panels and from outside a metallic, amplified voice warned him that this was a police operation and he was to come out slowly with his hands raised. He turned his head and saw the look of panic that crossed Ben's face.

"Is this to do with you, mate?" he wanted to know.

Jake shook his head. "I reckon this is all on you, sorry."

"Ah fuck it, no way!" Ben closed the distance between them and before Jake could get the door unlatched Ben had the belt around his neck and was using it to pull him back. "Don't even think about it, sunshine. They need a fucking warrant to come in here. And if they try without it, you're collateral damage. Sorry, buddy."

Jake scrabbled with useless fingers against the thick band of leather constricting his airway. All he could see in his mind's eye was the face of their first known victim, Wade, as they throttled the air out of him on camera. He stopped fighting and let his limbs go loose and pliable. When Ben relaxed his grip in response, he rammed both elbows back hard into the man's chest then, as he let go of the belt, reached for the door again.

"Step away from the doors and windows!" the amplified voice ordered and Jake didn't even stop to think. He threw himself to the floor and the glass erupted inward moments later, cascading over him like an icefall.

"What the fuck did you think you were doing, Chivis?" Cordiline demanded, the large vein at his temple still standing out like a warning flare as he stalked around the apartment some fifteen minutes later, with Ben looking sullen, in handcuffs, on the sofa, while the white-overalled forensics team were still combing through Ben's IT and his camera equipment. Jake was nursing a few small splinter wounds and a sore throat from the belt, but was otherwise unharmed.

"I recognized him at the bar. From the memory I picked up in Jim's apartment. I had to at least find out where he lived, and I saw an opportunity to gather evidence, so I took it," he told the inspector calmly.

Cordiline made a disgusted noise. "You keep riding in to play hero on your own, you're going to end up dead. Get out of here. Go find your crazy boyfriend and be at my office first thing tomorrow to give a statement."

Jake frowned at him. "I thought Mari was with you."

"He left the other suspect's apartment before we raided him," Cordiline replied, shaking his head. "I was surprised he wasn't here first. He usually is."

"Damn it, John. If he's been hurt, I'm holding you responsible!" Jake was on his feet and moving toward the street before he could stop him.

"Jake, hold up. He's carrying a wire and a tracking device," Cordiline called after him. "We can find him faster than you can."

"Boss, we've got the videos," one of the investigators called over, from where he was kneeling beside an open laptop. "And a whole shitload more stuff you might want to take a good look at."

"Good work, Cal." Cordiline looked grim but satisfied. "Take Mr. Chivis down to the van, will you, and find out where the hell Dr. Gale has gone."

Chapter Twenty-Eight

The alarm had already been raised by one of the lavatory attendants by the time Jake arrived at the location pinpointed by Cordiline's tracking team, and there was a rapid response vehicle parked outside with its lights still flashing. He was out of the van and through the doors of the public conveniences before the vehicle had even come to a halt.

Mari was sitting up when he got inside. His cheek was scraped and bruised, and his nose bleeding, but he was otherwise very much intact. Two paramedics, one male and one female, were fussing over him, asking if he wanted to be taken to the hospital, but Mari was shaking his head with his usual stubborn determination not to be hustled around. His expression brightened for a moment as he spotted Jake, then he got a look in his eyes that hurt to the core. It was somewhere between shock, sadness and embarrassment, hitting none of them fully. Jake took two steps, wrapped his arms around Mari and held him tight. In the background he heard the uniformed officer who had accompanied him into the gents' explaining the situation to the paramedics.

"Is it over?" Mari whispered against his cheek.

"The cops have both of them, Ilmari," Jake murmured back, rocking him, overcome with relief that he was safe.

"That's not what I meant," Mari said, in a small voice that made him ache deep inside.

"Oh." Jake didn't know how to answer. "Are you sure you're okay? Maybe you should go to A&E."

"Shhh," Mari breathed. "I'm fine. It was just a dizzy spell, that's all. The paramedics gave me oxygen. It was very nice. I'll be perfectly all right."

There was no convincing Mari to go to the hospital so Jake offered to get a cab, but Mari insisted that wasn't necessary, that it was only a short distance to Jake's flat. They walked in silence as Jake turned over in his head a million things he wanted to say and discarded each. He wanted to ask Mari if he was angry, he wanted to ask if he was walking back to his flat in order to officially break up. He wanted to ask if Mari hated him, but he wasn't sure if he really wanted the answers, so he didn't ask any of them.

By the time they were standing outside the entrance to his building, he couldn't stand it any longer.

"Are we okay?" he asked.

"I don't know. Are we?" Mari looked at him, his eyes so wide and anxious Jake's heart kicked him in the ribs.

"Do you want us to be?" He hardly dared to breathe.

Mari cupped both hands around Jake's face and pulled his lips onto his mouth. There was a fierceness to the kiss that shook Jake and sent his head reeling, not knowing if this was a reclaiming or a last goodbye.

When Mari finally let go, Jake just stared at him in utter bewilderment.

"Is that a yes or a no?" he asked.

"Idiot!" Mari huffed, shaking his head. "I love you, Jake Chivis. There, you made me say it. What do you imagine it means?"

All the tension left Jake's body in one sudden rush, like his bones would melt, and he folded around Mari. He kissed him again, just as fiercely, although after a moment he softened it to something more sensual. He was breathless when their lips parted again and he wanted to rush Mari upstairs and get his clothes off, but before he could, a wolf whistle from a cluster of bar patrons spilling out of the party inside caught his attention.

Jake looked at the bar and back at Mari. "Hold on to that thought," he said, detouring into the crowd and pulling Mari along with him.

"Jake…"

"This will just take a minute, then we'll leave, I promise," Jake said, weaving his way through the throng toward the stairs and down into the dungeons below. He didn't go far, just enough to spot his target.

"Colm," Jake called. When he got the man's attention, he slung his arm around Mari's shoulders, then flipped the smirking Dom off and hustled Mari toward the stairs.

"What on earth was that about?" Mari asked, although evidently he had some idea, because he sounded amused.

"Fucker told me you were out of my league," Jake muttered, tightening his fingers around Mari's.

"Did he?" Mari was trying not to chuckle but there was a bubble of humor in his voice as he pulled Jake to a halt and turned around before they reached the stairs.

"What are you doing?" Jake asked. He had visions of having to break up a fight between his less-than-burly boyfriend and the rather more muscular Colm before Mari got too badly hurt. Not a good mental image, no matter how it turned out.

To his relief Mari didn't wade in and start throwing fists. He ran up two steps, putting him above head height, and put two fingers in his mouth, whistling like a hill shepherd. Every head turned their way, including Colm's. Once everyone's attention was focused on him, Mari pulled Jake up onto his step, then folded both arms around him and drew him close from lips to knees. Mari planted a long, slow, hungry kiss on him that soon had the whole basement whooping, cheering and shouting ribald encouragement. Jake was pretty sure that Mari had made his point when his lover gripped him tight, balling his fists into Jake's jacket, and turning their bodies so that Jake's back was to their audience. He let go of his jacket and from the corner of his eye he saw Mari lift both hands, with the middle fingers extended. Loud laughter and good natured ribbing greeted Mari's expression of defiance.

Jake slid both hands down Mari's back and over his arse, pulling and lifting at the same time until Mari wrapped his long legs around his waist. They broke the kiss off and Jake grinned, glancing over his shoulder to throw a smug look Colm's way. Colm held up both hands in surrender then laughed and applauded good-naturedly with the rest.

The crowded bar was a blur on the way out. Jake carried him all the way up two flights of stairs.

"I want you, Chivis." Mari's lips moved against his ear, the words a growl of need as Jake let him down to wrestle with the front door. "You know, all the time that Ed was trying to get into my pants, all I could think was, if it had been you suggesting it, we'd have been naked and on the floor already."

Jake managed a strained laugh. "That statement simultaneously makes me want to rip your clothes off *and* go beat the shit out of someone. What are you doing to me?" He got the door open at last and pulled Mari inside. As soon as it was closed behind them, Jake pushed him up against it and kissed him with ravenous hunger for the touch of his lips.

"I'm sorry about last night," he breathed into Mari's mouth, running his hands up and down his flanks and grinding against him. It was totally unfair to apologize to him like that, but at the moment he would take any edge he could get.

"Last night?" Mari gasped against his lips as he undulated with Jake's body, pinning him to the wall and grinding down hard on him. "What happened last night? I can't remember anything but this."

Mari's fingers combed roughly through Jake's hair, pulling his lips onto that soft, warm mouth. It was a good thing Jake wasn't still carrying him, because his knees went positively watery at that kiss. Some small part of his brain tried to ask if he hadn't meant to talk to Mari first, but it was silenced in a rising tide of passion. He couldn't remember what he'd been so angry about before.

Sliding his hands under the bottom of Mari's shirt, he cupped his ribs and chest while Mari squeezed his ass and thrust his tongue into his mouth. Mari's urgency was contagious and Jake tugged at his jacket, dropping it on the floor and pulling his hooded sweatshirt up and off, as Mari did the same for him. By the time they were reaching for each other's hips it was like a race to see who could get the other naked faster.

A buckle popped, ties were tugged loose, his zipper dropped and their breathing quickened in synchronicity as their pants descended. Mari slid his hands into Jake's boxers and gripped his backside as Jake rode the heat of his lover's mouth with his lips, a soft moan escaping as Jake's hands roamed over bare flesh.

When they were down to nothing but underwear, Jake broke off the kiss long enough to pull Mari toward the bedroom. The floor or the sofa would do, but he needed to be able to spread out and he didn't want to have to stop for lube. As soon as they were across the threshold Jake spilled Mari across the bed and dropped on him like a hawk diving on a mouse.

Mari's hands were everywhere, stroking and gripping and pulling at him. Whatever had gotten into him, there was no denying how turned on he was, his mewls of desire fraught with need. The way he moved and bucked against him put steel in Jake's cock and it made him throb to feel Mari just as hard.

"Oh, my days, fuck me!" Mari whimpered, and his gaze was melting cobalt fire, looking up at Jake in absolute desperation. "Please! I never wanted anything so much. I am so unworthy of you, Jake Chivis. But—"

Jake silenced him, covering Mari's frantic lips with his own. As they parted he breathed a soft, "Ssshhhhhh."

Mari was huffing under him, his hands still pulling Jake against him. He spread his legs wider, stroking his bare feet up the backs of Jake's thighs, drawing him down like a spider.

"I need you."

Aware that it was probably not a good idea to go as fast as Mari was demanding, Jake still reached down and pulled off his underwear, noting as he did that they were a plain navy-blue pair, in soft cotton. It was ridiculous but he felt better that Mari hadn't worn sexy undies for his undercover operation. A wiggle and he was out of his boxers and back between Mari's thighs. He kissed him hard, reaching out blindly to snag the lube, then slicked up his cock and pressed slippery fingers between Mari's cheeks, rubbing in teasing circles.

"Stroke yourself, baby," Jake murmured over the tender skin of Mari's throat. "This is going to feel so good."

Mari wrapped the fingers of his right hand around his long, lean cock and began to ease the silken hood of his foreskin back and forth over the glistening, blood-flushed tip. The other hand reached back up into Jake's hair, pulling his lips back down for another kiss and when they broke apart his breathing was more ragged, less controlled than before. His slim, sculpted body writhed constantly under Jake, hips bucking, thrusting his erection into the circle of his stroking fingers. Fair hair spilled like tendrils of spun sugar over his face as he squirmed and undulated, eternally restless. For once he was quiet though, just uttering the occasional groan when Jake's fingers, or his own, got him too stimulated for absolute, breathy silence.

Despite all the squirms and moans and breathless need, Jake could sense the small thread of anxiety in Mari and knew he was fearful that his body would betray him again. Without the long build up, without the bondage and submission, could he still do it? Jake thought he could and he pressed two fingers into him with no hesitation. Mari was tight, so very tight, but his body didn't clamp down, he didn't go rigid or fall prey to his usual anxiety and frustration. He tipped his head back on the pillow and groaned as Jake's fingers curled inside him and flexed over his hot spot.

Before Mari had any time to think about it, Jake smoothly withdrew his fingers and guided the head of his cock to Mari's ring, applying light pressure on the crown with his thumb as he slowly let his hips sink. The little 'O' of muscle gave way and the heat and tightness engulfed his sensitive cock head. Even knowing now that it was possible to get inside him, he wasn't sure which of them was more relieved or more breathless at the way it felt.

Mari twisted under him, turning his head for a moment and staring at the wall. Jake thought he was holding his breath, as if he was waiting for something. Long, gold tinted lashes fanned his cheeks as his eyes closed, then he exhaled a tremulous rush of air and a whimper of sound escaped with the breath.

His hand stilled for a moment or two on his cock, then he was moving again, humming softly to himself like a wordless mantra for calm. He didn't push Jake away though. Didn't tell him to stop.

Slow and steady, Jake let his weight carry him deeper. He resisted the urge to plunge ahead, at least for a few moments. Mari might like certain kinds of pain but he didn't want to push too far, too fast, and ruin things. The sudden freeze and clench of muscles didn't come, and once he was settled and just rocking slowly, he brushed a gentle kiss against the corner of Mari's mouth.

"Open your eyes," he whispered. "Show me that you're okay."

"I'm scared that if I look it will be real." Mari exhaled. "And if I think it's real then it will break the spell that's letting me do this. As long as it feels like a dream, I can do it."

He did turn his head though, seeking out Jake's lips with his and returning the kiss rather less chastely. His long legs encircled Jake's hips, taking possession, and he arched his back, pushing down onto him, in time with the slow roll of Jake's body between his thighs.

Jake slid a hand under his shoulder and the other caressed his hip, wrapping him in a loose embrace as they kissed and moved together.

Baby steps, he reminded himself.

When Mari was ready for it to be real it would be. Until then, Jake was more than happy to be his fantasy. The fingers digging into his back and the way Mari bucked told Jake he wanted more and he increased the pace, taking him harder and faster, and — *oh god* — did it feel amazing.

The rhythm of their bodies, locked together, conjured a low, hungry, feline sound from his lover's throat again and Mari's hand, moving back and forth along the length of his cock, fell into time with Jake's thrusts. As Jake kissed him, Mari pushed his tongue into his mouth and his hum of pleasure increased in volume and intensity.

"Ohh, Ja-a-ake!" Mari crooned, the fingertips of his left hand tracing the circles of his back tattoo like it was a mandala, helping him to focus and relax. Jake knew that the tattoo had been his guardian but he'd never imagined that its protection might extend to those he loved as well. It was a comforting thought.

Jake pressed his hands down on the mattress, leaning up. Mari still had his eyes closed, his lips were glossy, reddened from their passionate kisses, and there was a hint of a flush on his cheeks. He was so gorgeous, so beautiful. Jake glanced down, watching the way Mari's hand worked his cock, the toned muscles of his stomach quivered and their bodies met and meshed together.

"That looks as amazing as it feels," Jake breathed. "So fucking good…"

Mari's shimmering lashes fluttered and, at last, the near translucent lids slid back to unveil the full glory of his astonishing, clear, ice-blue eyes. His pupils were wide and black, leaching some darkness into the iridescent irises so that they seemed a rich cobalt at their hearts, fading out to ice-blue at the edges. Mari stared up at him without blinking, poised between dream and reality, still stroking and tracing with his restless fingers as he gazed back at Jake.

"You are amazing," he panted. "I am so crazy about you, Chivis. I just wanted you to know that."

Jake lowered his head until their lips just barely touched.

"I love you, Ilmari," he whispered, sealing the words in with a passionate kiss as he drove into him again and again.

Mari craned his neck upward, kissing him hard in response. Those long legs locked Jake in, pulling him down fiercely. His slim body shuddered and he moaned his longing into Jake's mouth.

"Ohhhhh! Harder! Harder!"

Jake nipped the side of his throat and dug his knees into the mattress, driving into his lover as hard and fast as he demanded. Tying him up and getting into him had been exciting, and hot, but doing him like this was somehow more intimate, yet every bit as scorching.

He pushed one hand into Mari's hair, running his fingers along his scalp, and sucked at the spot he'd just nipped hard. His own breathing was ragged and the tension was building in his balls.

"Don't stop. Don't stop. Don't stop," Mari was chanting, as if he could somehow control the situation just by saying the words. His hips rose and fell, rubbing his rigid cock against Jake's belly as they ground together harder and faster. His fingers clawed down Jake's back over and over, pulling their bodies as close as possible. "Oh, my stars! Jake! So close! I'm. So. Very. *Ohhhhhh*!"

"That's it, so good, babe. Come for me, sweetheart." Jake murmured breathless, seductive encouragement in his ear. He pulled the lobe between his teeth and nipped him there too, never once breaking the rapid, driving tempo of his hips.

The pressure of his teeth on Mari's flesh seemed to have a galvanizing effect, because he jerked and spasmed like a wild thing around Jake's thrusting cock when he nibbled at his ear. His breath was coming fast and hard, in violent huffs of desperation as he thrashed and bucked, pushing his hips and his sexy backside down hard on Jake's dick. Mari's cock leaked a streamer of wetness across his belly that said more than anything how close he was.

"Uuhhhhh, mmmmhhhh, make me come. Make me come," he was pleading and Jake could not be sure if that plea was directed at him or some higher power.

Jake reached down with one arm and hooked it behind Mari's knee, drawing it up so he was nearly bent double. Sweat beaded at the nape of his neck and on his back. Jake was so close to coming that he had to clamp down on the urge, making himself focus on the slap, slap, slap of their bodies and the slick sounds they made rubbing together.

The shift in position allowed him to rub up against Mari's sweet spot more vigorously and his mate threw himself back down on the bed, uttering a strangled yelp. Mari gripped the bedcovers to either side of his glistening, sweat-slick body and his ass muscles tightened in violent spasms around Jake's shaft, milking and squeezing. His cry became a whimpering sound as his bobbing cock twitched and swelled, then spurted hard, four, five, six times in all, soaking his chest and belly and leaving him breathless and utterly spent.

The only reason Jake was able to hold back at all was that he didn't want to miss watching him come like a fountain, but within moments there was no more holding back the tide. He rolled down over Mari as the first spine-tingling wave hit him and grunted softly as he wrapped his arms around him, burying his face into the side of Mari's neck as the orgasm pulsed through him. It was one of those really good ones, where his toes curled and he saw flashes of light behind his closed lids, then couldn't move to save his life for several moments afterward.

Mari didn't seem to mind. He managed to pry one hand up from the duvet cover and stroked his trembling fingers through Jake's hair, turning his head so that their lips touched.

"Oh, sweet fucking stars, Chivis. I think I could very easily fall in love with you all over again," he gasped.

Jake kissed him tenderly and lifted one hand to comb his fingers through Mari's hair.

"You didn't tense up," he pointed out, smiling at him. "That's twice now."

"No." Mari looked up at him with a dreamy, grateful smile. "Yes. Because you took me to another place. I was ready for you. So ready that—I don't know— nothing else mattered but me and you. And it was amazing. Later, it'll hurt, maybe. But I don't care."

"Not sure if that's what it was," Jake said, caressing his thumb over his cheekbone. "I've seen you super horny before, and even after all kinds of build-up you couldn't relax. Whatever changed, I'm glad."

"I am too," Mari told him, his expression sincere. "For most of my life I've not given a damn what anyone thought of me, but I don't feel that way around you, Jake Chivis. I want to be all you need."

"You're already that," Jake said, and smiled sleepily.

"I am?" Mari sounded surprised but not displeased with this.

"Would I put up with you if you weren't?" Jake teased him.

"Cheeky, much!" Mari poked him in the chest with a forefinger.

Jake caught his hand and lightly bit the tip of his finger, then sucked it and winked at him, letting it pop from his mouth. He pushed himself up, which sent all kinds of sweet aftershocks through him and grinned down at Mari.

"You are all I need, Ilmari, and I love you like crazy." He kissed Mari's forehead, the tip of his nose, and his lips, then rolled off him with a groan and a happy grin.

Mari caught his arm. "And where do you think you're going?"

Jake turned his head to look at him. "Nowhere. Gonna get cleaned up, maybe grab some water. Are you staying tonight?"

"Just try to throw me out and see what that gets you." Mari chuckled, prying himself up from the sweat damp sheets to lean over Jake and plant a lingering kiss on his mouth again.

It was a sweet, soft kiss that swiftly gained heat and even though Jake had thought he was well and truly done for the night, he found he wasn't that done after all.

Chapter Twenty-Nine

Mari thought that Cordiline looked like he'd not got much sleep the previous night, as he and Jake were shepherded into the close confines of the DI's untidy office. Jake leaned on the back of the chair in front of Cordiline's desk while he propped up the wall to their right, arms folded across his chest. Neither he nor Jake had slept much in the last twelve hours either, but that did not make him any more sympathetic to the DI's cause.

"Did you arrest them?" he demanded. Jake fired him a warning look but Mari ignored it.

"My team are working through the information that you provided, Dr. Gale. The suspects we apprehended last night are still in custody. It's looking likely that we will charge Benjamin Warrington today with the murder of James Daniel Sullivan and three other men, and Brian Edward Temple as an accessory to murder." Cordiline looked at him squarely, a silent message in his stormy blue eyes to not make matters harder by arguing.

"Likely?" Mari huffed with an element of disbelief. "Not certainly? After everything we went through?"

"It's just cop speak, Mari. They've got enough evidence for a case against them. They aren't going to let them slip through their fingers. Are you?" He directed the question at Cordiline.

"I can't discuss that with—"

"Oh, stop. It's too late for that," Jake said.

Cordiline flushed at his hairline and it was the first time Mari had ever seen the detective look at Jake with anything but barely hidden lust. He was well and truly angry. Mari diffused the hostilities for a moment.

"Can we not fight for a few minutes? I have something to say to the detective here."

"Go ahead," Cordiline instructed, when Jake didn't immediately argue anyway.

"I've been thinking over what happened when I was with Ed the other night," Mari told him, pushing away from the wall and stalking the little office for a moment before coming back to stand in front of Cordiline. "I wasn't myself, and for a while I just put it down to anxiety. But it was more than that. Ed did something to me in the bar the night we first met up. If I'd not bought my own drink I'd have believed he spiked it. When he left, I felt as if I was waking up out of a weird dream and it was the same again last night. I think—this is going to sound freaky but bear me out—I think he's exerting some kind of spooky influence over his victims."

Cordiline stared at him for a moment and Mari waited for him to make a flippant remark, but he didn't do anything of the sort.

"That explains a couple of things," he murmured, and made a small note on his case file.

"Is that all you have to say?" Jake asked, visibly incredulous.

"Nope." Cordiline folded his arms and glared back at him. "It's not. Just what the fuck did you think you were doing last night, huh? You could have really fucked things up."

Jake gave a one-sided shrug. "I'm not a cop anymore. I don't have to play by the same rules."

Mari rolled his eyes because if he'd tried a counter like that, Jake would have called him on it for sure. He held his tongue though. It wasn't worth the argument after last night, when he'd thought he would never hold Jake in his arms again.

"You don't *have* to do anything at all," Cordiline said darkly. "You had no reason to be there. If you thought you recognized the perpetrator then you should have contacted us and let us deal with it. If things had gone down differently —" Cordiline stopped, and swallowed his words, lowering his hands to the desk for a moment, unclenching his fists. For a short while he stood with his head bowed, trying to compose himself.

"Inspector," Mari said, opting for a more gentle approach. "Things didn't happen differently. It's okay. And Jake was a policeman. He knows how to handle himself. We got a result."

Cordiline looked up at him with a frustrated frown.

"Dr. Gale, I shouldn't need to remind you that you are not a member of Her Majesty's Constabulary," he said tersely. "Yes, you certainly played your part, and I am grateful, but I have to advise you — yet again — that it is not your place to play cops and robbers on a murder case. Not yours and not Mr. Chivis' place, either."

"Yeah, only, you wouldn't have even suspected it was a murder case if it wasn't for Mari," Jake pointed out.

Mari tried not to appear smug and sensed that he was probably failing. Cordiline looked from Jake's defiant features to his own and back again with a shake of his head.

"If he'd decided that he wanted to kill last night we could have been bringing you out in a body bag, Jake," the detective pointed out.

Jake sighed. "He wasn't out looking for someone to kill. He was looking to get laid. I was only going to go back to his flat so I knew where it was, but I saw an opportunity to get you the evidence you needed, so I took it. Yes, it was a risk, but a calculated one."

"Jake understands what he's doing, Inspector," Mari added, keeping his tone polite and just about the right side of deferential. "He's had training in situations like this, I'm sure." Mari looked at Jake. "You have? Yes?"

"He worked in arson investigation and homicide, not undercover," Cordiline said.

Jake lifted an eyebrow. "Still checking up on me?"

"Someone has to." The words were out before Cordiline was able to censor them and he flushed again. "If I have a rogue cop on my patch then it's in my interests to find out what he's up to before that backfires on me, wouldn't you say? If something had gone wrong last night—"

"You keep coming back to that. Nothing went wrong," Mari interrupted, frustrated with this line of inquiry. "They didn't kill unless the victims were looking for a way out. We discovered that. And Jake isn't suicidal. Between us, we bagged you a brace of bad guys. You should be grateful."

"The department *is* grateful for your assistance, Dr. Gale," Cordiline said.

"Uh huh, but not mine," Jake said. "And actually, Ben tried to strangle me, so I'd say that their motives aren't totally altruistic."

"In fairness, he figured you'd stitched him up," Mari reminded him.

"Whose side are you on? The fact remains, though, they're behind bars thanks to me. And him." Jake nodded in his direction and Mari snorted in quiet disgust.

Cordiline had the good grace to look down as he said, "Your involvement with this case is unofficial and will remain so."

"Can't let 'em know a rogue yank is catching your bad guys, huh?" Jake looked amused.

"Not exactly," Cordiline evaded.

Mari had held his tongue, so far, as this exchange had gone on, but now he said, "You're afraid that something bad will happen to him, and you won't be able to stop it."

Cordiline's eyes flashed with brief, defensive anger but the flush in his cheeks betrayed him and Mari nodded. "I might not always recognize what's right under my nose but I'm not wrong about that, am I? We both know how you feel about him."

"Shut up," Cordiline told him softly but with no less vehemence. "That's not why you're here. That's not why either of you are here. I've been told to inform you that, if you interfere unofficially in a Met case again, you will both be prosecuted. My superiors are less than happy about it."

"Fuck right off!" Mari laughed, with an incredulous shake of his head. "We solved your case. That's just sour grapes!"

"No, it's not," Cordiline said, dangerously calm. "You left in the middle of an undercover op before gaining a confession. Which could have been forgiven if you'd not taken off your mic to have sex with the suspect."

The blood drained from his face with his previous good humor, and all three of them went very still.

"That is not what happened," he said at last, rather less forcefully. He looked at Jake, whose expression gave nothing away, as usual. "It's not! I told you what happened. He had me kind of hypnotized. I didn't go with him though, Jake. I left Ed's flat to come and make sure you were safe as soon as you'd contacted me. I didn't want Mr. Walls-Have-Ears here listening in on us if I had to speak to you, is all. That is not what happened!"

Cordiline's lips twitched. "I can replay the recording, if you need your memory refreshed. You took the mic off and got cozy with the suspect about five minutes before Chivis contacted you."

Mari's blood ran cold at the accusation. He couldn't even deny taking off the wristband. He had done it deliberately enough, and not even thought about the reasons why. Had Ed realized what it was? Though what did that matter if Cordiline didn't even believe him.

"That's enough, John." Jake broke in quietly. "You have the evidence we were able to get for you and the perps in custody. If you need us for anything else, call." Jake stood. "We're leaving."

Cordiline rose with him, the amusement fading from his blue-gray eyes. He nodded, ignoring the lethal glare that Mari was burning his face off with. He held out his hand and when Jake did not shake it, he just patted him on the arm amiably.

"Be careful, son," he said. "You're right. You got enough evidence for us to hold them, and we can still get enough out of their laptops to make charges stick. You're a good man, Jake, but I'd hate to be watching SOCO zip you into a body bag if one of these experiments backfires. Just take care."

Mari inhaled a rapid breath and opened his mouth, but Jake just looked at him and he closed it again without a word.

Jake bypassed the lift and took the stairs and Mari followed in a silent fume. It wasn't until they were outside that Jake finally spoke, but what he said was not what Mari expected.

"The other night when you went to meet the suspect on your own, I just want you to know, if you had told me about it, if you had told me about your plan to meet with him to get information, I wouldn't have tried to stop you. I would have gone with you, to make sure you were safe, but I wouldn't have got in your way. I'm not trying to control you, Mari."

"I didn't want to sleep with him," Mari said, still aggravated. "Ed, I mean. I just wanted to find out what he was doing."

Jake stopped walking and looked at him. "I didn't say you did."

"You didn't have to. Your friend back there said enough for both of you. Yes, I took the wristband off. I was worried that things were getting out of control, and if he didn't give me any option, I didn't want them listening to it. Okay? That's all. But it didn't. I don't even know why I'm telling you this." Mari stopped too and turned to look back at him. He was shaking, all of a sudden scared again at how easily his happiness could turn to dust.

Jake put warm hands on his shoulders but didn't grab him and shake him like he had the other night when he was angry—he just squeezed and gave him a gentle nudge.

"Stop. It." Jake squeezed again to emphasis the words. "I didn't accuse you of anything. I'm trying to apologize here and you're ruining it."

Mari stared back at him for a moment and uttered another incredulous huff, then shook his head once or twice because he couldn't find the right words for a while.

"Wonders will never cease," he murmured at last, bringing his hands up to cup Jake's face. He touched his lips to Jake's soft, warm mouth and kissed him hard.

When they pulled apart again, Jake smiled at him.

"You think I'm stupid or something? It's not like I couldn't tell Cordiline's been dying to drop that bomb on me since last night. Besides, it would be hypocritical of me to get pissed at you when I went home with the other suspect. Not that I was intending anything to happen there either."

"So, we're good?" Mari queried tentatively. "Score draw, or whatever the soccer term is?"

"We're better than good," Jake agreed, his hands still caressing Mari's arms through the sleeves of his hooded jacket. The warmth of his touch felt like spring coming on after a cold winter.

They walked on for a while in comfortable silence, arm in arm. Mari leaned close to him, still deep in thought.

"It confused me, last night," he said after a while. "Ed—he was an odd fish. He said a lot of weird stuff about being able to see my aura. Mystical bollocks, you know? But he seemed really sure, like he believed it. At first, in the pub the other night, I just thought he was bonkers, but last night... I'm not sure, Jake."

"In what way aren't you sure?" Jake asked with a crooked grin that made him scowl.

"Don't tease me."

"I'm not teasing, you sound like you're working something out in your head. What's going on in there?" Jake stopped and tapped his skull with one finger.

"I meant what I said to you about not wanting to sleep with him," Mari huffed and carried on walking, forcing Jake to keep pace with him.

"And I told you that I believed you. What's bugging you, Ilmari?"

"It was like—" Mari clenched his teeth for a moment, trying to remember, because recalling the events of the previous evening felt like pushing through cotton candy to get to the truth. "Every time he got close to me, it felt like my self-control unraveled a bit. I didn't lead him on. And he wasn't attractive to me in any way. When he touched me, though—" He shuddered.

"What?" Jake sounded more serious now and he came to a halt, looking back at him, biting his lips as he struggled to remember what had seemed so important when he'd started speaking.

"It was like he switched something on in me. Or off, even. I wasn't myself, when he was touching me. It was like he was pushing me toward something, and when he touched me, I almost wanted to go there. It was creepy. And now, I can't remember it clearly. It's as if he's pulled a screen around the past and shut it away. I have to really struggle to remember."

Jake's eyebrows rose toward his hairline but he didn't ridicule Mari's explanation out of hand.

"This was only when he was touching you?" he queried, for clarification.

"I think so, yes. My head was pretty clear while I was walking around the apartment. He had loads of candles burning. Horrible-smelling things. At first I thought it was those. I wondered if it was something in the candle smoke messing with my head. But now I don't think so. When he went to the kitchen and I interfaced with his laptop, my head was totally clear."

Jake frowned thoughtfully for a moment.

"What do you know about Water Elementals?" he asked at last.

"Not much." Mari shrugged. "One of my great-uncles was supposed to have been one, but he died before I was born. I never met him. This healer my mother is meant to be going to is one, though. I think she figured I'd be impressed by that."

"I looked into the abilities of other Elementals when we were investigating Birthright," Jake told him and slid one arm through his again as they resumed their walk home. "The very powerful Water Elementals are supposed to be able to manipulate emotional energy."

"You think Ed is an Elemental?" The thought had occurred to him too, but having Jake say it firmed up the idea in his own mind.

"He could be. And it would explain how easily they were able to encourage their victims to do what they wanted, if he's able to manipulate their feelings somehow. Think about the videos for a moment. None of those guys put up a fight when they were tied to the bed, did they? They didn't even resist much when Ben started to choke them. It was only at the end when their bodily instincts toward survival kicked in that they struggled. Any person, knowing that they were dying, would react in the same way. We're hardwired to try and live, Mari. Even suicidal people are."

"You think he was mind-controlling them, sleepwalking them to their own deaths?" Mari shivered as the true horror of that understanding took a hold him. "All my days! That's horrible. Did I have a narrow escape?"

"Not mind control exactly, emotional manipulation. Still, it's close enough and from the sound of it, you were strong enough to resist what he was doing to you, even if he's fogged your memories of it slightly," Jake said, still looking thoughtful. "It might be worth mentioning it to Cordiline though. It could change his view of what happened to the other men, if they were coerced into either the sex or the suicide pact. At the moment, Ed is only an accessory to murder. This information changes things a bit."

"Damn. Do we have to talk to him now? I think he's had more than enough of us today." Mari heaved a sigh.

"Let's get it over with," Jake said stoically.

Chapter Thirty

"We both have the day off. We should go do something," Jake suggested, a little over an hour later as they were leaving the Albany Street station for the second time that day.

Predictably, John Cordiline had not been pleased to see them, but he did record Mari's account of his experiences with Ed and promise that they would take this into consideration when they were drawing up their case against him. Mari had cheered him up by volunteering to testify against the man in court, if necessary, and Jake was enormously proud of him.

"Like, what?"

"I don't know. Something. We should celebrate."

"What are we celebrating?" Mari glanced at him with a quizzical smirk.

"That we're both alive, unhurt, and the bad guys are in jail?"

"That sounds like something to drink to, admittedly." Mari chuckled. "Let me check in on Mama and we can decide."

Tonka bounced all over them as Mari unlocked the front door and let them into the hallway. From the day room, Anni called out, "Is that you, darling?"

"No, just me!" Mari responded cheekily. "And Jake."

She peered around the door with a bright smile. "How lovely. Come and have some breakfast."

"Thank you." Jake made a soft sound and snapped his fingers at Tonka. The enthusiastic Staffie settled down and trotted at his heels like he belonged to him while he followed her, and the smell of bacon and toast, into the kitchen.

"I swear that dog is never as well behaved when you aren't here," Mari commented as they settled in the sunny day room and helped themselves to food and coffee.

"We have an understanding," Jake told him.

"Apparently so." Anni chuckled, watching the way that Tonka parked at his feet and looked up at Jake with unconditional adoration. "A glowing endorsement. I hope my son is appreciating you as well as my dog, Jake Chivis."

"Mama!" Mari stared at her, aghast. "I am not anybody's puppy."

She blew him a kiss. "Ilmari. You will never be any man's dog. And Jake wouldn't treat you that way, which is why Tonka and I like him so much."

"You say that like I don't." Mari pouted at her.

"You need to show him," she replied.

"You need to stop telling me how to run my own life, Mother." He laughed, shaking his hair back from his eyes again and turning his gaze on Jake. "Jake knows how I feel about him. Right?"

Jake took a bite of the toast he'd just slathered in jam and washed it down with a sip of his coffee. "You have feelings?"

"Huh!" Mari stole the rest of his toast and made a great show of demolishing the whole slice. "Don't tell the world."

"Shush, the pair of you." Anni laughed at them. "And don't talk with your mouth full, Ilmari. You are both perfect just as you are. For one another."

"The oracle has spoken," Mari said with a sigh. He buttered another slice.

Jake smiled at her. "I think so. At least I hope so. He gets uncomfortable with the 'L' word, but it is fun to see him squirm around it."

"Make him squirm, Jake. It's good for him," she advised.

"Mama!" Mari objected. "Whose side are you on? No, don't answer that question. I don't think I could bear the betrayal."

Jake grinned as Mari shamelessly tore off a bite-size piece of toast and fed it to Tonka under the table.

"I had some news yesterday," Anni told him, still smiling as she watched him trying to avoid the inevitable. "And in a sense, I'm glad you two are looking after one another. I went to see the healer that Mr. Barnard referred me to. And I want to go ahead with this trial."

"That's brilliant. Yes? You're happy?" Mari asked, and even though he was smiling Jake could hear the hesitation in his voice.

"It's a chance. Like all of them," she said, very matter-of-fact.

"That sounds like another reason to celebrate, I'd say," Jake put in. "Mari and I were trying to decide what to do today. Maybe you'd like to go out with us?"

"That would be lovely, but I don't want to cramp your style," she said.

"We're not going skateboarding, Mama." Mari laughed and Jake laughed with him, loving the glitter of genuine mirth that was back in his lover's bright eyes.

* * * *

After a little discussion, they went to Greenwich so that Tonka could run in the park and Mari could show Jake the Dateline and the Cutty Sark and buy him lunch at a very nice restaurant overlooking the river. It was turning out to be a beautiful, early spring day, bright and crisp, like the embodiment of a new beginning. Mari loved to see how Jake doted on his Mama. He was charming and polite but never in such a way that it seemed he was pandering to her seniority or her illness. Jake was just naturally a gentleman. Mari had never known such a consummate gent in all his life, and was very glad to be able to call this one his own. All in all, it was a very pleasant day for all of them, in stark contrast to the last week of upheaval and intrigue. Walking down the hill through the park from the observatory, with the City of London spread out before them, arms linked with his mother on one side and Jake on the other, and Tonka racing around, chasing squirrels, Mari could not remember a time since his childhood when he had felt so content.

"Every day should be like this," he said, with a sigh.

Jake slid one arm around his waist and kissed his cheek. "I have to agree. It's been a great day. Not only was the company good, but it's been really nice not to have to worry about every last thing I've touched."

"It's working then?" Mari turned his head to look at Jake, both proud and pleased with his lover. "You *can* turn the control on and off. Fantastic! I just need to figure out how to do the same. Not to get carried away when I interface with a system. Maybe one day we can just be normal."

"Pah!" his mother said in tones of disgust. "Normal is over-rated. Who wants that?"

"Normal is relative. If the past month is any indication, I'd say we are very normal, compared to some of the whack-jobs we've met," Jake added.

Mama nudged him. "See. Listen to your smart young man."

"I do listen to him, Mama." Mari chuckled darkly. "We're not as insane as we could be. That's a ringing endorsement right there. When do you start your new experiment? Or am I not allowed to talk about that?"

"You're not allowed to *worry* about it," she corrected. "I'll be fine. You and Jake look after one another."

"I'm not comforted by your attempts at flannel," he said with a pointed look.

Anni sighed. "It's as we thought. The new treatment isn't a drug trial, Ilmari. It's more...experimental. I was going to tell you eventually, but I wanted some time to think it over."

Mari raised an eyebrow, trying to keep the worry off his face. They had been here before. Mama had a penchant for paddling uncharted waters when it came to the battle against her nemesis. He could not say that he entirely approved but he knew, in the end, he would support her, whatever she chose. It was why they worked so well together.

"You've hired a magician? He's going to levitate the cancer out of your system?" he said with as straight a face as he could manage.

"Don't be facetious," she warned.

"I do it so well," he teased. "Is your mysterious Water Elemental going to stay a secret then?"

Anni was silent for several seconds, which did not bode well for whatever it was that she was jumping into. At last, she sighed again, and said, "There is empirical evidence that this healer has had success in eliminating diseased cells, but touch therapy has never been used to treat a blood cancer like mine before. These are uncharted waters, for now."

"Mama," Mari sighed. "We've been here."

"It's not like Paris," she objected. "He *was* a charlatan. This one has proven results. Survivors."

"I should hope so!" Mari huffed. "How much is he costing?"

"*She*," Mama corrected him, then told them a number that made Mari splutter and Jake choke.

"I don't earn that in a year, Mama!"

"What exactly is this person's success rate, and do they expect payment if it doesn't work?" Jake asked practically.

"She's tackled different diseases and she has a success rate that's comparable to most of the drug trials, without some of the less palatable side effects of drugs and radiation," Anni explained, warming to her topic. "She operates on a half and half basis. A payment secures her services and the rest is payable once the treatment is completed." She hesitated then added, "It won't be a hospital appointment. I have to go to her sanctuary."

"Sanctuary! Don't tell me, she lives on a mountain in the Himalayas with a herd of magical Yaks and a tree frog Familiar with an unpronounceable name." Mari was shaking his head, unable to quite overcome his natural skepticism.

"No. Actually, she lives in Camden. She has a block just off the High Street that she's converted into a healing retreat. I can walk to my sessions and back," Anni said.

"Well, that's almost civilization, I suppose," Mari remarked. "I can think of worse places to fritter away a quarter of a million quid."

"I'm glad you find it agreeable. At least you won't have to shepherd me to every session," she said.

He blinked at her for a moment. "You're going on your own? Is that wise?"

"Of course I am, and of course it is. You have a job to be getting on with, and a life. I'm a grown up, as you sometimes forget."

"But you're not well," he protested, then wanted to kick himself for stating the obvious.

"That's precisely why I'm doing this, Ilmarinen. What exactly do you think you can prevent by escorting me everywhere, like I'm at death's door?"

"Mama, I'm trying to be practical. What if you get sick while you're out? What if you can't carry on with the treatment?"

"Then I'll call you. Stop fussing, Mari. I will be fine. It's only two afternoons a week, for a few months. You can get on with your life and when it's done I'll be good as new," Anni insisted.

Anxiety tightened his chest like a band of iron, but there was no arguing with her when she got a plan in her mind and he just held his hands up at last. It was not as if he hadn't heard this inspirational speech before.

"I love you, Mama," he said quietly.

"I love you too, Ilmari. Don't fret," she admonished and pulled away. She set a steely eye on Jake, adding, "I expect you to look after him when I'm having treatment."

Jake nodded. "I'll do my best."

* * * *

Later, when they were curled around one another in Mari's bed, his still-agitated lover murmured, "She's been plotting this since she met you. She's confident you'll take her side. My mother is devious."

Jake brushed a stray lock of hair from Mari's eyes. "You really think so? She sounded like this was something she'd just found out about. Besides, how would she know if I'd even be around or not?"

"She must have been talking to this woman for some time," Mari deliberated aloud.

"Oh, come on." Jake sighed, watching him with an amiable smile. "She just wants to be well again. She is not doing any of this to make you feel like she doesn't need you."

Mari folded his hands over Jake's chest and rested his chin on the back of one of them, looking up at him with a narrow-eyed stare. "She's got you where she wants you," he said, though he sounded less annoyed and more resigned.

Jake combed his fingers into Mari's hair and kissed him. "Is that such a bad thing?"

Mari didn't answer that and Jake smoothed a thumb over his cheek.

"She'll be fine. Let her get on with it," he said softly. "It's not as if we're a million miles away if anything goes wrong."

Mari bent his head for a moment, his fair hair brushing like silk over Jake's ribcage as he weighed his words. When he looked up again Jake saw a shimmer of emotion in those jewel-bright eyes.

"I'm not ready to lose her," he confessed, and Jake pulled him close.

"You aren't going to lose her, Ilmari. She's a fighter. And...whatever happens, I will be here for you, you know that, right?"

Mari clung to him for a while, in silence, his head resting on Jake's chest. Jake stroked his hair, listening to his breathing as it slowed and grew less ragged.

"When I found out that she was seriously ill, I... Don't be mad at me, Jake, but I made plans to take my own life. If something happened to her, I mean." Mari didn't look up at him, and Jake's hands stilled on his silky hair for a moment. He felt that his heart might stop if Mari said that he still felt that way. The idea of losing him just wrenched his soul apart. "I didn't want to be alone again," Mari clarified, the words heavy with emotion. "After Tomas... I didn't think I would ever have anyone in my life like that again."

"You will never have to be alone," Jake said to him, once he was able to speak, and he meant it from the heart. "I will be here for you as long as you need me, Ilmarinen Gale. You will never push me away. I promise."

301

Mari glanced up at him, his expression curious, as if he was measuring the veracity of that vow, before settling down again with his head on Jake's chest. He stroked his fingers through the dark hair that dusted Jake's torso between his nipples and Jake resumed the comfortable caressing of his scalp, his pulse settling into a steadier rhythm when he realized that Mari wasn't about to reject him.

"That means a lot to me, but it's not why I'm telling you this," Mari murmured. "When I was trying to get Ed to say something incriminating, pretending I wanted his help to end it, he didn't believe me. He said he could see there was past darkness in my aura but that I didn't really want a way out. I think he was right. Something has changed in me, and I think that something is you."

"I'm glad to hear it," Jake said, kissing the top of his head. "It's going to be okay, Mari. Whatever happens, whatever things have happened in the past, I will always love you. We both have a lot to live for."

Once Jake was breathing more steadily, his chest rising and falling beneath him with the even cadences of sleep, Mari closed his eyes tight against the prickle of happy tears. He would not cry, not now. Yes, he had made stupid choices and even worse mistakes, before Jake came into his life, but they were consigned to the ruin of his former life and they could stay there for all he cared. His past was dead and buried. He had spent too long, and too much of himself, chasing an impossible dream with Tomas, and the lengths he had gone to in his desire to please a man who cared nothing for him had almost destroyed him. He knew he had been a fool for love, and fear of making a fool of himself again had been what held him back from telling Jake how much he meant to him. This felt right though. He had never truly felt happy before. Jake Chivis made him happier than he had ever been.

Right now the only things he wanted were his mama's good health and this chance at a future with his beloved Jake by his side. Lulled by the steady rhythm of his lover's heartbeat, Mari held him closer and silently vowed that he would let nothing else come between them, ever.

Yes. We both have so much to live for.

Want to see more from Bellora Quinn? Here's a taster for you to enjoy!

Quinn's Gambit

Bellora Quinn and Angel Martinez

Excerpt

Surely just a kiss, an embrace… These things can only be beneficial. Valerian let his hands slide down the lovely human boy's back. He leaned in to press his lips against those full, lush ones offered up to him so willingly…

Perhaps it was the human scent or the way the boy ground against him a bit too eagerly. None of it was right or familiar, all of the foreign human-ness grating on his nerves. He pulled away and turned to face the window, arms crossed over his chest.

"I'm sorry. This isn't working."

"You telling me this was a waste of my time? You drag me all the way up here for nothing? Time's money, big boy."

Val ground his back teeth together, fighting his temper. "I neither break nor bend my promises. Your money is there, on the bureau. You may take it and leave me."

"Hey." The sharp voice calmed to something more soothing. A gentle hand caressed his arm. "I didn't mean it like that. Just gotta be careful, you know? We don't have to do anything. I have clients that just wanna talk or cuddle. I have one who just wants someone to hold him while he cries."

Is that what I'll soon be reduced to? Paying someone to comfort me? "I spoke harshly. I apologize. But I have... It was a mistake. Please. I occupied your time. The money is yours. I simply need to be alone now."

"Okay. I get it. But you change your mind, you call me, yeah?" The boy shoved the roll of cash into the pocket of his threadbare jeans. "Give me a chance to see if those yummy pointed elf ears are as sensitive as they say."

With a grin and a wink, he swaggered out of the room. A moment later, the door to the apartment clicked shut. Val leaned his forehead against the cool glass, gazing down at the late evening traffic ten floors below. He could open the window. Lean out. Tumble to the waiting pavement.

Val heaved a weary sigh. A human would die, but with his bone structure, he was likely to survive — in a good deal of pain, but still alive. Living alone had begun to wear on him, nothing more. Perhaps he should have a roommate. It wasn't the same as having a *senrist* of young males waiting for him, but at least it would be someone with whom to converse. Gods, but he missed them. He had tried to describe the *senrist* to his human work partner once. The closest parallel he could pull up had been a harem, but it didn't begin to convey the love and devotion he had once been so privileged to have.

There were days he felt better, days when he thought, perhaps, he could adjust. Then something like this would happen to remind him that this was not his world. He would never belong here. The city bustled below him, sunlit streets and people hurrying about their days. Life—all around him life—while every day he died a bit more inside.

* * * *

Quinn sat on the sunny park bench watching ducks paddle around in the pond a few feet away. He had been sitting enjoying the warm weather and waiting for just over an hour when a young mother walked by with a toddler clutching her hand. An older boy tagged along beside them. Both kids had ice cream cones, the little girl with most of hers on her hands and face and down the front of her shirt, but she was still adorable in springy, golden pigtails.

Quinn watched as the family made their way down the path toward the footbridge that crossed the duck pond. They seemed completely unaware of the dark shape moving under the water, tracking their progress. Just before they reached the bridge, the dark shape resolved, lurching up out of the water. A tangle of weed, muck and pond scum streamed down a huge face twisted into a monstrous grimace, and the creature gave a low, menacing growl.

"Shit!" Quinn muttered and shot off the bench. This was not supposed to happen.

The mother and children screamed, their ice cream cones flying as they raced away from the bridge in the other direction. Quinn knew they were headed directly toward a cul-de-sac that ended in high shrubs, a fence and nowhere to run.

The monster lumbered out of the pond, growling, gnashing its pointed teeth, arms outstretched as it went after the terrified family. Quinn was faster, though, and raced down the path, darting between the monster and its intended prey. The woman had just figured out she had run right into a dead end and was trapped. She clutched the crying kids and they huddled together, terrified.

"Don't worry. I'll protect you!" Quinn yelled, boldly turning toward the reeking beast. He raised his staff, muttering an indecipherable incantation. The end of the staff began to glow brightly and he pointed it at the pond monster. "Begone! Leave these people alone, foul beast!"

The creature hesitated, then took a few more menacing steps.

"I said, begone!" Quinn shouted, brandishing the staff. "I warn you…if I release the fireball from my staff, you will not survive it, fell creature!" *Begone… Fell creature… God, I feel so cheesy saying stuff like that.*

The swamp monster came to a shambling halt. Groaning, it lifted its gray-green, seaweed-draped arm to shield itself from the light that glowed bright from the end of the staff. With a cry that sounded as if it were afraid and in pain, it started to back away. Quinn followed, keeping the staff thrust forward, driving the creature back. At last it fled, shuffling back to the pond and sinking into the murky water.

Quinn breathed a sigh of relief and let the energy drain out of the spell. The glow at the end of the staff winked out. He turned back to the shaken family.

"It's okay. It's gone now. It won't bother you again," he said in his most confident and soothing voice.

"Oh, God, thank you! Thank you so much! I don't know what we would have done if you hadn't been here." Tears of relief shimmered in the woman's eyes now that it looked like she and her children were safe.

"You don't look like a wizard," the boy said, looking up at Quinn with huge round eyes. "You look like my brother, Robbie. He's in high school and thinks he's too good to play games anymore."

Quinn managed a smile. "I'm a little older than that. Every wizard was young once, though. Good thing I was here today or that troll would have had you guys for lunch."

"You'd think those people from AURA would make sure beasts like that were locked up! I don't know how I can repay you," the mother gushed, already reaching into her pocketbook.

Quinn held his hand up. "No, no, I couldn't. It's no more than anyone would have done. It's quite all right," he said humbly.

"I insist, please. At least let me buy you lunch." She pressed the bills into his hand.

Quinn hesitated and finally closed his hand around the money. Bowing his head graciously, he made the cash disappear, this time with sleight of hand rather than real magic.

"Let me escort you past the pond so I know you've made it safely out of the park. Then I'll go back and see if I can hold the monster until AURA gets here," Quinn said.

He led the grateful family away, over the bridge and back toward the street, making sure they were in a more populous area before he took his leave. On his way back to the pond, he stopped at a hot dog cart and bought four footlongs with some of the money the woman had given him.

The pond's surface was smooth as glass when he returned, no sign of the monster or people anywhere. He waited, listening. He walked up the path about twenty yards, checking for any pedestrians, then walked back. "All right, coast is clear," he said to empty air.

The 'monster', who wasn't a troll at all but a boggle, rose up out of the depths, face split in a gruesome smile.

Quinn put a hand on his hip and looked at him sternly. "I thought we agreed you'd wait until I gave you the signal?"

"Aw, c'mon, Quinten. That was the most fun I've had in ages!" the boggle said.

"I said no marks with kids, Groof! They'll probably have nightmares for months!"

"Oh, listen to you, Mr. Moral High Ground." Groof snorted, which sent a spray of pond water from his nostrils. "What about that octogenarian you signaled on last week? He could have had a heart attack. Besides, the old ones don't run nearly as fast." He laughed, a wet sound, as if mud was stuck in his throat.

Quinn sighed. "Next time, *wait for the signal*, Groof. Here..." He tossed the hot dogs one at a time, still wrapped in paper, into Groof's open maw, saving the last for himself. He tried not to grimace as the boggle chewed open-mouthed and his black tongue licked not just his lips but also his chin, cheeks and nostrils after swallowing each one. Groof was cool as far as boggles went and he was a pretty good partner, but his eating habits made Quinn a little queasy.

"Mmm... Extra mustard and onions, just like I wanted. You are a good friend, Quinten," Groof rumbled with a happy chortle.

"Yeah, yeah... All right. See you tomorrow." Quinn sent him an airy wave over his shoulder as he hefted his backpack and started in on his own hot dog on his way out of the park.

About the Authors

Bellora Quinn

Originally hailing from Detroit Michigan, Bellora now resides on the sunny Gulf Coast of Florida where a herd of Dachshunds keeps her entertained. She got her start in writing at the dawn of the internet when she discovered PbEMs (Play by email) and found a passion for collaborative writing and steamy hot erotica. Soap Opera like blogs soon followed and eventually full novels.

The majority of her stories are in the M/M genre with urban fantasy or paranormal settings and many with a strong BDSM flavour.

Sadie Rose Bermingham

A storyteller since before she started school, Sadie also enjoys reading, photography, live music and long walks on the beach.

Sadie has worked as a bookseller, a pedigree editor for the racing industry and a local and family history researcher. Originally from the north of England, she has been working her way across the UK ever since. She currently resides on the south east coast with her long term partner, where she hopes to buy a mobile home and establish a whippet farm.

Bellora and Sadie love to hear from readers. You can find their contact information, website details and author profile page at http://www.pride-publishing.com.